THE GIRL IN THE LIBRARY

A Mystery

J. A. Tattle

For my parents and puppy, with gratitude.
And all pets, especially the tiny terrors:
furry little bundles of determination much beyond their size
and stature,
who witnessed the beginning of this book but not the end

1

In a small town near a big city, a well-mown field opens every weekend, in appropriate seasons and weather permitting, for the county Farmers' Market. Sun almost always shines onto two rows of white-canopied market stalls standing aside the grass like chess pieces awaiting play. By September, the sunlight casts long shadows.

Ben Mahoney, a city tourist who enjoys driving into the country on weekends with his wife and dog, is wandering between the tents full of produce vendors, crafts, and vintage bric-a-brac. Insects drone pleasantly nearby.

He is enjoying the fresh air and asphalt-free inertia of his surroundings when his attention is jostled by an unexpected smell. Somehow, in the clean outdoor air, there is a faint whiff of papery mildew, post-war concrete, and aged Naugahyde.

It takes a moment, but then Ben grasps it: something nearby smells like his grandfather's basement. Pausing in the grassy aisle, Ben looks around and finds one of the tables holds a large cardboard box. Curiosity is an instinct over which Ben has little control and he wanders toward the box without caution.

The box is a large shipping carton and commercial printing on the cardboard declares its original intention to hold thirty-six boxed Trimline handset telephones ready for retail sale. "*Scandalously easy to use*" informs the printing on the box. "*The dial comes right to you. Extra long cords.*"

Ben's twenty-first-century nose wriggles in amusement at these 1960s innovations. He pops open the box flaps and a beam of sunlight reaches in and glints across a large number of oddly shaped glass bulbs, coated in fine dust.

Ben, pulling out one of the bulbs, clears some dust with his thumb, and holds it in strong sun at the side of the tent. It is almost a tube, filled with metal filaments, with sharp little prongs sticking out of the bottom.

Instinctively, Ben turns away from the gaze of Harry, the junk dealer, who is engaging with another customer. Harry is a burgeoning acquaintance of Ben's, given Ben's fondness for weekend trips to the country and vintage mechanical nick-knacks.

Ben smiles to himself: *these, are interesting, and Harry probably does not know what he has...* Prodding the box flap down with one finger, Ben sees two things written on it: *$40* in fresh black marker and, under a layer of dust, *Bob.*

Ben gently returns the bulb to the box and levers the box flaps closed. Lifting it up, Ben turns toward Harry, who, sensing a sale, shifts his attention.

"Hi Ben"

"Harry," replies Ben congenially, nodding once, "how much?"

"Box says forty dollars, Ben."

"My wife's seven months pregnant, Harry, and she's going to kill me when she sees this."

"Steampunk kids'll give me forty."

Ben, feigning inspection of the country market grounds, made exaggerated glances to the left and to the right: "I don't see any Steampunk kids, Harry. Are you going to haul this heavy box of fragile bulbs" — Ben was too honest to call them lightbulbs, even while bargaining — "around until you find some Steampunks?"

Harry, indeed tired of the unexplainable cargo, paused a moment in thought, "thirty-five."

"Twenty."

In the distance, Jen, who could sense when her husband was up to no good, began an approach. She waddled somewhat now, and had their ever-protective sheltie dog underfoot, but even so, both Harry and Ben calculated they had mere moments to strike a deal.

"Thirty."

"Done."

Ben, nestling the box against the table, pulled out his wallet and retrieved a ten and twenty, which Harry snatched from his hands the moment Jen arrived, sealing the box's fate.

"Howdy Jen. When's the baby due?" said Harry with an air both innocent and light.

Jen nodded politely enough, but tightly, and turned to her husband. "We're here to buy things we need!" The dog fixed Ben with a look of chagrin. She patted her belly, "we need stuff" she gently pointed a finger into his chest "To Be Ready."

Harry looked at Ben with a degree of sympathy and guilt and said to Jen, "This your first then?"

"Yes."

"Aw, it's easy as pie you two. Don't worry, eight weeks is plenty of time" and Jen's astute and professionally trained mind immediately noticed the inconsistency between Harry's ignorant opening gambit and his accurate knowledge of her due date. "You'll get everything sorted," said Harry, who in addition to being an antiques and junk salesman, was father to two and grandfather to five. He knew that was not entirely true, but also knew it was the right thing to say.

And Jen, sensing a tingle of energy in her husband, and a carefulness in the way he grasped that box, knew better than to ask him questions about it in front of Harry. He had clearly paid something less than $40; *not worth fighting over.*

"Well, if you've bought that we might as well give up and go." Ben received another chagrined look from the dog. "We can't fit anything else in the car."

And with that she turned, trundling towards the parking lot, ever-loyal Cassie trailing behind. Ben smiled and, nodding goodbye to Harry, hauled the box to his waist and quickly caught up to her.

Harry watched them progressing across the grass towards their (*ridiculous looking*, in his opinion) mini hatchback: sweater-clad Ben and plaid-jacketed Jen Mahoney, thirty-somethings, whip-smart beauty of a dog, about to have their first baby. It reminded him, wistfully, of starting his own family (back when he was all of nineteen). Oddly, the fashions still seemed the same (he shook his head a bit at that). After a moment of relief spent eyeing the empty place previously home to Ben's find, Harry did not think again of the box or its strange contents.

In the parking lot, Jen pulled out her set of keys and popped the hatchback while holding Cassie by the collar with a light command to "stay girl." Normally the hatch going up was a sure indication for Cassie to leap in. Ben deposited the box to one side and adjusted it to make a nominal spot for the dog.

"Up girl."

Cassie flopped, disgruntled, next to the box, which took up so much room. And smelled of darkness.

2

They stopped, as Ben was now trained to assume they must, about thirty minutes later and halfway back to the city. Annie's Apple Hut was one of the better options on this road, in terms of coffee and bathrooms. Also, apple-laden baked goods.

Jen trundled off while Ben got in line, ordering two decaf coffees and six apple fritters. Parking the steaming coffees and pack of donuts on a picnic table outside, he let Cassie out of the car.

Jen returned, checking the time, and then dropping her phone back in her pocket; she eyed the box in the open hatchback. Lately, her mind was too focused on checklists and plans to engage with things like Ben's purchase. She strongly suspected it was in no way relevant to their home life or useful to the baby. Some newfangled process in her rapidly evolving brain automatically assigned it a low priority.

However, she could see the box side through the open hatch and chuckled at the old *"Extra long cords"* advertising copy. She sipped her coffee and picked up a donut, "so what is it then?" Biting into the donut she watched Ben put his coffee down (a sure sign he was about to start explaining things energetically with his hands; she was very fond of his hands).

"I think…" he paused and scratched his chin. "I think they might be some sort of primitive computer memory."

"They?"

Ben got up, went to the box, and retrieved one of the bulbs and brought it back to the picnic table. While Jen absorbed the energizing cinnamon sugar of the donut and warmth of the coffee, Ben held the bulb in his fingers, analyzing and talking.

"It looks something like a type of memory invented in the late 1940s called a Selectron tube. I haven't seen one before in real life — it's been years since I've seen a picture even. Although I have to say it seems much more compact than I think they were, and the assembly is more refined. More mid-century."

Jen used a sugar free hand to pull out her phone, googling "Selectron tube." A picture popped up and she could sort of see what he meant.

"What do we do with it? Are they worth anything?"

"Real Selectron tubes are probably worth a fortune. All that early stuff is now." On that, Jen added "value" to her query and started scrolling the results.

"Jesus, thirty thousand dollars!" Her eyes boggled a bit, but Ben quickly deflated her hopes.

"These can't be worth that. If I had to guess they are from the fifties or sixties."

Jen nodded, "Like the box."

"Like the box."

"And there are so many of them that whatever they are, I doubt they are rare. I think they must be some sort of corporate R&D for a specific application. All I can think to do is maybe try to figure out how they work…"

Putting the tube down carefully, resting it in the gap between planks in the picnic table, Ben leaned back, appraising his quarry. "I suspect I will need to ask Sam at work." He narrowed his eyes, starting to formulate a plan of attack.

"Sam is in IT?"

"No, Sam is faculty. He's cross appointed to history and interested in historic technology — he's done some work with old legacy hardware."

Jen cleaned the sugary glaze off her fingers using a napkin and plucked the bulb off the table, breaking Ben's focus. Not knowing anything about old computer hardware, Jen tried to imagine how this could possibly relate to the kind of memory in her desktop or on her phone.

However, what she lacked in computer engineering knowledge, she might make up for with investigator skills. She passed it between her hands, turning it, while Ben resumed sipping on his coffee. He was right about the workmanship. It was vintage, but somehow did not feel antique.

"There are numbers here, stamped on the glass."

"Really?"

"Yep. Seven, zero, one, zero, one, two." She repeated it: "Seventy, ten, twelve."

"Hmmm," they mumbled in unison.

They binned their coffee cups, bundled the dog into the back, and stowed the remaining donuts on the dashboard. With good traffic they made it home to their downtown condo underground parking in twenty minutes, by which time Jen needed to pee again and they rushed up the elevator, leaving the box in the car.

3

Three days later Ben walked home from work, deked down to the car, and retrieved the box. Hauling it upstairs, he unlocked the apartment door and plonked his keys and the box on the kitchen counter. It almost filled the granite work surface. Looking around their condo, he concluded it would not fit in the hall closet, even if that were not already packed with shoes, boots, and outerwear.

They had about eight-hundred square feet to work with and not a lot of options for storing hundreds of globular technologies from the last century. He walked into the miniscule room that had, until recently, been their shared office, and put the box on the floor, before returning to the kitchen.

He grabbed a snack sitting on one of the two bar stools at the counter and thought for a couple of minutes, then went into the bedroom and through to their shared closet — a walk-in, but not spacious. The top shelf held maybe thirty stacked shoe boxes. He started tapping on their fronts and any sounding hollow, he carefully extracted. After a couple of minutes, he had ten empty boxes. Presumably, their previous occupants were clogging up the front hall closet floor.

Spotting Jen's yoga mat, he grabbed the mat and went back to his floor-bound treasure from the weekend with what shoe boxes he could carry. He unrolled the mat and went to retrieve his laptop and a dust cloth.

Ten minutes later he was happily sitting cross-legged on the mat, laptop open to a spreadsheet, with eighteen dusted bulbs sitting in three shoe boxes. Jen arrived home an hour later with Cassie trotting beside her (Cassie spent Wednesdays at doggie daycare, getting some mid-week air and exercise).

She unleashed the dog, poured some kibble into Cassie's bowl, and deposited her purse and police accoutrements on the coffee table. She then arrived at the door to the tiny room and observed her husband, sitting cross-legged with his box.

"Not in here!"

"What? It's the only place with space...?"

"We have to stop thinking of it as where we dump stuff. It's her room now. And that box smells like mildew."

Unlike Ben, Jen did not have happy memories of sepulchral basements. Jen looked around at the yellow, freshly painted walls, the assembled crib. They had not accomplished much more than that and her mental checklist started rolling immediately.

"We need a rocking chair, a change table and a chest of drawers, at minimum." She wandered back towards the kitchen.

"What do you feel like?" Ben called out into the other room.

"Pizza. Again. She wants lots of salty olives. And peanut butter cookies."

He was not entirely surprised by this request and pulled out his phone, clicking the app for their local pizza place. He hit a couple buttons to order their usual: thin crust, light cheese, ham, green olives — he clicked for extra olives — and herbed tomatoes. On impulse he clicked for extra oregano too. *Ready in 20 minutes.*

"Big day?" he asked.

She nodded and assented with "hmm." "Cleared a bunch of outstanding paperwork. Sumeet is much relieved. He's starting to get a little panicky about the mat leave. Never had a partner 'abandon' him. Temporarily, as I pointed out." She settled on the couch and put her feet up, removing her purse from the coffee table. "Bring your stuff in here." He shifted the boxes onto the coffee table and living room floor then propped his computer on a cushioned lap desk on the couch.

"I'll go get the pizza." He handed her the remote and gave her a peck on the head before leaving.

"And the cookies," she implored, just as he reached the door.

"And the cookies."

* * *

Ben exited the elevator and crossed the ceramic and grey wood pseudo-gallery of their condo lobby. He pushed through the glass and metal front doors of the security vestibule and a cool autumn breeze worked its magic on his muscles and mood.

Despite the snack, his stomach grumbled in anticipation of pizza. Jen was not the only one gaining weight during the pregnancy. Their midtown street was quiet at this hour as many of the surrounding buildings held commercial offices, which also supported two coffee shops and the ever-busy pizza parlour around the corner.

He stopped in at the closest coffee shop, which was glowing a comfortable yellow light onto the darkening sidewalk as sunlight receded behind the tall buildings. It was hosting just a few beverage-sipping, laptop-clicking stragglers over the dinner hour.

By some miracle — or perhaps sympathetic planning by the manager, who had noticed an uptick in demand for peanut butter cookies a few months earlier — there were three of said gigantic cookies sitting alone under a Perspex dome on the counter.

He bought the lot, carrying the paper bag in hand around the corner to the pizza parlour, where their order was waiting on top of yet another plastic display case, this one full of pizza slices. He checked the receipt taped to the box to make sure it was his, thanking the guy behind the counter, and then retraced his steps home.

Jen heard him fumbling with his keys and opened the door for him. She also grabbed the box, with cookies resting on top, out of his hands and promptly fell upon its contents like a beast successful in hunting on the plains.

She had put two plates, napkins, and cutlery on the kitchen counter while he was gone, and two glasses of their favourite fruity sparkling water were on the coffee table. Their streaming service was paused at the opening credits of a British rural crime series they were working their way through, an episode each weeknight.

Slices in hand, they settled on the couch, chomping happily ("it's especially good tonight," to which Ben replied: "extra oregano") and falling into fictional tribulations a world away from their urban North American existence. It was not long before Ben had finished three slices and woke up his laptop.

Jen was still eating pizza, very contently, but eyeing the paper bag of cookies. Convinced she had already solved the episode they were watching (as was only fitting, given she was a detective), she ignored the show for a minute and asked her husband the obvious question: "What are you doing?"

"I'm going through all of them. Doing a count. Checking to see if they all have numbers on them and if any are a different type. So far they all have numbers. Different numbers, in what appears to be one or more sequences. And the bulbs are very uniform. I think they are industrially produced, which is baffling, because I've searched online and can find no known commercially produced memory that matches."

"Hence the shoe boxes."

"Yep, to divide them and rough sort. I need some more." He got up and retrieved three empty boxes from the closet. Jen clasped the paper bag to her chest, adjusted her feet on the coffee table, and began munching on one of the giant cookies.

For forty minutes Ben typed away inputting each number off every bulb he pulled out and sorted. They all started "70" so he shoe-boxed them based on the digits following. Most on the top layer had been 701 although a few 700s were in there, followed by 8 or 9, so each of those got their own box, then 7007s, 7006s, 7005s.

When he pulled out a 7004, staring at five basically full shoe boxes (the 701s seemed relatively empty), he got up and went foraging in the closet, emerging with four more boxes. By the time the show ended, Ben was into the 7001s and not many remained in the bottom of the big box.

When the credits music started, Cassie knew this was the moment for action. She rolled out of her bed, shook out her coat and trotted over to Ben expectantly. A puppy or lesser dog might have whimpered, but Cassie had long ago assessed Ben and determined he was not an idiot. He would understand there were things that needed attending to.

And he did. Getting up, he picked up the leash and the baggie roll, decided on a jacket, clasped Cassie's leash in place, and grabbed his keys, leaving the apartment and locking the door behind him.

Jen flicked over to the news and hauled herself off the sofa, taking plates, cutlery, napkins, and glasses into the kitchen and depositing them where needed. She disassembled and flattened the pizza box and tucked it next to the paper recycling bin.

She wiped down the small counter and returned to the living area, standing for a moment looking at the ten shoeboxes staring up at her. The bulbs were basically evenly distributed, with tens of bulbs in each box.

Ben had lined them up in sequential order and other than the unfinished box only the second and the tenth looked lighter than the others; the tenth by about half. She picked it up and counted the bulbs: sixteen. She picked up the second box and counted the bulbs: twenty-eight.

A story on the news caught her attention and she sat down. However, a wheel started turning in the back reaches of her mind. She was familiar with this particular wheel. It was mostly a process that happened at work and she knew it meant something important was rising to the surface. Her brain had already, or was about to, figure something out. The key was not to force it. She turned her attention to the news broadcast, but a twitchy feeling kept drawing her right eye to Ben's laptop screen.

She looked at it. Lines and lines of numbers typed in as he pulled bulbs out of the box, all starting "70" and several running in little bursts of sequence. She cursored to the topmost box and hit the Sort button. The column of data started at 700105 and she began to scroll down, quickly. She hit end digits 131 and then it jumped to 201 and her brain practically tried to scream the answer, but the cursor kept moving. It was when 228 jumped to 301 that she understood.

4

B en and Cassie returned home, and he opened the door to discover his wife standing triumphant in the middle of the living room. Cassie paused a moment to assess the situation and decided to observe from her dog bed in the corner.

"What is it?" Ben wondered if she had somehow finished furnishing the nursery in the twenty-odd minutes spent outside with the dog.

"Dates."

"What?" He was baffled.

"The numbers on the tubes. They're dates." She picked up his laptop and propped it open on the kitchen counter and began to show him. After the initial realization, she had finished distributing the remaining bulbs into their boxes and typing those numbers into the spreadsheet. There had been five at the very bottom of the big box that started 69: 691227, 691228, 691229, 691230, and 691231. With the list sorted in sequence these were now at the top and their presence further confirmed her theory.

"There's a bulb for every day of every month in 1970 up to the 16th of October, plus five bulbs for the last five days of 1969."

Ben kissed her. One for each day. As an IT administrator, that pattern was immediately familiar to him. He picked a bulb up: "they could be some kind of back-up. I wish I could get a sense of how much data they could handle." He put it back and looked at the spreadsheet, saving and closing it.

"It's odd though. In 1970 they had magnetic tape backups by then. Floppy disks even. And if it is supposed to be working memory," (how working memory would need to be stamped with days he could not imagine) "I am pretty sure 1970 is literally the birth year of RAM."

He did not doubt that she was right, but he was surprised. Instinctively, he had assumed they were dealing with something ten, maybe twenty years older than that. "I've got to show it to someone who knows more. And I've got to take a shower." He went towards the bathroom, determined to stick his head in the shower spray and ruminate.

Jen left the boxes in the living room without worrying Cassie would disturb anything because she was too well behaved, picked up a bit of other clutter, and went to turn off the light in the nursery. She looked around and the room did feel empty. Once they had the rocking chair she would be less anxious. That was all she needed, really, a rocking chair like the one her grandmother had. She flicked the switch and made ready for bed.

❊ ❊ ❊

On Thursday morning Ben woke early, got ready for the day, and took the five 1969 bulbs, wrapped them in tissue, placed them in a plastic pencil box and placed that in his bag. He wondered why five 1969 bulbs should be in with all the 1970 ones. And why 1970 stopped at October 16th.

When Jen awoke she suggested he take the dog out while she made pancakes and bacon. They were sitting at the little glass table by the living room window, pancakes finished, general plans and obligations for the day outlined (as much to themselves as to each other), and orange juice and coffee in hand, as Ben struggled for a moment to articulate something.

"I think I should show the bulbs to Sam Eide at work..."

"Sam the professor?"

"Yes. But I think we know too little, so far, and I don't want to waste his time."

"Hmmm. Good point." Jen was experienced in the difficulties of investigation cooperation and Ben was not wrong. "I'm more than a little curious at this point though."

He was relieved to hear her say that, because he was curious too, despite the impracticalities of engaging with a thoroughly useless distraction so close to the baby's arrival.

"And the date thing might help, eventually" she continued. "Well, we should go back to the market this week-end anyway to look for a rocking chair. We can ask Harry what he knows about the box."

That was it. That was the appropriate next step. They finished off their coffees in unison and silent agreement.

"I have to go" he stood up and kissed her on top of her head. Jen stayed sitting as the front door closed behind him. She resolutely finished her large orange juice, which was full of folate.

She gathered the breakfast dishes and deposited them in the washer with the dinner dishes of the night before, then tied off the garbage and recycling. She took both out into the hallway and to the garbage chute room and sent them hurtling into the basement with a few button clicks. Back in the apartment, she pulled the pizza box out again. She would have to take that down to the first floor herself. Cardboard of any size could not go down the chute as it caused the thing to jam.

For that matter, the big mildew box could go out too. It was empty now and with her hormones, she could smell how the basement odour was permeating the condo. She went over and took a look, hesitating for a second. What if they needed to fingerprint it? She chuckled at the thought. Lifting viable prints off the thing (and somehow matching them to ... what, exactly?) was highly unlikely. This was hardly a criminal investigation. She could not imagine it mattered to throw it out. But she decided to maybe treat it a bit like evidence; evidence, at least, of where it had come from.

She could see writing on the top under the dust — "Bob" — so she took out her phone and snapped a photo or two. Other than the freshly written "$40" (and she could guess who wrote that) and the advertising copy printed directly on the cardboard, there were no other marks on it or inside it. She started breaking the box down with her usual ritual, which involved popping out the bottom, pulling off any plastic packing tape that probably should not go into recycling, and cutting up the panels.

And here she observed something odd. There was no plastic packing tape on the box. The bottom was glue assembled by the manufacturer and there was no tape on the top to close the flaps. They had been interfolded shut, but they clearly had never been taped or sealed in any way. And she had already noticed there were no shipping labels and no residue of any labels that had been removed, no abrasions on the cardboard at all. So, this extra-large shipping box — glued to assembled volume at a factory somewhere, presumably the telephone factory — had never been taped shut and never been shipped anywhere. And yet, here it stood, fifty-odd years later, in their condo living room.

She flattened it out, sliced it into panels with an X-Acto blade she kept on hand for the purpose, and took a few more photos of all the box panel printing, double checking that the interiors were empty. Grabbing her purse and other stuff, she tucked the pizza box and the smelly cardboard under her arm and set off for the downstairs recycling room and then to work.

Once out on the sidewalk, with her arms free, she pulled out her phone and texted her husband:

Threw out your smelly box. But took pics. Thing had never been shipped. Or sealed shut. And glue assembled at the factory. Where'd they make phones?

A few minutes later his reply pinged into her hand.

Pic good. Phone question interesting.

An association started to rattle around in the back of Ben's brain.

5

On Sunday they woke early, as agreed the night before. If Jen was going to get a rocking chair they needed to beat the city antique shop owners and interior designers out to the county market.

The evening before Jen made some muffaletta sandwiches, letting them marinate, tightly wrapped, in the spicy oils and pickling juices overnight. In the morning, she put those and some fruity soda waters in a tiny cooler bag. They also brought a wine bottle tote filled with five thermal metal water bottles (two decaf coffees and three waters; one for Cassie, who had a travel water bowl and kibble container). Lastly, there was a box of five muffins; Ben had already eaten one by the time Jen was out of the shower.

As soon as they hit green space outside the city, they stopped and let Cassie out of the back so she could do her business and they could stretch their legs and breathe some fresh air. It was just turning 8 AM.

"So, what are we looking for again? In the rocking chair?"

"Windsor style" Jen said, naively certain that would get the idea across.

"What does that mean?" Ben said, baffled.

"You know, old, wooden, with spindles up the back — tall back. Has to have good arm rests though. Well positioned. That is the tricky part."

"Hmmm" he tried to form a picture in his mind.

Back in the car, they set off again. Green fields, resplendent weed-covered ditches, and nice rows of trees — some leaves turning colour — zipped past. It was calming. They started these weekend trips two or three years ago, well before they were pregnant, because they hoped this was where they were headed. They would leave the city and get a house out where it was green and quiet. Presumably, the horrible city commuting would start then, but it would be worth it.

Neither of them was from the area — they each arrived for university — and over the years they latched onto day-trip destinations and took the car out to explore the possibilities. They were looking for a community that suited them, long term. For a year now they always headed in the same direction, past the city boundary and into the real *'county'* territory out beyond Annie's Apple Hut.

Ben turned down the numbered road leading to the grassy field behind the arena that hosted the weekly market. Pick-up trucks and vans were driven into the market space along two tracks and tents were being set up in front of each to form the impromptu outdoor mall. Jen began scanning what she could see being unloaded, looking for furniture.

"Bathroom break?"

"Good idea."

Ben pulled the car around and parked on a gravel patch close to the door of the arena at the far end of the field. They got out and tied Cassie to a railing near the building entrance and went inside to a low-roofed lobby. The washrooms were down hallways to the left and right, while ahead were old oil-painted wood and glass doors leading to a vast arena.

The arena was empty except for piles of folded tables and stacks of chairs, and a number of large peg-boards on wheels. The explanation for this assemblage was obvious once Jen turned down the hallway to the bathroom.

On the walls, cork announcement boards were covered with the scheduling and competition rules for the Fall Fair. She scanned them as she walked: *Children's Drawing Competition (Kindergarten)*, *Poetry Competition (Grades 5-7)*, *Best Jam (Adults)*, *Best Cake (Teens)*, *Best Needlework*. Mentally she added *(Old Ladies)* as the age classification for that one, although she might have been surprised by the people at that very moment dedicating themselves to winning said category.

Jen liked this, communities organizing themselves and gently propelling people to accomplish things in life; to develop a little more than they might otherwise. As a police officer, she often saw the opposite outcome and it was depressing. For her daughter, she wanted a community like this one.

A few minutes later and they met up again where they had tied up the dog, and walked out into the field. "You take the left and I'll take the right and we'll reconvene when we reach the middle. We're looking for a rocking chair, chest of drawers if it's in good condition and a changing table" (although she was sure they would just end up going to Ikea for that).

Ben accepted his orders without question. Jen was Mission Lead on this one, no doubt. Their perambulations began. Each tent had an assortment of portable display tables arranged in a U-shape or square on which were wares for sale. Any larger items, like furniture, could be displayed either at the front near the aisle or at the back where people had to walk around to see them properly.

Other than the food — local honey, fruit and berries, herbs and garden vegetables, some cheese stalls — there was a definite pattern to the household goods on display. An infinite array of mid-century china sets could be seen, and to a lesser extent old electric small appliances and cookware, some still in decent condition and good value.

Jen counted seven sets of octagonal living room side tables and probably fifty table lamps of similar vintage. They were observing a great turnover: a post-war generation with expendable income, acquisitive in a booming manufacturing economy, was transitioning to the great beyond. And leaving everything they had bought, unimaginable quantities of it, behind them.

Jen was careful to look for furniture at the back of each tent stall and even on the trucks that were not completely unloaded. She started talking to the vendors, inquiring about chairs and small tables. One explained that they would clear a house out and it was often the chairs and tables that got snatched up by the city dealers on the very first sale weekend. This late in the summer most of the stock had been picked over and there had not been many new house clearance opportunities in the last two months. There was a seasonality to it.

Meanwhile, Ben had gotten distracted by a stall that had some genuine antiques — and increasingly rare ones at that, as it was mostly farm equipment and nineteenth-century farmhouse furnishings. He was fascinated by an old vegetable slicing machine. And there was an ice-cream churn. Jen came up by his side.

"You sure we don't need an ice cream churn?" He placed his hands on it hopefully.

"Yes, I'm sure."

She put a hand on his arm and pulled him over to a cluster of plastic chairs where some pre-teens were selling cubes of watermelon in solo cups. They bought two and sat down. Jen explained that all the good tables and chairs had probably been snatched up by interior designers weeks before.

"Should we check antique shops in the city?"

"No, no, it'll be ridiculously expensive. We'll just get a chair at Ikea." She was noticeably deflated, and he did not like for her to feel that way.

"We'll check the last few stalls and then go talk to Harry."

6

Harry, nodding at their arrival, vaguely worried he would be getting the huge useless box back, continued polishing up an old glass and chrome ashtray. The gesture made him seem like a saloon barkeep.

"Hi Harry" they said in unison.

"Hullo"

"Harry, I'm trying to make sense of those bulb thingies I bought last week," Harry's brow unfurled at that, "where did they come from?"

"Ah. House clearance. An old widow. The estate lawyer brought me in back in the spring. It was in the basement." He tapped his right hand against his brow and squinted his eyes, checking the recesses of his memory for residual information "mmm, 589 Unity Street was the house. The name was ...." — he struggled — "ah, Micklethwaite! Believe it or not. Mrs. Micklethwaite. That's her china over there," he gestured at some gold trimmed, stylized wheat-sheaf china sitting in a box near the front of his main table. "How she got it, I've no idea" he said, not talking about the china. He shook his head and splayed his palms as a sign of defeat, putting the ashtray down in the process.

Ben and Jen looked at each other: *a name and an address. Not bad.* Jen handed Cassie's leash to Ben, a sign he interpreted, correctly, that she was heading off to the washroom. After she was a few paces away, Ben took out his wallet and retrieved a business card.

"Harry, you got a pen?"

"Sure thing." Harry handed him the pen he used for writing up receipts when required.

"Listen, Jen really, really wants an old rocking chair for the nursery, and we can't find one." Ben was crossing out the university contact information on his card and writing in his personal phone and email.

"What kind?"

Ben was not going to say 'Windsor Chair' to Harry. He did not quite know what it meant, and he did not want Harry to think they were annoying city people who used fancy jargon, which was ironic, because as an experienced old guy who often dealt in furniture, Harry knew what a Windsor chair was.

"I think she wants one that reminds her of her grandmother's" he flipped the card over and wrote *Windsor Rocking Chair* on the back. Then he handed it to Harry "If you get a line on one, will you let me know?"

Harry took the card, looking at it. *Ben Mahoney, MScAC, Systems Manager, IT Department.* At the university, no less. He tucked it into a little metal receipt box he kept handy, "No problem."

They nodded at each other and Ben headed back to the car, Cassie trotting alongside with a smile because she was absolutely sure they were at the beginning of an adventure. As he walked, Ben plonked "589 Unity Street" into Maps on his phone. It was not that far, and it was on the way into town.

When they were both back in the car, Ben suggested driving by 589 Unity on the way to checking out the town before having their sandwich lunch in the town square park. Jen agreed.

They turned onto the county road, going farther away from the highway and on roads they had not used before. Despite the rural-feeling green fields and ditches of the fairgrounds on their left, on their right it quickly transitioned to 1950s and 60s split-level ranch houses and smaller bungalows. Generally, they were in good condition, some with modern additions or other renovations, and most enjoying the benefit of mature trees and well-tended lawns.

After a couple of turns into the subdivision they were on Unity Street and rolling slowly past 589. The roof over the garage was removed down to the trusses and studs and it was clearly undergoing a major renovation. Ben said *"it does look like grandpa's house"* under his breath and chuckled.

Jen, not understanding what he meant, ignored him. The lawn was patchy even away from the renovation activity and there were sharp raw branches where a once gigantic overgrown bush had been ruthlessly cut back.

"The siding and windows look a little rough" Jen said, and they did. Mentally stripping back the changes wrought by the construction crew, they both guessed that a year ago this was a run-down old house, probably inhabited by someone elderly and isolated. It was not a happy thought.

Rolling on and arriving at the intersection for the main drag, Ben turned. Within moments they saw the town square park and a classic small-town streetscape of two- and three-story brick commercial buildings. There was an old, very upright, red brick town hall, cupola still intact on top, in the middle of the north side of the park. Ben took the car around the perimeter so they could check it all out, and then parked near a picturesque gazebo surrounded by tables and park benches.

They got out, popping the hatch but putting Cassie on a leash until they could tell if she was allowed to go gambolling around by herself. They also grabbed the bottle tote, remaining muffins, the cooler bag, and Cassie's portable bowls.

They set up camp at one of the tables and served Cassie her lunch before unpacking the cooler. The sandwiches, messy as they were tasty, required a few minutes of determined concentration but as Ben moved to pour them both coffees, Jen pulled out her phone.

Saying nothing, she typed *Micklethwaite obituary* and the name of the county town into google. The very first link, from the county paper, started to provide answers. She skimmed it quickly and when convinced it was relevant went back to the beginning and started to read it aloud:

"MICKLETHWAITE, Deborah Ann (nee MacDonald). Peacefully after a brief illness on Wednesday, November 15th, 2017 at Crestview Nursing Home. Deborah, in her 94th year, beloved wife of the late Robert and devoted aunt to nephew Rob Micklethwaite (Sandra) and niece Sophia Simpkins (Donald). She will be missed by five great-nieces and nephews and two great-great nephews. Predeceased by sister Patricia Thomason. Services Glenwood Chapel on Friday, November 17th from 10-11 AM. Interment Glenwood Cemetery."

"'*wife of the late Robert*' ... 'Bob' written on the box?"

"We may be on to something," Jen concurred. She put *Robert Micklethwaite obituary* into Google, but it was clear the first handful of additional results were meaningless. She tried *Bob Micklethwaite obituary* and added the county town but again the only relevant thing that came up was Deborah's own notice. Backing up to her first search results and scrolling down, she noticed obsolete address and telephone listings for *D Micklethwaite, 589 Unity Street*. They seemed to have the right widow.

"Well, if he died more than ten, fifteen years ago, the obit won't be on the Internet," Ben noted. "It would be good to know when he passed. Where is Glenwood Cemetery?"

Jen mapped it, grasping his assumption that Deborah would be buried with her husband, "a slight detour on the way home. The office is closed now though." She clicked on the website link to see what their options were for getting more information.

Conveniently, there was a menu item *Find a Grave* and that led to a database screen. She entered Micklethwaite and dozens of names popped up, Deborah was near the top and three Roberts were found alphabetically filed down the list. Next to each name was a section, row, and plot coordinate. She navigated backwards and found a link for a cemetery map on the main page. "I think we can find the burial, if we go there."

At that moment two Golden Retrievers, running free in the wind — clearly locals — came up to say a brief hello to Cassie before racing off, as retrievers are wont to do, to the vast green pasture of the rest of the park. Cassie perked up at this and turned expectant eyes towards Ben and Jen. They relented and the next hour was spent in off-leash stick chasing, squirrel chasing, pats, and belly rubs. As they packed up to go, Cassie looked around thinking she could get used to this rather nice park. Even the retrievers.

❊ ❊ ❊

Cassie was not long in the car before the hatch opened again. She wiggled her tail with glee and panted happily. This was proving to be a glorious day. She looked around. They were in one of the parks that had big stones everywhere. Those were different, but they were not bad parks. Up until the early summer, Jen had often taken Cassie running along the asphalt trail of one such park not too far from home. They hadn't been to it since the Big Change started happening though, which was okay.

The key thing to remember about these parks is that you are not allowed to pee on the stones. It was tempting — there were corners everywhere, but she knew it was wrong. And it wasn't just a rule she followed; she could tell other dogs weren't allowed to do it either.

The other thing was some people in these parks could be very upset, or sometimes just sad. Those tended to be the ones that weren't walking on the trails though. They were out in the lawns, near a stone and standing still.

Once, before they lived with Ben, they'd gone on a long trip and Cassie had met a nice old lady and then the three of them had gone to a stone park and Jen and the old lady had been a bit upset and a bit sad. Trotting and sniffing among the stones, Cassie could sometimes still sense the sad upsetness standing there, from sometime before.

Jen was talking: "Okay, this should be section D. It's a big tear drop shape. We need Row 17 Plot 21 but the map didn't say which way the rows run or which side the plot numbers start on. I think I should go up the left and you go up the right. We count off seventeen rows and then work in towards the middle, reading all the stones in that row and surrounding it. If it is not there, we go up to the north side and count seventeen rows down towards here. If that doesn't work, we might have to give up."

Cassie was left off leash and when Ben and Jen split up and started walking away, she decided the best thing to do was run back and forth between them, stopping to investigate anything particularly interesting she should find. She could tell there was no one else in the cemetery but the three of them so she indulged in the kind of yipping and barking she could not get away with in the city, excitedly announcing her arrival as she skittered toward Ben and Jen in turn. She found a good stick and delivered it to Ben, who threw it up the trackway cars travelled on.

When she returned with it, Ben and Jen were together again and looking at a stone with great interest. Cassie dropped the stick and trotted over. Just as she reached them, something happened. Something that hadn't happened in a long time.

All the hairs down Cassie's neck stood on end and the muscles in her face tensed and her eyes flared open and she found herself looking left and right to see if something was there. She smelled a faint whiff of danger. A predator had been here. And it was strongest right in front of the very stone Jen and Ben were staring at. She backed onto her haunches and growled at it:

Deborah Ann MacDonald
March 8th, 1924 – November 15th, 2017
Wife of
Robert Micklethwaite
February 5th, 1923 – October 14th, 1970

"It can't be a coincidence."

They took their suddenly ferocious dog by the collar and quickly headed back to the car, baffled at what she could be reacting too. It was not the dog that had their attention though, a fact they might have regretted if they'd had the capacity to understand. What they were focused on was Bob Micklethwaite's death date.

"No, no. Can't be a coincidence. We must have Bob's tubes. What was the date on the last one again?" he asked Jen, who would have a better memory of her discovery from earlier in the week.

"October 16th"

"That's weird, two days *after* he died. I suddenly find myself extremely interested in the life and career of Bob Micklethwaite."

"Me too" said Jen "I'd look into him at work, but it's too early — the databases don't go back that far. We'll have to think of something else."

The sun was low in the sky by the time they crested the hill above the city, and all the concrete below was transformed into terracotta. It had been a good day. The dog was tuckered out in the back. Being out in the country was restorative and trying to figure out what Ben's ridiculous bulbs were was not a bad distraction for nervously expecting first-time parents.

They got back to the condo and set about roasting a chicken and washing and peeling some russets for mashed potatoes. Once the chicken started to brown, and the pot on the stove was bubbling away, Cassie parked herself at the kitchen entrance (practically in front of the stove, given the compact design) and stared, salivating in the direction of the warm and wonderful odors. The Scary Smell from the stone park fell towards the back of her consciousness and she once again concluded this was the Best Day Ever.

Jen sat on a bar stool, one foot dangling into the dog's fur. With Ben's laptop open, she pulled up the website for the county newspaper that had published Deborah Micklethwaite's obituary. She navigated the various sections and columns and determined their online obituaries only went back about eight years. She found a contact address for the obituaries and pulled out her phone, sending a quick email.

Hi,

How would I go about getting a copy of an obituary from 1970?

Thank you,

Jen Mahoney

She pocketed her phone and closed the laptop, removing it to the coffee table to make space to finish the potatoes and carve the chicken.

7

On Wednesday night they decided to go to Ikea. There would be Swedish meatball and potato dinners once they got there, but first they had to battle the traffic, which was no small thing on the arterial roadways of the city at evening rush hour. But fight they did, and a mere hour and ten minutes after leaving their parking spot, they won. They had arrived. To the Ikea parking lot.

Which was extremely crowded. But after circling and waiting they parked and joined the throng of fellow shoppers entering the store. With a bit of fast action on the stairs they made it into the cafeteria line and could eventually be found, quite haggard, but seated comfortably with full trays of the meatball dinners.

Ben had succumbed to the display of Swedish pastries at the cafeteria check-out and grabbed a much-needed package of green marzipan logs dipped in chocolate called *Sötsak Dammsugare*. They carbohydrated and rehydrated and then set out for the furniture display floor.

"If we get the dresser and the change table tonight we can start unpacking the baby shower haul from the linen closet and then start filling the linen closet with diapers and laundry supplies. And we can do a list of what is outstanding once we have everything in its proper place."

"Yep."

They arrived at the baby and child section. There were six changing tables to choose from, some in multiple colours. Ben fished a Sötsak Dammsugare out of the package and downed it like it was medicine to make his brain work. Jen started comparing. She eliminated the cheapest one immediately because it had only one shelf for storage and she was hoping for a nice painted finish.

The next two had lots of open shelving beneath. Ben held the tag and read the product blurb: "Apparently the open shelves make it easy to grab things with one hand while you hold the baby on with the other." He mimed this, testing their theory, and realized for the first time that he would very shortly be caring for a being so fragile and defenseless she always needed to have protection around her, and you could never let go. As the sugar started working, Ben's instincts to make a good choice kicked it. They would both be spending a lot of time using this table over the next two years.

"Well, these two are basically the same. Ninety bucks extra gets us four drawers instead of two shelves. Lots of storage," Ben completed his pitch.

"You know what though we can't vacuum under either because they have no feet, just those little plastic blob things." With Cassie, this was a very worthwhile consideration.

"Well, these two have feet." One was a very nice simple-looking two-shelf number at a very reasonable price. The other had an open shelf but also two bureau drawers.

"Hmmm, this one with the drawers says it converts to a chest after potty training. It's a hundred bucks more, but that would be worth it if we could get more use out of it later. And it has a matching furniture line with other pieces."

"Done."

Decision made, they were very proud of themselves. Now they just had to fight their way downstairs, retrieve it from the giant warehouse, make it through the cashier line up, battle the traffic home, and assemble it.

Four hours later they gave up on the last stage. It was midnight and they left the partially assembled chest on the floor in the nursery and crawled into bed. Ben spoke softly: "I think on Sunday we should go out to the country and not go shopping. We should just take Cassie to that park she loved. And buy some pie."

"Sounds like a plan," Jen whispered back, and kissed him on the chin.

8

It was late in the workday on Thursday when an email ding emanated from Jen's phone.

Hi Jen,

Apologies for the delayed reply. Back issues of the newspaper are available to the public on microfilm in the Local History reference section of the county library. The county historical and genealogical society has prepared an index of obituaries and you can check it out _here_. If you find the one you are looking for, I can scan it and send it to you for a fee of $15, or, if you are local, you can just go into the library and make a copy for free (bring a USB key).

Hope that helps.

Best,

Tonya

Jen headed home. She reached the condo and took Cassie out for a walk, picking up things to eat on the way back, including some peanut butter, brown sugar, and chocolate chips. She was just starting to prepare dinner when a text arrived from Ben:

Malware on the network. Late night.

She texted back:

There'll be peanut butter chocolate chip cookies when you get home. Good luck.

Eight blocks away Ben took the opened package of slightly stale Sötsak Dammsugare out of his backpack and ate the precious remaining three, then cracked his knuckles, got up, and entered the virtual fray.

Jen settled down and finished a nice stir fry made with leftover chicken and a healthy assortment of vegetables. She put a movie on and started baking the cookies. By the end of the movie, she had a couple dozen cookies in Tupperware and left a plateful on the counter, taking two in a napkin back to the couch. She pulled out her tablet and brought up the link Tonya had sent her earlier.

The local history and genealogy website was surprisingly detailed and informative. Volunteers posted indexes and transcriptions that provided a lot of information on those who had called the county home. She had seen profiles in criminal investigations containing less information.

The obituary indexes were subdivided by year, so she clicked on 1970. Scrolling down she found Bob Micklethwaite and there were four separate entries next to his name: *DN 10/15/1970 p4, FN 10/16/1970 p4, O 10/16/1970 p4 see also FA 10/17/1970 p1*. Further perusal of the page revealed the codes: there was a death notice the day after he died, a funeral notice and obituary the next day, and on the day following he was mentioned in an article in the main part of the paper. It sounded like they might be able to find out quite a bit about Bob's life and career with a trip to the county library. Sunday might not be just about Cassie-time and pie after all.

❊ ❊ ❊

Ben slept in on Saturday, but Jen got up early and took Cassie to the vet for a checkup. There was going to be a trip to the groomer and a professional deep clean of the condo in the next four weeks because she suspected vacuuming would soon thereafter drop off the priority list for a while.

When they got back, Ben was up. He was standing at their bookshelves putting away an old photo album no one had looked at in years. On top of the shelves were the ten shoeboxes of bulbs. It was not a great look for the living room but for now they were out of the way.

He turned, still bleary eyed, but awake enough to crouch down and pinch-pat Cassie's jowls when she rushed up to report on their early morning adventures ("who's a good girl!?!").

"How about brunch? You hungry or did you have a big breakfast?"

"I could do brunch," Jen had had a substantial breakfast three hours earlier but could definitely eat some more.

"Okay." He went and jumped in the shower.

They checked local restaurant traffic on a couple of apps and found a hotel restaurant around the corner they could probably get into and set off walking. They were seated quickly. It was in an expansive old 1960s dining room with huge plate glass windows looking out on the pool deck a story below and concrete terraces filled with plants and small trees.

Ben ordered Eggs Benedict and Jen chose Eggs Florentine, with a large orange juice.

"How'd the malware battle go?"

"Eh," he dismissed it with a gesture of his hand and a shrug, after two days he was tired of it.

Jen chuckled, "I thought I was the one that had to deal with criminals."

Ben looked rueful, "not these days…"

Coffee arrived on a tray, a generous French Press big enough for two and immaculate white china cups and saucers. Ben poured, as Jen would be hard pressed to lean across the table. He held the large, round cup in both hands and drained most of it, revelling in the calm warmth of the cup radiating into his hands and arms.

"Ah, that is good. I feel like a person again."

"Don't worry, we'll feed you and everything will be *all better*."

And somewhat miraculously the waiter arrived at that very moment and deftly deposited their breakfasts. "Our luck is turning," Ben observed. The eggs were expertly done and extremely tasty. As Ben started eating (the ravenous one, for once), Jen filled him in on her progress in their recreational investigation.

"I emailed the county paper to see about an obit for Bob Micklethwaite. They directed me to the county library and the local historical society website. There seems to be not only an obit, but some sort of article about three days after he died. All we have to do is go to the library and look at it on microfilm."

"Where's the library?"

She pulled out her phone and opened the Maps. The county library was already entered and showing as a blue dot. She held out the phone to Ben so he could see the location.

"Hmm. Not too far from the park."

Jen pocketed the phone and the conversation turned to other things. They strolled back to the condo about 2:30, took Cassie out, and when they got back, Jen was yawning.

9

It was a crystalline Sunday morning with a cloudless powdery blue sky. Everything basked in the clarity of white autumn light. The fine details of leaves, fences, and fretwork on houses in the distance resolved into focus. Jen snapped some shots of the landscape on her phone as they travelled.

They left later than usual and took a similar picnic to the one enjoyed last time. Ben decided to stay on the highway past their usual turn off and they came into the town from a different direction, seeing some older nineteenth-century homes and churches.

Cassie was ecstatic when they popped the hatch and she realized where she was. With a leap she was off, racing in circles, stopping to smell every tree and lamppost. They set up the picnic (including bowls for Cassie, which were ignored for the better part of an hour) and took their time tucking in.

Jen got up to find a washroom and discovered they were in the basement of the old town hall building, accessible from outside down a short ramp. The hall was brick, two stories plus the half-story basement, in a vertical design that must have been fifty feet to the roof line. There was a low-pitched gable and the cupola on top of that. How impressive it must have seemed on completion in the 1860s, just as the town came into its possibilities.

Jen decided to look inside and walked up the cement front steps, entering through a beautiful old white-painted door. The meeting room and council chambers on the second floor were blocked off with a velvet rope across the mahogany stairway but the foyer of the main floor was quite large and on the walls were interesting old wooden plaques covered in hand-painted gold and black script.

The plaques were lists of municipal office holders. The mayors had the most impressive board and amongst the eighty or so names on the board a Micklethwaite caught Jen's glance immediately. It was another Robert, mayor 1887-92 and 1896-99. *Well, that explains the density of Micklethwaites in Glenwood Cemetery*, thought Jen. They were an old county family.

There were several other interesting old names no longer much heard of and Jen wondered about their origins. Other than the inevitable Smiths, Thompsons and Millers, she recognized only one: Cadworth. Jen had an instructor at Police College named Peter Cadworth and wondered if there was a connection.

To the right was a plaque headed *Sherriff*, which surprised Jen. This was hardly the wild west. Quickly, she realized that as the first settlers to the area had been from the United Kingdom this moniker reflected the county sheriff tradition brought from the Old World — more Robin Hood than Wyatt Earp. Come to think of it, the cowboy sheriffs must trace back to that origin too.

After a dozen or so names on that board, there was a break and another heading, *Chief*. In the beginning these were probably chief constables but by the twentieth century they became what she would recognize as the modern administrative and managerial overlords of the county police.

There was another Cadworth on this board — one much more recent — Richard, and he held a long stretch from 1961 to 1989. After him there were five chiefs in rapid succession. Finally, the list ended when the current Chief of Police took over ten years ago, her name added with a start date only.

Including the board for Chief Librarians, she was one of only a few women listed anywhere in the room. For a moment Jen stood, wondering why two centuries had passed before that happened and pondering the state of the world about to welcome her daughter, then she went back outside to play with Cassie.

10

T hey packed up the lunch gear and decided to walk over to the library, which proved to be a picturesque trip up a beautiful old street. Large red brick houses — mansions, really — stood behind expanses of lawn and floral borders, some with wrought iron fencing and gates. Ahead, the street ended in a T-junction and this held an old classical stone courthouse. There were brackets with banners hanging from the light posts and these announced not only the county library, but the museum and municipal art gallery. As they got closer they could see that the library was housed in a modern addition stuck onto the back and side of the courthouse, while placard signs directed pedestrians seeking the museum and gallery to the historic entrance at the front. They went around the back and Ben tied Cassie to a railing near the library entrance.

They pushed through the doors into an atrium vestibule with slate tiled steps and an accessible elevator servicing the main and upper levels, appended to the old building fabric. Spotting a circulation desk, they walked through the empty queue and a librarian came over to meet them. Jen, explaining they were looking for microfilms of the county paper, received directions to the second floor.

The second floor was the lovingly revived Victorian courthouse library. Among the antique shelves and hefty bound volumes there was also a bank of brand new computers, some with attached platens for scanning. A woman in her sixties sat at an old courthouse desk and with grey hair in a bun, glasses fixed to the end of her nose, she was unquestionably the Reference Librarian. They went over, already walking more quietly and deferentially than they had since they were children.

"Hi. We are looking for the county newspaper on microfilm?"

The librarian stood up, "do you have a specific date?" she asked, walking towards a corner that held several metal cabinets.

"We do," Jen took out her phone "I used the online indexes: October 1970 — the 15th, 16th, and 17th."

The librarian unfurled a drawer in one of the cabinets and ran a finger down the line of boxes in the middle, "well those should all be on this reel." She closed the drawer, "come over here and I'll get you set up on a machine. Did you bring a USB key by any chance?"

"We did," Ben pulled one from his pocket.

"Good. It is quite easy to save an image once you get the knack of the software. I'll give you a tutorial."

The librarian sat down at a computer with an attached scanning apparatus and loaded the reel onto the two winding wheels, showing them how to weave the film under and around rollers and through the plates. She clicked a switch on the back of the scanner and opened a program on the desktop. They could see particles of dust magnified many times on the computer monitor. Then a black band as the film began to roll forward. Once a newspaper image was on the screen, the librarian stopped the film, manipulated the image orientation, and autocorrected the focus and exposure.

"Here is the zoom button, and these can be used to tweak exposure and focus" she said, using the cursor to point at features in the software program "you crop using the green box and then scan to USB with this button. It is set to make a jpeg at 400 dpi."

The librarian picked up the box the film had come in and looked at the dates, "this runs September 1st to October 31st, so your target is about three quarters of the way through," she hit a fast forward button and very rapidly whirled the reel towards the end, when she stopped they were on page three of October 16th. "Do you think you can manage?"

Ben answered, "expect so" and as the librarian got up, Ben sat down.

"Thank you!" Jen said brightly to the librarian when she turned to go back to her desk.

"What page is the obit on?" Ben asked.

"Four. Should be the next one." Ben hit the slow forward button and the next page was revealed. The Funerals list was visible first and they could see: *MICKLETHWAITE, Robert. 2 PM Saturday, October 17th, Glenwood Cemetery Chapel.*

With a bit of vertical nudging to the sliding glass plate they found the obituary, filed alphabetically near the bottom of the same page:

MICKLETHWAITE, Robert. Tragically Wednesday, October 14th, 1970. Bob, in his 48th year, beloved husband of Deborah and devoted uncle to Rob Micklethwaite and Sophia Thomason. Predeceased by parents Robert Sr. and Hannah and brother Samuel. Funeral to be announced.

"Not very informative. Hopefully the article has more." Ben scrolled through the remaining pages of that issue and they arrived at the below-the-fold front page of the Saturday paper, where a full-sized headline caught their attention:

Local Engineer Dies in Fiery Crash

Residents of Main Street were awoken just before midnight on Wednesday to the sound of a horrific crash in the gully behind the Presbyterian Church. Engineer Bob Micklethwaite, 47, well known and liked by so many of his townsmen, died instantly when his vehicle breached the barrier at the bottom of Croft's Hill, went airborne, and then impacted the gully at high speed, resulting in a fiery explosion. Initial investigation by the county police indicates the cause is likely a failure of the vehicle's brakes on slick road conditions but it will be difficult to prove this given the extensive damage. Micklethwaite was a Second World War veteran, Highlanders, and long-time employee of the phone company and the research and development labs...

They both reached this point of the article simultaneously and Ben, flexing his fingers in recognition and frustration, exclaimed loudly: "Of course! The phone company labs! They were not far from here and had one of the most advanced research programs of their day. I should have guessed from the phones on the box..." He was slightly disappointed in his own associative ineptitude but nonetheless excited to have figured out where the bulbs probably came from.

"Hmmm, we should keep reading, maybe it will say more about what he did."

...working there for 25 years, progressing through the ranks from Research Assistant in the Physics and Computing Lab back in the 50s to Chief Operations Manager of the Southwest Central Office. Bob oversaw the implementation of all the significant changes which have led to such great improvement in the efficiency and reliability of our phone communications in the last 20 years. Rory McCormack, communications liaison for the company, extends heartfelt condolences to Bob's family and commented that he was "a truly innovative and dedicated employee who will be greatly missed by everyone he interacted with at our corporate head office and, I am sure, by all staff at the Southwestern operations facility.

At this point the column reached the end of the page and wrapped around to continue at a point higher up above the headline:

The Legion has announced they will hold a wake in celebration of Bob's life on Saturday night after the funeral. Bob is survived by his wife Deborah and nephew Rob. His parents both passed about 20 years ago, in the years following his brother Samuel's death at the Invasion of Normandy.

They looked at each other, struck slightly dumb by these developments. In seeking an explanation for Ben's enigmatic old technology, they had not expected to stumble upon a sequence of family tragedies. "We'd better make a copy. Can you expand the zoom to get the whole thing?"

Ben did so, and as the machine whirred to pull more of the front page within the green cropping box, a large picture started emerging in the middle, above the fold. A chill went through Jen. Twice in her career she (and everyone in her unit) had been seconded to Missing Persons and in an instant she knew what that picture had to be.

11

"**B**en, can you move it up and sideways for a minute?" He did so, hearing the sudden pitch-change in her voice. As his hand moved the platen apparatus to adjust the view, the large school portrait of a young girl prominently and clearly positioned in the middle of the front page was fully revealed and a very large headline appeared.

No Progress in Missing Girl Case

More than a week has passed since Julie McNally, 11, was last seen at the county fair. Police Chief Dick Cadworth briefed the press Friday afternoon, confirming expanded searches will be held this weekend. The police are asking everyone who possibly can to report to the town Fire Hall at 9 AM on Saturday and/or Sunday to participate in an organized search of the fairgrounds, surrounding fields and the creek gully.

When the girl was identified as missing last Friday at around 8 PM, four hours after she was seen near the hog pens, scent dogs were brought in to try to track her. However, given the large number of people on the grounds and the nature of activities, this effort was not successful.

Chief Cadworth assured townsfolk that every possible course of action is being undertaken. All fair employees and volunteers, and all carnival workers, have been identified and interviewed. The police have completely searched all buildings, vehicles and trailers on the fairgrounds and parts of any rides in which the girl could have become entrapped. Many fair attendees provided their recollections of the girl from that afternoon.

Given the lapse in time, there is acute concern for the girl's safety. The mayor has suggested to the Chief that the regional police be brought in and her parents emphatically support this request. They see no way she would or could have left the town of her own accord, particularly given her age. The girl had no access to money other than the small amount she spent at the fair that afternoon and is generally considered shy, bookish, and unlikely to have friends who would have facilitated her running away.

Her poem won the Poetry (Grades 5-7) competition which was blindly adjudicated on Wednesday. The judges were struck quite sensitively when the identities of the winners were revealed. Sharon Thorpe, Chief Librarian, and Wendy Croft, one of the English teachers at the high school, were on the judging panel. They both expressed extreme concern about the girl's fate and are anxious given the investigation has produced no leads thus far.

Jen shuddered slightly. There was enough information in that article to suspect the situation had ended with a very bad outcome. Ben, naïve about the probabilities of recovering a child lost for more than a week, simply asked "I wonder what happened?"

"We'll have to look it up online to find out, unless you want to sit here for hours reading through the paper?"

"No. Online it is." He extracted the USB key from the computer and pocketed it, then hit the rewind button and the machine zipped to life, returning the unwound reel to its original state rather aggressively. They placed the reel back in the box and headed over to the Reference Librarian to return it.

"Did I hear you mention the phone company labs?" the librarian inquired.

"Yes, you did. We seem to have come into possession of some of their old technology," Ben offered by way of explanation.

"Well, there's an exhibit on them, *Age of Innovation*, currently running in the County Museum next door, in case you are interested."

"We are indeed, thanks for that," Ben said, meaning both the suggestion and the microfilm reel, which he deposited on the desk "Jen, you want to check it out?"

"Sure." Jen paused for a minute, but her police instinct propelled her on: "do you know about the Julie McNally case? We saw it," she gestured back to the computer with a tilt of her head, as if the newspaper was still displayed there, "and wondered what happened."

"Ah, of course, October 1970, you would see it," the librarian said with a bitter wistfulness. "She was a friend of mine. Used to spend a lot of time reading in that window seat over there," she said, gesturing to the large window with a deep sill and a cushion that looked out over a newly landscaped park behind the building. "They never found her. Not a trace. I'll go to my grave without knowing what happened. Her father did. Her mother's still alive though."

Jen said "I am very sorry to bring it up. And sorry it happened."

"Oh I wouldn't worry about bringing it up. Her disappearance will never be forgotten. It hangs over this town, in perpetuity."

They were much more somber while descending the stairs and making their way outside, unsettled by the tragedies brought to the surface by this brief research excursion. Cassie noticed their downcast demeanour at once, was reminded of the anxiety felt on the cemetery trip, and decided she better be on alert to possible dangers (that was her job, after all).

They unleashed her from the railing and trotted her around to the front of the historic building where she was promptly tied up again near the original building entrance. Ben and Jen went inside.

There was a desk to the left which held several pamphlets for the gallery and museum exhibits, as well as a box requesting small donations for admittance. A chair behind the desk was currently empty.

They dropped five dollars into the box and picked up the *Age of Innovation* pamphlet and, on determining the gallery was upstairs while the museum operated on the main floor and basement, they walked through a large set of double doors, one of which was propped open.

They found themselves in a nice old room with the same windows as in the reference section of the library, but this room was decorated in shades of cream and dove-grey and had very sedate lighting.

Jen cracked the pamphlet:

The Telephone came to our community in 1919, when the burgeoning population growth and increasing popularity of the new technology led to the establishment of both the Southwestern Exchange (later the Central Office) and shortly thereafter, the nearby research and development facility.

The first exhibit was a glass case holding an early metal and wood Candlestick telephone which had no dial. Next to it sat a large panel with metal lined holes, near to which were cords like oversized audio connectors.

"Those'll be manual switch boards" said Ben, finding himself in something close to his element. "You couldn't dial a number yet, but by picking the handset off the stand, you were connected to an operator who connected your circuit to the local destination circuit once you said the number you wanted." Ben had managed, from his own memory, to reproduce the gist of the descriptive text for the display.

They moved onto the next case, which showed two phones. One was similar to the previously displayed phone, except it had a rotary dial and the second, which was labelled a *French Phone*, no longer had the stand and had the earpiece and speaking piece arranged in the plastic handset (like her grandmother's phone, as Jen remembered from childhood). While clunky in retrospect, that earpiece and mouthpiece arrangement was like the cell phone in her pocket.

The museum display narrative continued:

The next innovation was the invention of Dial Service. The rotary dial was invented by Almon Brown Strowger in 1891, although it subsequently took many years to create versions of the technology that worked for ordinary customers. The user lifted the handset, selected a digit with one finger and rotated the dial through to the stop position and then released the dial. As the spring-loaded dial recoiled to resting position, it generated a sequence of electrical pulses representing the digit. The user then entered the next digit in the desired phone number and the process was repeated until the entire phone number had been dialled and transmitted to the Telephone Exchange and displayed on an indicator. The Southwestern Exchange still relied on telephone operators to complete the circuit between the caller and the recipient at this point. However, the operator only needed to connect the circuit and no longer had to monitor and ring the lines as dial and ring tones now informed the caller of transmission status. While this was much more efficient, the exponential growth in telephone installation and use meant many local women were employed as Operators from the 1920s to 1950s.

And above the caption was a series of pictures showing women working in the local exchange in each decade.

Even after the invention of Dial Service, the electrical pulses were not processed fully automatically for many decades. Our local research facility was established in 1921 and contributed extensively over the next forty years to the development of the true Electronic Switching Systems which would ultimately make most phone operators obsolete and enable long distance direct dialing by the 1970s. Work in our lab even included early digital technologies, particularly in the period just after the Second World War.

Ben murmured in satisfaction at that, "I'm sure our bulbs have something to do with this lab activity."

He took out his phone and started snapping pictures of the text in the museum display, as a way of making notes. They progressed through several more cases and descriptive boards when a kid — clearly a student on work study — popped his head in through the doors.

"Hello. Sorry I wasn't at the desk earlier, would you like a tour?" He seemed eager to finally have something to do, so they took him up on his offer and moved back towards the entrance doors.

The kid began a much-rehearsed tour presentation:

"This complex was built in 1911 in a Beaux-Arts style designed by noted local architect Anderson Jeffries, using limestone from nearby quarries. A larger, more modern building was needed to replace the functions then housed in the red-brick Palladian town hall and jail, which is still standing in Town Hall Square Park. This building served as the County Court House from 1912 until 1968 and as the town jail from 1912 until 1985."

"The library had one small room in the Court House from 1918 but was able to substantially expand in 1968 and 1985 and again more recently with a modern renovation that you can see by going around to the back of the building. The building is now entirely dedicated to historical and cultural functions."

The student paused to catch his breath.

"How much of the exhibit have you already seen? I can go through that or we can go down to the basement and look at the permanent local history exhibit."

"Eh, we've seen this," said Ben, allowing Jen to assume he had everything he needed.

Their guide turned and led them single-file down a narrow enclosed staircase with cold stone floors and heavy-seeming walls.

"The basement is constructed with triple thick stone walls as it served as the county jail for seventy-three years. We still have six jail cells as part of the exhibit space."

They reached the bottom and found themselves in a large room with six cells, doors open, against the south west wall, and glass display cases arranged elsewhere. Cordons defined individual exhibits containing furniture and other historical objects as well as photographs displayed on boards hanging from the ceiling.

"Archaeological investigations within the county boundaries unearthed a partial mastodon (unfortunately no longer in exhibitable condition) and some artifacts indicating indigenous settlements near where the creek intersects with the river." Here, their guide paused at one display case and they could see arrow heads, pottery fragments, and a dusty old model of the landscape with interesting excavated features labelled, long ago, on now-yellowed typescript tags. It smelled of mothballs.

"European settlement increased in the early nineteenth century when many families arrived from the United Kingdom, in particular from Yorkshire, Lincolnshire, and Nottinghamshire. " The student continued, at a bit of a drone, while they wandered around the room, paying more direct attention to any exhibit that caught their interest.

After a half hour they had seen pretty much everything and popped inside a jail cell to see what it was like, looking out the minuscule windows and experiencing a whiff of claustrophobia. Once the spiel was finished, they followed the student back up the narrow stairs and were quickly outside again.

They collected Cassie and made their way back to the car. Cassie flopped with her nose pointed out of the hatchback rear window, looking somewhat forlornly at the park as they moved away and turned onto the main street. In the distance Cassie recognized Harry, who was crossing the road at a slow jog.

12

Harry opened the door to the Legion and went inside. Joe Russo had died of cancer on Tuesday and the boys were getting together for a send-off. He had been at high school with Joe, who was not young, and the death was expected. Everyone knew the disease had been particularly brutal and so the mood inside was an odd combination of grief for a comrade fallen too soon and relief the battle was over.

He got a beer and went and joined a cluster of tables. Before long they were happily reminiscing (really, as Gary Sommerson would gleefully tell his wife later, "shooting the shit"), mostly about football games won and lost forty or fifty years earlier. Somehow, as the stories meandered back around to what each had done after their high school athletic careers ended, it emerged that some spent long years working for the phone company.

"Things have changed so much now. Glad I didn't have to stick around and learn the new stuff. Can't teach an old dog new tricks!" said Bill Emmerfelt, who was slightly younger than Harry.

"No, no, all computers now — they don't need any people, let alone us," said John Thurlow. "Yep. It was Bob Micklethwaite that started everything down that track." He waved a hand to the side, mentally positioning all these technology changes in a space they no longer paid attention to, and then he paused. "Funny, we had his wake here," he calculated for a moment, "fifty years ago. 'Round this time of year, too." Harry's ears perked up at that name.

"Car accident, wasn't it?" asked Gary.

"Yep. Strangest thing. He was the most mechanically skilled guy I ever met and then one day his breaks fail and Boom! Dead in the gully on a rainy night."

"Bob Micklethwaite you say?" asked Harry. "I handled the estate clean-up for a Mrs. Micklethwaite back in the spring, any relation?"

"Aye, she was his widow," said John.

"You know, I found the oddest thing in her basement," continued Harry, with a pause, catching their attention. "It was this gigantic box filled with glass bulbs."

John Thurlow smacked his thigh and exclaimed: "The bulbs! She still had them?"

Everyone looked at John, anticipating an explanation, which came after he relished the attention for a moment. "Those were Bob's special project. I was the one that packed them in that box after he died and took it and some other stuff over to her house," John said, still proud of his long-ago act of consideration.

Harry thought for a moment. "You know, I sold that box to this kid who's in IT at the university and he's trying to figure out what they were for."

John nodded, but on thinking it through, shook his head cautiously: "I don't know exactly."

Harry continued "Well, I have his contact info, can I send him your email and explain that you collected them in that box and knew Bob?"

"Sure, happy to help if I can," said John, swigging on his beer.

❊ ❊ ❊

As Harry was having his somewhat enlightening discussion at the Legion, Ben and Jen were stopped at Annie's Apple Hut, selecting from among the racks of pies. After careful consideration, they settled on a large dutch apple and six raspberry tarts. At the last minute they picked up six mixed blueberry and cherry tarts as well.

"That should last a day or two," Ben said, meaning to be realistic, rather than offensive.

"Hey! Eating for two here" said Jen, who knew he had just spoken without thinking and made mocking expressions of offence, causing Ben to throw up his hands. They got back in the car and were home in a reasonable amount of time. Jen decanted two tarts on a plate and set up camp on the couch.

Ben happened to be in the bedroom when an email pinged onto his phone. It was from Harry: *Hello Ben, I ran into a guy at the Legion today who knew Bob Micklethwaite, Mrs. Micklethwaite's husband. They worked together at the Central Office and get this, he is the one who collected the bulbs after Bob died and gave them to his widow. His name is John Thurlow …*

The email continued with John's contact details and Harry's sign off. Ben stood in the dim room for a moment and composed and sent a reply to Harry, and then he went out into the living room.

"Hey, Harry's found a guy who worked with Bob Micklethwaite and knows about the bulbs."

"No kidding?"

"Yeah, I am just sending him my number," which he did, inviting John Thurlow to call him when it was convenient. Then he went to the kitchen and cut a slice of the dutch apple pie, heating it up in the microwave and adding a scoop of vanilla ice cream. It was a blissful hour of couch surfing and dessert eating. Jen had gotten up to clean the dishes and tidy the kitchen when Ben's phone rang.

"Hi. This is John Thurlow. Is that Ben?"

"Yes, thanks for calling. Harry mentioned you know about these bulb things?"

"I do. A little bit. It was a long time ago though, and I didn't really understand the details, even when Bob explained it at the time. What would you like to know?"

"Well, we noticed that the bulbs have dates on them and there seem to be two for the days after Bob died. Do you know how that could be possible?"

"Yep. You see he had this rig that was connected into the core of the circuits. It had a bunch of timers and switches and held maybe a dozen or more of those bulbs in two rows. Bob would set them up and change a row out every week or two, I think. I didn't know they had dates on them, but that would make sense. Maybe one for each day? Fourteen bulbs for two weeks? He always did it before he left for the weekend on Friday. A couple days after he died I took all of them out of the rig and put them in the box with the others and then took that to Mrs. Micklethwaite."

"Okay, so that explains that. What did he tell you the rig was doing?"

"He was hoping to use it to better understand local phone traffic, I think. Maybe try to set up a system to charge usage billing, kinda like what we have now with the cell phones. He was way ahead of his time, Bob Micklethwaite. Anyway, he was recording something about the local circuit traffic on the bulbs."

"How did he read them?"

"Hmm. I never saw that he did anything with them, other than collect them in that box. I expect he would need to take them to where he got the bulbs to start with, in order to read them, and that was the R&D labs. Bob had worked there for years. I remember that the bulbs themselves were some sort of castoff from a project that failed. They'd manufactured a bunch of them, sometime after the war, but they didn't work right — or maybe something else didn't work right in the project, and they didn't go forward with it, but they'd already made a bunch of bulbs. Anyway, Bob was using them to record data. I am pretty sure about that. No one really needed the data though, so no one got around to reading them. They were his pet project and maybe no one from Head Office really knew about it, especially after he died…"

13

On Monday Ben awoke with a plan for pitching the bulbs as a research project to Sam Eide fully formed in his mind. He definitely knew enough about them to justify spending some time on it. Sam would probably be interested if he thought he could write a journal article after any investigation or experiments they conducted, and it seemed, at least to Ben, that was likely.

As these thoughts were percolating through his just-awakened brain, Jen was stirring beside him and slowly, subconsciously, hatching her own investigative compulsion.

When she awoke disgruntled, she initially attributed it to the pregnancy, but after resolutely putting one foot in front of the other to get herself up and to work, the feeling persisted. She was anxious, even angry about something, and it did not take too long to figure out what: Julie McNally.

There was a little girl out there, completely defenceless, and no one knew where she was. Whatever had happened to her, it was clear she received no justice.

Sitting at her desk, she opened an interface to the Missing Persons register and entered the details she knew. The database kicked up the profile and the newspaper article they had copied on the weekend proved to be fundamentally correct.

She then accessed the investigation file database to see what the regional police had been able to do when they were brought in; she assumed, correctly that the town police records for that far back had never been uploaded to the central system. The file was a little sparse given the year of disappearance and the fact that not all original paperwork had been scanned.

There was an investigation summary indicating the regional police had arrived late on the Friday (so the article in the Saturday paper was slightly behind events, including coverage only up to the chief's press conference that morning).

They immediately reviewed the casework up to that point and there was a summary sheet: two hundred forty-eight interviews conducted, fifteen persons of interest identified (ten carnival employees, three with criminal records, and five people local to the county, including one with previously identified predatory tendencies towards children). All but three of whom had been eliminated by alibis.

The summary report noted the local police had not succeeded in identifying any strangers to the community who may have attended the fair on the Friday and pointed out this was an urgent investigative priority.

While the summary sheet was in the computer, as well as some investigators' notes, none of the actual interviews appeared, although there was a note to the effect that the town police had provided photostat copies.

Jen concluded this key paperwork might still be in central storage and as she worked for an affiliated police division, she could simply send a request in. Whatever dusty remnants could still be found would be brought up from the vaults somewhere. She did just that, filling out an electronic requisition. Having expended five or ten minutes on this, she needed to get on with her day, but she felt better for trying to do something.

❊ ❊ ❊

Meanwhile, Ben sent an email to Sam Eide:
I've found something you might be interested in. Old phone company R&D labs technology (50s-60s, probably). You got any time this week to check it out?

Sam did not answer for several hours but when he did, they set a time for Tuesday, after work.

14

It was a quarter to six in the evening on Tuesday when Sam Eide turned up at Ben's office, mildly curious. He started off with a broad grin and appropriate pleasantries:

"I understand congratulations are in order?"

"Indeed. We are expecting a new arrival in November."

"Great to hear."

Ben pulled the plastic pencil case holding the 1969 bulbs out of a drawer and popped the lid, rustling aside some of the tissue. Sam leaned over and peered in: "Hmmm, what have we got here … Can I?" he asked gesturing with a hand that sought to pick one up.

"Sure. They were created in the phone company research and development labs just outside the city, sometime after the war. This guy told me they were part of some project that failed. However, an engineer and operations manager named Bob Micklethwaite took the bulbs and repurposed them — and, get this — he was using them to record data about traffic on the phone circuits in the late 1960s and into 1970."

"Why did he stop in 1970? Did they start with disks at that point?"

"No. He died, suddenly, in a car accident."

"Ouch."

Sam rolled the bulb between his fingers much as Jen had done three weeks before. Ben continued:

"Each bulb has been rubber stamped with a date, and John — he's the guy that knew Bob — says they were inserted in a rig with timers that was connected into the phone circuits, so it seems that they were making a daily data haul. They definitely hold data of some kind."

"How'd they read them?"

"That is where I am stumped. Apparently, to read them, John thinks Bob would have taken them back to the R&D facility. However, John says he never saw him take them anywhere; they were just put in this large box, which is what I bought. John did not think the guys at head office really knew what Bob was up to or that he really needed to do anything with the data he was collecting."

"Well, we've got some white papers — even some corporate archives from that lab — in the department library. They were donated when the lab was shut down and sold off about twenty years ago. Let me take a couple photos to work with."

"You can take the box if you want — I have plenty more at home."

"Great, I'll let you know what I find."

Ben packed up for the day and headed home. When he got to the condo, Jen was cooking. It smelled good: sage and onions and something roasting. And a plum and almond torte was just out of the oven. It was a bit unusual for her to tuck into so much cooking on a Monday, especially since they still had a lot of pies and tarts to work through, but he was not going to question it, extra pastries were never a bad thing.

15

The file arrived from storage to Jen's office on Wednesday late in the afternoon. She finished out the workday and cracked it open. It contained a couple of hundred interviews, reports, and memos, photocopied double-sided and bull-clipped to a cover sheet indicating they were sent over from the town police.

Almost fifty years old, the graphite was slaking off in places and the sheets were yellowed. Jen decided it would be good to scan it and then work from an electronic copy. She went to the office copier, removed the bull clip and some staples and paper clips on other documents, and then scanned the entire thing cover to cover.

Back at her desk, she sent the scan into a queue for administrators to review, process into sections, and upload to the investigation file system. Once uploaded, she would be able to use a secure app on her phone or tablet to review the entire thing on her own time. Then, she ordered a pizza to be ready in half an hour and left. She picked Cassie up before going to get the pizza on her way home.

Ben was already eating a sandwich made from Monday night's roast when she came through the door with the pizza and the dog, which did not really matter given the accelerated rate they now ate any and all food in the apartment.

She put the pizza on the coffee table, washed her hands and grabbed some paper towels and then flopped on the couch and started on a slice. Ben gave Cassie some kibble, then joined her and took it upon himself to turn on the TV and pick something to watch. Once they were done eating, Cassie needed a walk and Ben got up to take her out.

While they were gone an automated message pinged onto Jen's phone:

the expanded investigation file had processed and was now available for viewing. She opened it up, skipping past the material reviewed earlier. The interviews were originally filed alphabetically by interviewee surname but there was also a timeline of all interviews conducted and Jen decided to review them in more of a chronological than alphabetical order.

The first interview was contained in the initial report of Julie McNally's disappearance. It was what a constable had recorded when her mother came into the police station at 8:45 PM on Friday, October 9th, 1970.

> Mrs. McNally has not seen her daughter, Julie, aged 11, since approximately 12:40 PM. Julie returned from school (half-day) for lunch before heading out to the fair...

It took Jen a minute to grasp that the start of the Fall Fair meant students were let out early that Friday.

> She was expected home around 6:30 for dinner which usually starts at 6:45 PM.

A note in the side margin in the constable's handwriting: *Mother very agitated. Convinced something is <u>wrong</u>.*

The main text continued:

> Mother has made a number of phone calls and determined that Julie is not with any friends or acquaintances. All her close friends returned from the fair for dinner. Julie was seen at the fair by several people. According to phone call Mrs. McNally had with ~~her~~ ^Julie's friend Loraine Sorenson: at around 4:00 PM Julie wanted to go to the animal pens but her friends wanted to get in more carnival rides before dinner. Julie left to go to the animal pens alone. Father went to fair around 7:35 and looked over the entire grounds but did not find her and called Mrs. McNally from arena around 8:30 indicating she should come in to file report while he drives around looking for his daughter.

The report listed her particulars: *4 feet 6 inches tall, 80 pounds, long brown hair, and gray eyes.* A small wallet sized photo was attached, probably offered directly from Mrs. McNally's pocketbook. It was clear the constable had taken it seriously, which surprised Jen, given that historically police had not understood the importance of investigating missing children immediately.

She guessed, correctly, that the constable was so alert because the fair was in town — a special occurrence that annually increased risky behaviour and accidents.

He had called his supervisor at 8:58, apparently while Mrs. McNally was filling out a sheet of information on the people she had already called looking for Julie. That sheet was attached to the report interview.

Additional marginal notes showed dispatch notified patrol officers at the fair at 9:01 PM that they had a missing child and gave her description. Another notation was entered in code to the effect that the reporting constable and another officer went to the fairgrounds to meet up with the patrol officers and begin an initial search and investigation.

The bottom of the report was signed by Marilyn McNally in a shaky script, on what Jen imagined had to be the worst day of her life.

∗ ∗ ∗

The patrol officers and constables from the station apparently conducted a rapid thirty minute search of the arena, barns, and the carnival rides to no avail, at which point a detective arrived and the investigation began in earnest. Based on what she could see, Jen guessed that he had ordered at least six other officers to systematically interview fair employees, using photocopied blow-ups of the wallet snapshot, to try to establish a timeline of sightings as well as rapidly identify any aberrant occurrences anyone had witnessed.

Three municipal employees with knowledge of the grounds — one with a set of master keys — were brought in to accompany three officers who spent the next two hours conducting an exhaustive search. By midnight they were convinced that wherever Julie McNally was, she was no longer at the fair. The interviewing had continued late into the night.

Around five on Saturday morning the decision was made to call in some scent dogs and by six every single town police officer and six of the seven secretaries and dispatchers were at the fairgrounds awaiting instructions (leaving only one person behind at the station to monitor the switch board). As the sun rose, providing light, Chief Cadworth quickly organized the group and asked them all to fan out, walking along every street and pathway — not just the routes back to her house — carefully looking for any sign of Julie.

At the same time, Chief Cadworth drove to the McNally residence to inform the parents they were sure Julie was not at the fairgrounds and to explain that scent dogs were coming in and they would need an article of Julie's clothing. Cadworth noted both McNallys were exhausted, and Mrs. McNally's brother was there. He decided not to interview them at that time and further interviews with both parents did not appear until farther down the list, later Saturday afternoon.

Looking back, Jen found some marginal notes on the scent dog requisition to the effect that the dogs had alerted near the hog pens but had not been able to trace the trail. The decision was made not to close the fair and that decision was later questioned by the regional police, who were worried about a compromised crime scene; this generated a written justification still included in the file.

The gist of it was that there was no evidence of a crime scene at the fairgrounds, although the town police acknowledged it could be an abduction site (if so, it was likely impossible to generate evidence from). The police needed information from those who had been at the fair the day before and half the county would come right to them if they left the fair open. Additionally, they wanted the carnival to continue as expected to ensure no one from that operation was unaccounted for or was known to have split town. All the carnies were out of town strangers, and already, clearly, the top suspects.

The justification provided to regional police also described how the county police station's women dispatchers and secretaries, including four part-timers and retired employees called in by the others, apparently set up a phalanx of tables across the fairground entrance and worked with ticket collectors.

They recorded every single person admitted to the fair after that point, showed each a picture of Julie and asked them four questions: (1) had they attended the fair on Friday, (2) had they seen Julie (and if so details were recorded) and (3) had they seen anything odd, or (4) did they know anything else about her whereabouts?

While these surveys had been used to identify several people whose later interviews appeared in the file, the questionnaires themselves (probably hundreds, even thousands of them) were not in the current scanned documents and Jen made a mental note that she might have to ask someone to dig them out. At that point Jen fell asleep on the couch.

16

And so it was, over the next week in the evenings, after chores were done and dinner was eaten, that Jen worked her way through the file, an hour or two at a time, making some notes as she went. Ben noticed she was up to something but decided not to bother her, thinking it might be work she had to finish before the baby arrived.

They successfully unpacked the baby shower gifts from the linen closet and Jen had compiled a long list of supplies for Ben to collect after work and tote home every day, much like a nesting bird.

In the five days after Julie disappeared the town police managed to get a reasonably clear picture of her movements up until about 4 PM on the Friday. After lunch, she went from her own house to Loraine Sorenson's house, five doors away (Jen mapped it — the street was not far from Unity Street where the Micklethwaites lived).

The two girls had walked along the expected route to the fair entrance where they met up with more girls walking into the fair from other directions. Loraine had been interviewed, with her parents, three times. The third interview was instigated by the Sorensons when Loraine spontaneously remembered additional details over the following week.

Loraine did not recall anyone odd from that day. No cars had passed them slowly, so far as she could remember. No one, let alone a strange boy or man, had stopped to speak to them.

The girls had walked around for about half an hour checking out the fair and letting their lunches settle, before they bought tickets and went on some rides. Loraine remembered the bumper car ride operator well and was slightly afraid of him.

He turned out to be a hard-drinking and smoking middle-aged man with very bad teeth but no criminal record. He was put through the ringer by the police, but had a sequence of strong alibis from constantly operating his ride before being tasked with an emergency fix to the Ferris wheel that commenced about 3:30 and took almost two hours.

The girls took a break from the rides around 2:45 and went towards the arena to get some candy. Loraine had gotten taffy and shared it with some of the others. She remembered that Julie bought a caramel apple.

While eating they walked through the arena to look at the exhibits (reading this brought to Jen's mind the competition notices and peg boards she saw on entering the arena weeks ago). The group of girls stopped and read Julie's poem posted on the poetry board. In recalling this, Loraine started crying uncontrollably and the interview came to a halt.

By noon on Saturday there was zero evidence of an accident and pretty much everyone on the investigation assumed they were dealing with abduction. As Loraine and the other girls had gone back to the rides while Julie went in the opposite direction, it was possible Julie had left the fairgrounds and been abducted walking home sometime between when she was last seen just before 4 PM and a later time, when she would have left to make it home for dinner.

Worse still, it was also possible she left the fair, not walked directly home, and something had happened in an unknown location. Given these possibilities, the investigation had focused for several hours on trying to determine if anyone had seen her leave the fairgrounds.

The exit from the fair was a set of turnstiles designed so that people could not sneak in for free. Those turnstiles were quite close to the entrance and monitored by the ticket sellers there. No one recalled seeing any girl of Julie's age come through the exit turnstile by herself.

They could not be sure she had not come through accompanied by other children or an adult, but each person was fairly sure they would have noticed a child leaving the fairgrounds alone because generally speaking they kept an eye out for safety issues. Given that she was no longer at the fairgrounds, it seemed she must have left with someone or in a group, either on foot or, possibly, in a vehicle from one of the service entrances.

It was not likely she had gotten over the boundary fence by herself. For one, it just did not seem like something she would try to do on a whim, and no one could come up with any other reason why she would need to climb it. It was chain link and quite high, with angled top extensions in most places — designed to protect expensive municipal equipment: snowplows, sanders, the Zamboni stored in the arena parking lot as well as to thwart the nighttime aspirations of teenaged vandals.

The service exits for vehicles were gated as another property security measure (many expensive trailers, farm equipment, and trucks came to the fair, as well as prize-winning animals). The three people who had manned the gate near the arena, through which the animal trailers passed, were absolutely positive that no trucks and only a few cars had left that day and none of them had a child passenger.

The field gate at the far end of the grounds, through which all the large carnival ride trailers and antique farm equipment passed, was not manned but this was because it was padlocked. All the heavy equipment had been brought in no later than the day before and then the access was closed and locked as required by the fair's insurers to eliminate the risk of vehicles or equipment running over fairgoers once they were milling about on the field.

They considered the possibility the padlock could have been tampered with or the abductor had a key. However, there was no evidence of this on the lock and if the kidnapper had driven across the field in a car to get to the gate, it would have been highly noticeable to many hundreds of people, including the nine people that were stuck at the top of the disabled Ferris wheel from about 3:25 until 5:00, who literally had nothing to do but watch all the human activity occurring on the field below them.

As much as the regional police would later criticize the town police for failing to identify strangers who had visited the fair on the Friday, it was clear they tried to do that. However, Jen spotted a major blind spot that may have crippled the investigation early on. As they questioned huge numbers of people at the fair, they unfortunately asked for descriptions of any suspicious person who had been observed attending the fair *alone*.

They had assumed an abductor would be a lone wolf, without considering the possibility of a pair (or group) of predators, who could more easily blend in. It was probably unsurprising that no isolated individual, particularly a stranger, had attended the opening day of the fair and that this inquiry had resulted in no leads.

On Thursday, a week later, Jen put her tablet down in the living room, went in and brushed her teeth and got ready for bed. She checked online to see if Cassie could go to the fair. Unfortunately, pets were not allowed on the fairgrounds.

"Would you feel like going to the county fair this weekend?" she asked her husband.

"Sounds good," he said, half asleep already.

Checking the weather, Saturday looked a good day to go, and Jen used her phone to book Cassie in for an extra session with their dog walker.

17

Fortunately, Saturday morning dawned with warm fall weather, although the pleasant day ensured that on arriving at the fair it took a good long while to find street parking but Ben enjoyed the autumn street scene as they walked on town sidewalks towards the grounds, with leaves dropping from the large old trees.

Jen was thinking how this was part of the route Julie McNally and her friends had taken so many years before. Once they arrived, she took a hard look at the gates and the entrance kiosks, spotting the exit turnstiles. They looked old and seemed likely to be the ones from 1970. Getting in line, they moved forward until it was their turn to pay the entrance fee and pass through into a space they recognized, but which had transformed into something entirely different.

To the left was the grassy expanse that typically hosted the market tents on Sundays. Now the entire field was completely full, with an arcade, carnival rides, and a long row of steam-powered farm equipment as well as hundreds, possibly thousands, of people.

In the distance Jen could see that the gate they normally drove through at the far end was indeed closed off and padlocked and for the first time she really paid attention to the high chain-link fences that surrounded the property. In front of them was the gravel parking lot for the arena, devoid of cars and playing host to food stands, almost entirely candy.

A sequence of cages and temporary fencing created a bunch of animal pens on the right side. Those pens continued on to a long, low set of barns and stables Jen had never really noticed before. These structures were clearly very old, possibly a hundred years or more, and likely were built at a time when the weekly market had included animals for sale.

The barns wrapped along the right side of the property around towards the back of the arena in an area Jen could not see from where she stood. A trackway ran through the pens from the back of the arena to a vehicle gate about fifty feet to the right of the pedestrian entrance.

Jen took the lead and they headed off towards the arcade and rides, stopping at a kiosk to buy a small packet of ride tickets (she would only be able to go on one or two of the more sedate options). What Jen really wanted, to start with, was a ride on the Ferris wheel. Leading Ben towards it, they stood on the ramp, currently empty as the wheel was full and the ride had just started.

"Are you sure this is okay? You're eight months pregnant." Instinctively, Ben did not like the idea of his wife getting on that contraption. "How old is this thing?" Ben asked the operator, causing Jen to smile to herself both at his protectiveness and because the answer to that question was exactly what she needed to know.

"It's 52 years old, but don't worry, very well maintained and refurbished and we've never had an accident at this fair," said the operator. Jen did not volunteer her knowledge of the fact that nine people had been trapped atop the thing for two hours on October 9th, 1970.

"It's safe so long as the weight limit isn't exceeded, and the safety bar can close." The operator eyed the two of them "I think you should be okay. To be honest we've had blokes with beer guts bigger than the two of you together and they've been fine. I'll check your clearances carefully once this ride comes to a stop and you get on."

Jen was determined to ride the Ferris wheel and pressed Ben's forearm, "it'll be fine, the views will be spectacular."

The operator concurred with Jen's statement and took three tickets from each of them, "best view of the town there is."

"Is it always set up here?" Jen asked.

"Yep. County tradition. You'll see why when you get to the top."

Moments later the operator pressed a lever, and the ride came to a stop, he disembarked the passengers from the carriage sitting level with the platform and motioned for Jen and Ben to climb in. They fit comfortably enough, even after he pressed the safety bar down, on which they could rest their hands.

The wheel jerked into motion and they rotated backwards, the carriage swaying gently. The next people were let off and a trickle of people joining the queue were in turn seated into the next available carriage. This continued and with a few progressions Jen could start observing from high up specifically what parts of the fairgrounds were visible from the Ferris wheel. Since they were the first people on for this ride, they stopped at every position on the wheel while the operator loaded people off and on.

The surrounding landscape was breathtaking when they reached the top. The spires of the town rising and receding into the distance. They recognized the cupola from the old town hall and could see the building that housed the library. Rolling hills, fields, and forests stretched out in all directions and the meandering path of the creek became apparent. More importantly, Jen realized how visible everything happening at the fair truly was to anyone at the top of the Ferris wheel.

The only exceptions were inside the buildings and the small area behind the arena which, even from this height and distance, was still blocked off by the massive size of the structure.

A few weathered wood cabins situated among the antique farm equipment were not open to view and there were some trailers associated with the carnival equipment and the arcade, but these were small spaces with people either entering and exiting continuously or standing in close proximity.

Any disturbance associated with a struggle, even between an adult and a small child would be highly noticeable both to crowds on the ground and anyone sitting still on the wheel. The last people in line sat down and the wheel started to turn smoothly, picking up speed. Ben clasped Jen's hand and she put her mental mission to one side, enjoying the experience.

"You know in five years, when she's big enough, we'll have to bring her here," Ben said, meaning their daughter.

Jen struggled to smile.

They went on the Merry-go-round as well, exhausting their pack of ten tickets, and then meandered through the arcade trying their luck at supposed games of skill. Ben won a pink teddy bear, which was great for the nursery, and Jen triumphantly plonked it into her tote.

An hour spent wandering among the tractors and threshers, and Ye Olde Poste Office, proved a nice respite from the modern world. Ben enjoyed a local enthusiast's presentation on how farm equipment rapidly evolved in the nineteenth century with the advent of industrialization; he started looking at the large steam-powered machinery with increased interest.

Slowly, they worked their way back around towards the arena and candy stands, stopping for peameal bacon on a bun and apple cider. The arena seemed the next logical step and they went inside, finding the oil painted doors, closed on their last visit, now wedged open, allowing the vast expanse of the space to open like a cathedral.

Near the doors several large peg boards as well as some blanket racks and clothes lines were covered in beautiful handmade patch-work quilts. These were the candidates and winners for the Best Quilt Prize — pinned triumphantly with sateen prize ribbons — but also included some quilts available for sale.

They found a small stack of cot quilts and on looking through it, near the bottom spotted a lovely lavender, pink, blue and white quilt. It was $150 and after a bit of discussion they decided to buy it as a worthy and practical heirloom.

A silver-haired lady came over to assist them. "Have you found something you like?"

"Yes, thank you, but we are not done looking around the fair yet and we probably shouldn't carry it around where it could get dirty..."

"Not a problem, I will put it on the reserve pile with your name and phone number and you can come back to pay and pick it up before you leave. We reserve for one day only." Jen wrote her name and number on the back of a business card Ben took from his wallet, and the lady took a straight pin and attached it to the quilt, which was then deposited in a blanket box beneath a table nearby.

"If you decide not to take the quilt, please call me so we can return it to the sale pile" and she handed over a card with her number written on the back, which Jen pocketed.

They then set off into the depths of the arena, where glass cases and tables were filled with a bounty of preserves and handsome, overly large vegetable specimens. Cases of cakes and pies transitioned to sales stands, such as the honey stall that was normally part of the weekly Farmers' Market. They had covered about half the arena and bought some jam when they decided to go out the back door and look at the animals.

The Zamboni gate was open in the rink-end sideboards and on passing through they were in a cinderblock corridor leading to a hallway under the stands and a large garage door and emergency fire exit. The garage door was up to make a large pass through to the outside but there were no people milling about.

It caught Jen's attention that this door was relatively new, both because it still had a shiny factory finish and because old hinge marks were visible in the paint on the wall to the left.

A much larger set of old barn doors had recently been removed and replaced with an industrial-sized rolling track door (that seemed to operate with a gearbox on the wall) and next to it, a new metal emergency pedestrian exit door, with some of the old door space now infilled with new cinder blocks, freshly painted.

Outside was a small parking lot which held an ambulance, a fire engine, a patrol car, and several generic sedans that probably belonged to fair officials and volunteers. The assemblage of emergency vehicles was part of a plan that would go into place in the event of a crisis or disaster at the fairgrounds. Jen wondered if there had been such a plan before Julie McNally went missing.

Ben and Jen passed behind these vehicles towards the open door at the end of a stable block that jutted out from the barns running the length of the fairground perimeter. Looking over her shoulder, Jen could not see the Ferris wheel from where they were currently standing.

Even before entering the barn, they were assailed by the smell of hay and dung. And once through the door they were at once presented with the backsides of eight horses, each either napping or chomping. They passed behind the horses and went through another doorway into a corner room that was really the end of the long barn. There was a table and shelves, and hooks for holding saddles and harnesses.

"This must be a tack room," said Ben.

On turning right, they went through another door and found not only stalls holding some cows, but larger pens for sheep and pigs. There were a bunch of adorable lambs frolicking or flopping and two incredibly huge hogs with litters of fat little piglets seemingly numbering in the hundreds. Gigantic ribbon rosebuds ("1st Place" and "2nd Place") were stuck to the door handles of these two pens. They stopped a moment or two to take it all in, glad their offspring would be less numerous.

The next barn was accessed by another door up ahead and they could hear from the squawking that it was the chicken coop. Ben was already sniffling somewhat. "I don't think I should go in there," he said. Jen, knowing his allergies could be severe, nodded and they turned around and headed back the way they had come.

Once back in the arena, they turned left and started walking down the aisle running parallel to the one they had already seen. The first thing they saw was needlework. Cushion covers, table linens, and some framed samplers were proudly displayed. The first prize was awarded to one Gary Linehan, much to Jen's surprise.

Then there were rows of knitting and finally the large aisle transitioned to things made of paper. These were the contenders for the school competitions.

They reached the high school poetry competition first. Terribly earnest rhyming couplets were presented, the individual pages showing a range of personalized fonts and paper colours. Some were surrounded with original graphics and a few hinted at intense, even dark, young urges, barely suppressed.

Ben chuckled in rueful recognition, "maybe we shouldn't pay too much attention to the angst of teenagers right now. We need to stay motivated." Jen laughed, both at his logic and the embarrassed flush of recognition that passed across his face.

They sped along, reaching more sedate high school essays. The titles alone imparted a firm impression of youthful idealism and a global consciousness much more developed than their own had been at that age. The essays were followed by the photography competition. It was a passable simulation of a nationally important modern art exhibit. Ben said: "it's the cameras — and the camera phones — everybody has one ready when a good shot arrives, and the cameras do all the work."

Then they reached paintings and other media pieces, which, it was a relief to discover, were easily recognizable for what they were: the enthusiastic but novice expressions of children and teenagers. It was a bit hard to imagine how the judges had decided from among the hodgepodge which warranted first, second and third prizes. The one exception was the pencil sketches. Here, there was a clear standout: a realistic and evocative portrait of an old woman.

"Now there's some talent," Jen commented, leaning in to read the label.

And then they arrived at the primary school poetry. Jen remembered Julie McNally's poem won this competition five days after she went missing, and that her friend Loraine had burst into tears when recounting how the girls stopped to read the poem the very afternoon Julie disappeared. Almost fifty years ago the girls were where Jen now stood, unaware of what was about to happen.

The poems were all handwritten. Kids were apparently still learning penmanship in school and there was an outside chance that in five years their daughter's education would have some faint resemblance to their own. Each entry had been carefully drafted on inscribed lines and given a calligraphic title. The eight-year-olds compensated for their still unsteady fine-motor skills with determined upstrokes and the occasional overdeveloped curlicue.

As they walked on, the writing from lower grades appeared and the effort involved became more obvious and adorable. Jen paused and could not help but hug her belly with a growing pride in the accomplishments of little ones. Ben, on the same wavelength, leaned over and kissed her on the temple.

They soon found themselves back in the quilt display near the entrance. A different grey-haired lady manned the table and they headed towards her to pay for the blanket.

"Hi, we've a cot quilt on hold," Jen said.

The lady smiled and opening the blanket box, asked: "name?"

"Jen Mahoney."

The lady fumbled and wrestled a bit with the armful of quilts in the box. "Hmmm. There isn't one under that name, but this one is not tagged," and she pulled out their distinctive white, blue, and purple selection from earlier.

"That's the one. Should have my name on a card pinned to it."

The lady flipped it over and unfolded it, checking carefully for the pinned-on card, but it was gone.

18

Jen was tired when they got back to the car and, after stowing the quilt, teddy bear and jam in the hatchback, climbed into the passenger seat and nodded off before Ben even left the parking spot. While she slept, the wheels continued turning in her mind. Slowly, some cogs rotated into place while others proved impossible to fit, pushing one set of possibilities to the background while other gears remained engaged and potentially implicated in what happened in October of 1970. She woke up groggily as the car descended into their parking garage but had shaken off any sleepiness by the time they were in the elevator. When they opened the apartment door, they found Cassie flopped in the warm spot under the window, clearly tuckered-out from her midday romp with the neighbourhood dog walking pack.

Cassie could tell they had gone somewhere interesting without her though and wondered where it was. Some sniffing indicated they had been out in the country. *And there had been bacon.* She was slightly miffed.

Jen took the cot quilt and teddy bear into the nursery and positioned them in the crib then went back to the kitchen and assessed their options for supper. It was not good.

"You want to go out?" she queried her husband.

"Sure, I've had a hankering for Thai all week."

They changed into clean, less casual clothes and started traversing the neighbourhood towards the good Thai place. The patio was closed for the season, but the dining room was warm, comfortable, and atmospherically lit.

In their now usual fashion, they semi-consciously over-ordered, getting a full appetizer platter and two entrees. With rice. And extra spring rolls. The waiter brought them drinks and the spring rolls, and they were rapidly munching away. Jen was a bit mentally absent, which Ben was starting to notice.

"How's work going?" he asked.

"Oh, it's fine, it's fine. You?"

"Same. Would you want to try to get away for a mini-break before the baby comes?" Jen assumed he meant a weekend at one of the inns they had tried over the years, no more than half a day's drive outside the city.

"Maybe. We might be taking our chances though. I wouldn't want to go into labour too far out in the country."

"True" Ben said, and still, Jen did not pick up the conversation like she normally might. He decided not to push it. It was not like her to nap for forty minutes in the car either. They enjoyed dinner nonetheless and after an hour or so were walking home, boxes of leftovers in hand. They finished off a season of the British crime drama, took care of some laundry and got into bed.

Lights off, Ben rolled over onto his back and glanced at his wife's profile silhouetted by ambient city light seeping into the darkness. She was looking at the ceiling and paying him absolutely no attention, which was mildly off-putting. Ben could tell she was thinking very intently.

The rotating wheels had done their work. Despite the huge (likely) crime scene presented by the county fair, with its vast expanse and thousands of people, Julie McNally's disappearance was not as intractable as it looked on paper. Now that Jen had seen the fairgrounds in action, she was confident certain possibilities needed to be scratched off the list and others deserved a high degree of focus. The fair was, in some ways, an exceptionally large locked room.

She believed the locals on the ground when they said they did not think Julie had left the fair alone, both because of the way the gates were arranged and because Jen thought that among the constant crowds on the sidewalks outside the fair, heading there or leaving, would have been somebody who knew Julie and would have reported seeing her. Jen had looked up the size of the local schools at the time, the population of the town, and knew the layout of Julie's neighbourhood. This was not an anonymous urban environment: it was a small town running very much to stereotype.

If Julie had not left alone, she had either left under her own volition, and probably with at least two other people, given that the police had so carefully looked for a lone fair attendee and none had been seen. Or, she had not left of her own free will, and must have been immobilized and concealed, and if that was the case, there were several logistical aspects to consider.

The first scenario would indicate a conspiracy, either of multiple people in the group Julie was in — Jen could not help but recall some of the horrific bullying cases of recent years — or, of at least one other person covering up for the fact they were aware of a single actor who had opportunity to interact with Julie and was without an alibi. And when it came to conspiracies like that, cold case detectives have an advantage over their active case brethren. Over time, particularly decades, people talk. Jen needed to spend some time on the Internet, checking for chatter.

19

On Tuesday night Ben said he would be home late, and Jen decanted the last of their Thai leftovers onto a plate, microwaved it, and settled in at the counter with her tablet. She typed "Julie McNally missing" into Google and got a wide range of results from around the world; scrolling through, nothing of obvious relevance appeared. Remembering how successful obituary searching relied on adding a location, she tried the name plus the county. This generated what looked like a handful of useful results.

The first few were posts to the forum of an encyclopedic website devoted to unsolved murders. The earliest post appeared in a long thread discussing a probable serial killer operating in the 1950s and 1960s along a major highway system not far away. A user named *LoriW* had joined the thread and posted details about Julie's disappearance asking others to comment on whether they thought she could be a victim in this series of killings.

The responses made for interesting reading.

> *EvilHunter15: Do you know about any searches for a body? Did they check near the highway?*

> *LoriW: The search focused on the fairgrounds and surrounding area, as far as I know. They searched the creek gully very thoroughly.*

> *EvilHunter15: Looked at it on Satellite view, this guy is known for dumping his victims off bridges close to the highway into water (I don't see any bridges near here), but other than that, he really did not try to conceal the bodies. I suppose they must have checked all Jane Does recovered since then against this case. If they recover a child everyone checks really thoroughly. I don't think there are any unidentified remains of anyone under 15 anywhere within two, three day's drive.*

> *LoriW: We are pretty sure no trace of her has ever been found. Not in the*

country.

A third commenter chimed in:

> *KittenBecky: 1970 seems a little late. Right now it looks like he stopped in summer 1965 (although maybe he just started concealing things at that point?). He never struck as close to the city as this though.*
>
> *EvilHunter15: Good point.*
>
> *Admin: Lori, you might want to start a new thread. It's really hard to do comparisons of historical crimes when there is no crime scene. Try the Missing Persons forum.*

And Jen thought to herself how true that abrupt admin dictum was, not just on this forum, but in real life. Without a crime scene or body, the case had gotten nowhere. Sure, they threw everything they had at it the first and second week, but from the investigation perspective, it was not certain a crime had been committed and Jen knew how quickly budgets and manpower start to weigh on police executive decision-making.

Whoever was responsible for Julie's disappearance managed not only to abduct her — quite possibly from within the fair's fenced and gated perimeter — but leave no trace whatsoever. Was there a very cunning and practiced criminal behind this? Or had they managed to commit the abduction spontaneously and somehow horrendous luck had been in their favour? Had it all followed some sort of plan? It seemed the complete absence of evidence spoke to an organized offender.

Jen could see from her search results that LoriW took the Admin's advice and started a dedicated thread on Julie's disappearance in the Missing Persons sub forum. EvilHunter and KittenBecky joined the new post, continuing the conversation.

After a cut and paste of the original post from the other thread to start, EvilHunter had encouraged LoriW to post links to everything that was available on the web. There was not much, just the public Missing Persons database entry and a few other almost incidental things including some newspaper coverage from websites whose online archival presence happened to go back far enough.

Jen checked the links and did some more searching and other than this forum activity, there was no chatter about the case on the web. None. No one had unburdened their heart or conscience (honestly or not) into the electronic void to hint they knew something about the disappearance or the perpetrators. There were essentially no online suggestions, anywhere, describing what Julie's fate had been. EvilHunter and KittenBecky noticed the same thing.

> *EvilHunter15: You know it is unusual for a case like this to have so little information or conversation online. It's strange.*
>
> *KittenBecky: Are you thinking cover-up?*
>
> *EvilHunter15: No, not that. Cover-up would probably generate even more commentary – assuming the abundance of conspiracy theorists were able to snag it at all. It's just really weird. OP, it does not really seem to match with any known serial activity at the time.*
>
> *LoriW: What do you think that means?*
>
> *EvilHunter15: I can't put my finger on it. Any chance her friends or family had something to do with it?*
>
> *LoriW: No. Definitely not. Her friends and family loved her. I am sure of it.*

And on reading that comment, Jen felt she had just encountered Loraine Sorenson.

20

Jen took a break from the computer and started cleaning the kitchen and ruminating. When everything was tidy, she unhooked Cassie's leash and dangled it for a few moments, inspiring Cassie to get up from the comforts of her bed and go for an evening walk earlier than usual. On leaving the condo lobby, Jen paused and let Cassie pick the direction. She chose left, and set off at a brisk trot, a furry little bundle of determination much beyond her size and stature.

They made another left turn and covered several blocks without pausing or sniffing before Cassie stopped at a mid-block cross walk. She looked up and implored Jen with her eyes to hit the crosswalk activation button, a command Jen obeyed. After a moment they were moving across towards the sidewalk on the far side, which was at the base of a concrete embankment topped with bushes, trees, and the wrought iron fencing surrounding the cemetery.

Cassie trundled up the sidewalk, which was rising to meet the grade at the top of the escarpment and Jen realized she was heading towards the cemetery gate and their old jogging trails. They had not been here in months due to the pregnancy.

"So, you miss these walks, do you girl?" Jen inquired.

Cassie glanced up and, in her fashion, grinned and nodded at Jen. On reaching the gate (fortunately open until twilight, about 8 PM this time of year) Cassie's tail started wagging. They went through the ornate portal and then Cassie stopped abruptly, sat on her haunches, and started flopping her tail against the ground, looking up at Jen expectantly.

"We're not jogging," Jen explained. She patted her belly for emphasis.

Cassie waggle-nodded her understanding, stood up, and once again set off at a trot, picking a trail in the middle of the grounds. Oddly, she was not sniffing or exploring. She slowed a bit, sensing Jen was putting some effort into the inclines. Then, Cassie stopped and once again sat on her haunches, flopping her tail against the ground several times, as if to make a point. Jen did not know what to make of her behaviour. She had never done this before. Cassie was trying to tell her something.

"C'mon girl, we have to get going, they are closing the gates soon."

Cassie looked up at Jen, but when Jen gave a little pull on the leash, she gave up and understood they needed to make their way out, exiting on the opposite side of the cemetery to the one they had entered on. Once on city sidewalks, Jen navigated home as efficiently as possible.

Back in the condo, Jen fed Cassie and took her tablet to the couch. She opened the case file and started reviewing everything said by or about Loraine Sorenson. If Jen were to take the next logical step, it was important to know who Loraine was and exactly what her actions had been during Julie's disappearance. Was Loraine a viable suspect? Could she know something about what happened and failed to disclose it?

Fundamentally, the group of Julie's friends were each other's alibis. Adults working the candy stands and carnival rides were able to provide limited, slightly non-specific information on the girls' movements. They had been seen buying candy at roughly the time they were supposed to be, and the apple seller was sure she had sold one to Julie herself.

The group of girls, without Julie, were then seen getting on rides shortly after four, a time that could be determined because several carnival workers had switched manning rides when the Ferris wheel stopped working and the Bumper car operator had gone over to work on repairs.

If the girls were responsible for Julie's disappearance, it had happened in a short window of time and they had somehow masterfully concealed her body without leaving the fairground. Or, if they otherwise knew something alarming, they had behaved as if everything was normal.

Either way, they acted with almost impossible sangfroid in the hours after her absence.

There was only one inconsistency in Loraine's account. Mrs. McNally, in recounting Julie's activity for the preceding days, stated that when she arrived home from her weekly hair appointment Thursday night, Julie was saying goodbye to someone on the phone. When she asked Julie who it was, her daughter had implied that it was Loraine. However, when the police questioned Loraine, she denied speaking to Julie on the phone on Thursday.

Even so, Jen was almost inclined to eliminate the girls as suspects and she signed up for an account on the cold case forum.

21

With a profile created, she was able to directly message Lori, and sent the following:

Hi Lori, I noticed your posting about the disappearance of Julie McNally. Are you still interested in this case? I recently came across it. Best, Jen

No sooner had she sent that off than Ben arrived home, and he was strangely dusty.

Jen looked him over: "what has happened to you?"

Ben looked sheepish, "oh, this. We are moving a bunch of equipment out of storage this week. Rush job. Incredibly dirty down there. I need to shower." He wandered into the bedroom, stripping off layers of dusty clothing as he went. He re-emerged, much cleaner, twenty minutes later.

"Sam and I are setting up a mini-lab in the basement. He's got some ideas about the tubes. It's technical though, so I'll spare you." Ben went to the fridge and poured something to drink, "are there leftovers?"

"Nope, I ate the rest of the Thai. Pizza?"

In one smooth motion Ben extracted his phone from his pocket and did a highly practised dance with his fingers. Pizza ordered, he grabbed a less dusty jacket from the closet, depositing house keys into his pocket as he slipped it on. He stooped down to put on his shoes and spoke upwards through his damp and disheveled hair: "How was your day?"

"Eh, not bad. She's been kicking up a storm all day." Ben came over and flopped for a moment on the couch. Jen deposited the tablet on the coffee table, the screen going to sleep just as Ben took a moment to rest his head against Jen's belly.

As if on cue, a one-two punch-kick combination emerged from within. "We may have an MMA fighter on our hands." He ran an arm around Jen's shoulders surreptitiously checking for fatigue or tension and gave her a few gentle pinches to loosen her neck before pecking her on the forehead and then rising to go get the pizza. He had not seen what was on her tablet.

Once he was out the door, she turned on the TV and spent a good five minutes perusing their options before settling on a rerun of a movie from the 1990s. Ben was back through the door in record time and plonked the pizza box next to the sleeping tablet, returning to the kitchen just to wash his hands and grab two plates and napkins. "You want anything to drink?"

"Sure, thanks, glass of water."

Ben filled one and placed it on the plates before bringing everything over. Jen took two small slices and left the rest for Ben, who nestled in very contently: "Ah. I love this movie. They don't make blockbusters like they used to."

"So, tell me about the tubes," Jen inquired.

"Well. Sam has figured out a whole bunch of stuff using old lab archives in the department library. The tubes are so early they only encode for digits zero to nine, so whatever is on there is numbers. Anyway, he has the specs for the original machine. It was really supposed to be more like working memory for a system they thought they'd create while developing mechanical switching, but they couldn't get it to work. Bob realized that if a tube was used once, because of a flaw, it recorded the data in a non-volatile way, reliably at least for one more read."

"Well, that is pretty cool."

"Indeed. Sam thinks we can take the original design and build a system that will read the stored charges off the tubes — the bits, half-bytes really — in positional order and hopefully recover the data. Probably can only get one shot at a clean read with each tube though, given the age, and there isn't really error correction built in or anything..."

"Well, you have to try. Obviously. It's there." She chuckled ever so slightly, poking fun at their geeky determination.

"Obviously," Ben grabbed a final slice of pizza out of the box and took a big bite, very satisfied with himself.

The movie was into a good action sequence at that point, and they let themselves get distracted. Jen's tablet stayed inert and black on the coffee table.

22

S am Eide was gifted with a mind for spotting patterns in data. He just needed to get the data to appear before his eyes. A week after Ben returned home covered in dust, Sam sat in the faculty building basement as late afternoon transitioned to evening, in their newly constructed closet-sized lab, and mounted the tube for 28 December 1969 into his recently built reading device. He had just finished tweaking it after an initial attempt destroyed the data from December 27th.

This time, after the read process was initiated, he had more luck. The charges on the tube, read as a sequence of 0s and 1s were almost instantly transformed into numerals with a special program he had already created.

After a couple of minutes, he had a huge stream of numbers sitting in a text file. He ran a checking algorithm against the raw data and the number file, and the results were good. There were as many bytes of data as expected and none of the reads had generated anything other than a 0-9 numeral. This was not proof that something had not gone wrong with the stored charges or that the read had not skipped anything, but it was the best result they could expect.

He sent Ben a text: *I have data.* Ben replied: *Almost home, email copy?* Sam replied: *Sure.* He sent the text file of numbers to Ben's work email.

No sooner had he done so than a little sequence of numbers in the first line popped out at Sam: 0001 followed several digits later by 0002. His eyes scanned forward, there was no 0003 or 0004 but there was a 0005 and it was the same number of digits apart — fourteen — from the 0002 as the 0002 was from the 0001. The 0001 was removed fourteen digits from the start of the file.

Sam copied the data to a new file and quickly broke the long stream of numbers up by inserting a line break after every eighteen characters. He was looking at lines with fourteen characters followed initially by three, but after a while only two, zeros. The zeros were followed by numbers, which, while they did not reliably increase one value per line, did run in ascending sequence.

He suspected he knew what the final four characters on each line were and confirmed it by scrolling down to a line ending 0059, which was followed not by 0060 but 0100. The last four digits must be time stamps. He scrolled down rapidly through the file and found that the data was created using a twenty-four hour clock, the last line ending 2359.

The fourteen digits starting each line also had little bursts of repetition, primarily in digits one to three and eight to ten. Testing a theory, Sam copied seven characters from the start of one line he found near the middle of the file and used Find to see if it appeared again.

It did, fourteen times, starting on a line timestamped 0906 in the morning and ending on one stamped 1745. Sometimes it was at the beginning of the line and sometimes it held position eight to fourteen. Sam quickly wrote a little program to get the data into a spreadsheet in separate columns, breaking it up into three digits, four digits, three digits, four digits, and the time stamp. He ran a quick analysis on the two three-digit columns and concluded they held only nine distinct three-digit numbers.

He was sure what the data was at that point, and ideas about what they could do with it started percolating happily through his mind. First things first: they might not have equal success with all the tubes. He loaded the next tube and repeated the entire process successfully, and then did the same for the two remaining tubes in his possession, creating four separate data files, each one named after the day stamped on its respective tube.

Mission accomplished for the night, he got up, closing and locking the office on his way out to dinner. Pulling out his phone, he sent a text to Ben: *I think what we have here is a primitive call log. This could be a really interesting — unprecedented — research data set for mid-century phone activity. Bring more tubes tomorrow.*

❋ ❋ ❋

Ben arrived at the basement lab, shoebox of bulbs in hand, at 5:07 Thursday night. He had mentioned to Jen that Sam had made a breakthrough and he would probably be home late again. On opening the data file the night before Ben saw the stream of numbers — the obvious timestamps — and understood what Sam meant when he said it was a primitive call log. He was not exactly sure what Sam felt he could do with it though, so it would be interesting to find out.

"Ben! Great. You've got the January bulbs there?" Sam began.

"Yep," Ben fished out the January 1st bulb and handed it and the box over.

"Okay, well, I'll show you how the reader works. And we should time how long it takes to do the transfer." Sam positioned the tube in the device and initiated the read, it whirred along for a few minutes and then the raw data and the decoded number files opened on the desktop they had salvaged and installed in this broom-closet of a lab. Sam ran the checking algorithm and determined it once again appeared to have generated a good dataset without obvious errors. He saved the files. All told, it took eleven minutes.

"Okay, so ten to fifteen minutes to read each tube and you've got what, a little under three hundred left?"

"About that, up to October 16th."

"We're looking at sixty hours down here to harvest the data." Sam paused and asked tentatively, "when is the baby due?"

"Little over two weeks," Ben replied.

Sam continued "I am guessing you don't really have sixty hours free right now."

"No, I suppose I don't," Ben was a little crestfallen as he instantly guessed someone with Sam's professional commitments probably did not have the time required either.

Sam, sensing his disappointment, tented his fingers under his chin and quickly continued, "well, it strikes me that this dataset would be really useful to anyone studying the history and sociology of phone use. And that is a hot topic right now, given the emergence of cell phones and the Internet, and some of the changes we have seen in the last couple decades. Several of my colleagues upstairs are working on cell phones and addiction, the sociology of contact networks, you name it... Of course, what they don't have is a historical dataset like this to compare to. I think what I should do is ask around and see if I can find a grad student who could do the data transfer and use the data for thesis work. What do you think?"

Ben paused for a moment; Jen had been surprisingly supportive of his weird fascination but of course he was expected to be with her for every available moment over the next two weeks. After that, they would be too busy and exhausted to care about anything else. Also, Sam had scrounged the tiny room to build the reading device, but they might not have it forever. There really was only one way forward, and that was even assuming they could find the right grad student, who also had time on their hands in the next couple of months and was willing to do it.

"That sounds like a good plan. How about I start bringing the tubes here, you see if you can get a student and we meet again at the beginning of next week. If possible, I'd like to hand this off before Jen goes into labour." Sam understood completely and said he would see what he could do.

23

When Ben said he would be with Sam on Thursday evening, Jen decided to make some pasta that could easily be reheated if he got home very late and stopped by the supermarket to pick up fresh spinach linguine and prepared meatballs in Bolognese. She puttered home and took Cassie out for a brief walk before cooking dinner. She had just finished eating when the email notification pinged onto her phone: Lori had replied to her message. Jen grabbed her tablet and logged in to the cold case forum.

Lori: *Hello. Yes, I am still interested in this case. It is very important to me. Can I ask what your interest is? Best, Lori*

Jen replied: *Hi Lori, I came across the case when I was out at the county library. I am a police officer but this is not part of an official inquiry. To be honest I am about to go on mat leave, but I did take a look at the investigation file.*

Jen left it at that, hoping Lori would reply, saying more about herself and what she knew. About half an hour later, long enough for Lori to consider options and realize this was the first active interest anyone from the police had shown in the fate of Julie McNally in decades, she did.

Lori: *I see. Well, Julie was a friend of mine. We were with her shortly before she disappeared, and I cannot believe all this time has passed and we don't know where she is or what happened to her. Do you have any ideas?*

Jen: *Well, I've looked at the investigation they did, and I actually went to the fair a couple of weeks ago and it seems very strange that no one saw anything.*

Lori (encouraged that Jen had seen the fairgrounds): *Do you live in the county? I am still here.*

Jen: *No, we're in the city.*

Lori (after thinking for a moment): *I'm coming into the city on Saturday, would you want to meet for coffee that afternoon?*

Jen: *I could do that, any chance you will be downtown or midtown?*

They tossed some logistical issues back and forth and settled on coffee at the hotel restaurant around the corner, which had good parking and was close to the off/on ramp that would take Lori back out of town. Jen would haul herself over there for 3:00 PM and Lori would arrive shortly thereafter, looking for the woman who was eight and half months pregnant.

24

On Friday night Ben suggested they go out to dinner and they met up at a steak house. They had just selected dessert when Jen thought this would be a good moment to fill Ben in on what she had been up to — investigating Julie McNally's disappearance — and to mention that she would be going out to basically interview a witness the next day.

However, Ben started talking first, explaining that he would spend most of Saturday at the university in the lab. Jen, who was a little tired and grumpy, decided then that she would tell her self-absorbed husband about the investigation later, if she thought he really needed to know.

❋ ❋ ❋

Saturday dawned crisply, with the definite twinge of winter in the air. Ben bustled off to the university early and, oddly to Jen, seemed exceptionally energized and self-satisfied. She was irritated by this, given the baby was due in two weeks and Ben seemed to feel he had all the time in the world to putter about with his weird and irrelevant distraction.

She stayed in bed and slept in, warm under the covers, if increasingly uncomfortable, given the size of her belly. Come to think of it, she was not at all convinced she should get out of bed and pursue her own extracurricular activities either.

But she did. At 10:50 she got up, showered, made some lunch, and took Cassie out. She had a nap on the couch at 1 PM and by 2:30 was leaving the apartment to trundle over to the hotel café. She found a comfortable table, well in sight of the entrance and ordered a decaf coffee and a slice of chocolate pecan pie.

Lori (Jen assumed it had to be Lori) showed up exactly on time. She was in her sixties, with blonde hair streaked with grey, cut shoulder length, comfortably and casually dressed but demonstrating a bit of bohemian style. Lori had practical shoes, a serviceable handbag and a rosy complexion with a certain grandmotherly demeanor Jen warmed to immediately.

"Are you Jen?"

"Yes," Jen moved to get up while extending her hand.

"Don't get up," Lori patted Jen's forearm gently while pressing her extended palm "you should stay off your feet as much as possible." Lori paused a moment "I am, or was, Loraine Sorenson. Wheatley now. I suppose I must have been in the file you read?"

"You were." Jen semi-surreptitiously pulled out her badge and presented it across the table to confirm her own identity to Lori, thereby establishing their in-real-life bona fides. A waiter came over and Lori ordered a pot of tea and a brownie. Jen decided to keep things light until the tea arrived and Lori would have something comforting at hand. They chatted about the traffic in midtown and the increasingly cold weather. Once the waiter had deposited the tea and brownie, Jen brought the conversation around to the fair.

"I was at the fair with my husband a couple of weeks ago. Has it changed much, are the grounds the same as they were back in 1970?"

"It has hardly changed at all. Parts of the county are practically set in aspic. You said you'd been to the library?"

"Yes."

"That's the one really good modernization we've had. Beautiful old building and renovation, isn't?" Jen nodded. "Julie would have loved that. She spent half her life at the library — arguably where she was happiest, I think."

"Was she generally happy?" Jen asked, tentatively.

"You know, I think she was. Very cerebral — but still generally fun to hang around with and she didn't seem stressed by anything that I can remember. She had this strong determination — she should have ended up an ambitious woman, a star reporter or news anchor. Somebody who should be coming due for a lifetime achievement award about now." Lori looked down for a moment, choked up.

"That was what she wanted to be, a journalist?" Jen asked.

"Oh yes. Definitely a writer of some sort. And she'd already written some columns for the local paper. They were well done even though she was so young."

"Had she just done those?" Jen felt an instinctive flicker that she might be onto something, this was a behaviour that set Julie apart and it might be significant.

"She'd started the year before, writing once or twice a month. I still have all her clippings; would you want copies?"

"Sure, thank you. She won the poetry competition that year?"

"Yes, she did." This memory really caused Lori to tear up. Jen gave her a minute and reached over with a consoling hand. Lori took a sip of tea, bit into her brownie, and suppressed a moment of despair.

"How was her relationship with her parents?"

"Oh fine, fine."

Jen prodded further: "was she rebellious?"

"Oh no, not at all. She was always a bit of a grown-up. Very responsible. Naturally cautious and quiet. Not at all gullible or easy to influence, I can't see that she would have gone along willingly with a stranger. I am sure her parents never worried about her judgement — her disappearance was a spectacularly brutal shock for them. Killed her father. Her mother is a shell of a person living at the old folk's home."

"It seems like a really strange situation. Complete vanishings with no signs of abduction and no recovery of ..." Jen paused to consider how to phrase it "...evidence over decades are rare. Other than the occasional case where people fall into a well or make it into the ocean — but then, we even have examples of those because evidence is sometimes eventually found. What do you think happened?" Jen asked.

"I have really no idea. Any idea I've had over the years just seems impossible when you start to break it down. If someone, you know, kidnapped her," Lori flinched, "how did they get her out of there? If they didn't, how come she hasn't been found? Even if she was abducted, there's still no sign of her and how would someone ensure she wouldn't be found for so long? There's a lot of land in the county, but it is not unused forest wilderness..."

Jen looked across the table at a woman who was truly baffled in her grief. She did not seem to be hiding anything either consciously or unconsciously. There was an undercurrent of intense frustration to her demeanour as well. No satisfaction, no sense of dramatic indulgence, no signs of ego.

"What do you remember about the day it happened?"

"Well, the morning was a school day except we were all excited that the fair was starting and it would be a half-day. Julie sat ahead of me in class and I noticed absolutely nothing out of the ordinary with her behaviour, from what I could see. We spoke briefly right at morning bell before taking our seats, about seeing a variety show on TV the night before. When the lunch bell rang we went out together and walked home with Sarah Carmine; she's the reference librarian now."

"Think I may have met her," Jen interjected briefly.

Lori nodded and paused for a minute, pulling up as much detail as she could muster after so long, her hands reflexively moving to further draw in what she was seeing in her mind. "We walked on the north sidewalk the whole way — it runs at the top of an incline and the road is below. The police really dwelt on that walk, trying to get me to remember every person we saw, cars that drove past, etc. but I really couldn't remember anything significant..."

"Did you pass anyone walking?"

"No. Which was expected. No one would really be walking that sidewalk in the other direction at that time. It basically only led from the school to downtown so everyone was going the other way, like we were, to get lunch, and then nobody was really headed to the school midday anyways because it was closing for the fair. I could not be sure that we hadn't passed anyone sitting on their porch, or what have you. And I couldn't be sure there wasn't anyone coming up any of the cross streets. Cars definitely passed — the road is the rural highway running into town, but I don't think any of them slowed down or did anything unusual."

"Well, the police canvassed all the houses along the route and no one reported being outside or seeing anyone from windows other than a general stream of children leaving the school."

"That makes sense. We got to Sarah's house first and she went in for lunch, then mine, then Julie continued on. I had macaroni and cheese with hotdog pieces. Used to be one of my favourites but I stopped eating it after that day. Mom gave me no juice and no dessert because she said I'd be eating sugary things all afternoon at the fair and hyper enough from that." Recollecting this moment of maternal authority brought a smile to both their faces.

"I left the house about twenty minutes to one and walked over to Julie's. Didn't need to go up and knock, she was already out the door and halfway down the sidewalk when I turned the corner. We back tracked my route a bit, heading south, and two blocks later met up with Sarah again, and Mary Rogers, and continued on. I am pretty sure there was zero car traffic anywhere in the neighbourhood up to that point, and the only person we saw was Old Man Benjamin weeding his garden. The police spoke to him at the time, but he's been dead for decades now.

"Anyway, once we were a block or so from the main street the car traffic definitely picked up and there were a lot of people about, many of whom I did not know. However — and I really, really wracked my brains at the time and since — I did not see anyone acting unusually. Nothing stuck out. Other than the fact it was the fair — and it was a totally typical fair opening day (I'd been to a few at that point and many more since) — it was just an ordinary, normal day. It retrospect I still find that completely bizarre, that this was a thing that happened, and in the middle of the most ordinary, almost idyllic day."

Lori paused at that, took a long sip of tea and bit resolutely into her brownie, chewing for a few moments.

"We got in line, there was a family in front of us, an older couple behind us and behind them I remember there were rowdy boys, but I didn't get the sense that any of them really noticed us, or were interested in us in any way. And I was a bit older than Julie, twelve then, and I suspect I was starting to get interested in whether anyone was paying me attention!" Lori chuckled, somewhat ruefully.

"Once we were in the fair, we walked around for a bit checking everything out and then hit some rides. I was scared of this one ride operator who had terrible teeth, but my parents assured me the police checked him out really thoroughly and cleared him with an alibi."

"They did," said Jen, imparting the reassuring impression she had a thorough grounding of the case.

"Anyway, after the rides we got snacks and headed to the arena for a bathroom break and to look at the exhibits," Lori let out a long sigh "we saw Julie's poem and read it, and wished her luck, because the prizes had not been awarded at that point. She would have liked getting that prize! The poem meant a lot to her. And then we went back out the front of the arena to go back on the rides, but Julie said she wanted to see the animals, which were in the opposite direction. Mary definitely didn't want to go back, so there were a few moments of foot-stomping, if you will, and then Julie split off from the group, amicably enough, and that was the last I saw her."

"Did you see if she went back into the arena or did she go towards the pens from the outside?"

"It seemed like she was going towards the pens on the outside, but I cannot be sure she didn't go back in the arena."

"Hmmm," Jen paused for a moment, to take in the story, which was remarkably consistent with what she'd read in the file "what about earlier in the week? Can you remember the weekend before, or maybe the school week starting from Monday? Perhaps you had some special preparations for the fair that might jog the memory?"

"You know, there were." Lori looked off into the distance, squinting. "The weekend before we'd gone to the cottage at the lake, to take advantage of the last of the warm weather and to start shutting it up for the season. The plan was for dad to finish that up the Sunday the fair started but he never made it back. My grandpa had to go out in November and drain the pipes and everything because my parents had forgotten with everything going on." Jen wondered at that, the level of Lori's parent's involvement, but she said nothing and just made a mental note to see if it would make sense once Lori revealed more.

"On Monday we had a morning assembly at school and the exhibits students had created were presented before they were taken over to the fair. The band played and the principal wished us the best of luck, saying he was sure we'd win lots of prizes, the usual ra-ra sort of thing. I sat with Julie and Sarah throughout the whole thing. Sarah and Mary ended up missing some classes that week because they were fair committee volunteers and helped take everything to the fairgrounds and set some things up, but Julie and I went from the assembly straight to English class."

"That's interesting — Julie didn't have any of these duties?"

"No, she didn't and she didn't want them either — it was Teacher's Pet kind of work and she actually preferred doing school work, thinking by herself, and while she wasn't rebellious, she wasn't totally devoted to authority figures the way Mary was — Mary's a government bureaucrat now." Lori smiled knowingly after saying that, a tiny upturn at the corner of her mouth. "Monday afternoon at school was normal as best I can remember."

"What about after school? Did you hang out at all in the evenings?"

"We did. Thinking back, we must have been at the park on either Monday or Tuesday evening because I remember having a discussion with Julie and Sarah about some of the exhibits people had created — some that were good and some that were terrible — while we whirled around on the roundabout at dusk. It had to be after the Monday assembly, I think, because by then we'd seen everything and it wouldn't have been Wednesday because that was the night we all watched... Oh what was it called!?!" Lori tapped her forehead trying to get the name of a long-forgotten show to pop forth, but it would not surface, "anyway, Wednesday and Thursday there was good TV, and since it was getting dark earlier at that point and we weren't really allowed out later, the park must have been earlier in the week."

"Do you remember anything else about the conversation you had at the roundabout?"

"No, not really, it was so long ago and of course it didn't seem important."

"Okay. Now, focusing on that fragment of conversation you remember talking about the exhibits students created, try kind of placing yourself back in the moment." Jen paused and let Lori think back.

"Are you girls alone in the park?"

Without hesitation Lori replied: "Yes. At least I thought we were at the time."

25

"How did you get home from the park?"

"We walked. All three of us. Up the hill and then up to the north sidewalk and basically the end leg of the same route we took home from school. Mary wasn't with us, so Sarah got home first, then me, then Julie alone around the corner to her house."

"Could someone have followed her then?"

"I suppose. I didn't notice anyone either on foot or in a car. And, I think if there had been, I would have remembered it later that week when the police were questioning me."

"Could there have been someone waiting for Julie around the corner that you couldn't see?"

Lori thought for a moment, trying to recall precisely the landscape and sightlines of her childhood. "I suppose so. But, if a stranger accosted Julie on that walk home, you have to think she would have mentioned it in the three or four days afterwards, don't you?"

"Probably. But you never know, and I just want to get a sense of any unaccounted for time when she was alone leading up to Friday."

"Sure, okay."

"You said you all watched TV on Wednesdays and Thursdays and if I remember in your statement you said you'd called Julie on the phone Wednesday night?"

"Yes. You see there was a musical guest star we were all interested in performing on that variety show, whatever it was called, so I phoned Julie up right after he performed, and we drooled over him a bit."

"Was it the same one you were talking about Friday morning?"

"Yes, it must have been."

"But you said you'd had that conversation about something you'd seen the night before?" Jen asked, not unkindly.

Lori's brow wrinkled. Confusion, then determination spread across her face as she tried to work it out without making mistakes. "I definitely called Julie just after we saw the performance on the show, which was on Wednesday night. Thursdays were dedicated to *Bewitched*. But, we definitely talked about it at the beginning of the day on Friday, so I guess we were just still talking about it two days later."

"Could you have called Julie on Thursday?"

"No. Definitely not. They kept asking me that at the time. You see our moms got home late on Thursdays because they went to the salon the same time Thursday afternoon, then it was dinner, then Bewitched, so generally we didn't bother each other Thursday after school so we had time to finish our homework, which was always due Friday."

"Even with the fair?"

"Yes, even with the fair we had homework assignments due that Friday. I am sure I didn't bother her on Thursday. It was kind of ironic because it was the same time our moms were gossiping like crazy at the hair salon."

"Your mothers were friends?"

"Yes. Our parents actually. They were friends even before we were born. Our dads were at school together. My mom still visits Mrs. McNally at the home. Fortunately, my mom is doing okay independently, still." Jen nodded, acknowledging the good fortune of having a healthy elderly parent.

"Who were some of the McNallys' other friends?"

"Well, I can't really remember her dad's fishing buddies or anything,

but for the women it was mom, Mrs. McNally and Mrs. Cadworth —
Francesca Cadworth. However, that friendship did not really survive the
strain."

Jen interjected before Lori continued: "I recognize that name. The
Chief was named Cadworth, wasn't he?"

"Yes, Francesca was his wife."

"I had an instructor at Police College named Peter Cadworth."

"That would be the son. He's younger than us, only a baby when
Julie disappeared. Anyway, Mom and Mrs. McNally couldn't really stand
Franny's company after Julie went missing and her husband failed
to find her. Dick Cadworth's reputation definitely suffered after Julie
disappeared."

Jen paused a moment at that. From what she had seen the
investigation looked competent enough, although she might have done
a few things differently. It was easy for the public to criticize the police
force without understanding what they were up against.

"It is a particularly hard case," Jen commented.

Lori, observing a bit of sensitivity, tread carefully "well, from what
I remember, mom and Mrs. McNally thought there were parts of the
investigation which went too slowly. Nothing much happened crime-wise
in the county before that and there was this sense Chief Cadworth was
in over his head. Then, in the decade or so that followed, a dubious gang
element kind of set up shop out in the motel strip near the highway. Biker
gangs and drugs. And Cadworth did not manage to really bring them to
heel. I wouldn't say they operated with impunity but it was not the good
old innocent days. A lot changed after Julie went missing in terms of the
sense of safety. Cadworth retired in good enough standing but the police
department was a bit of a mess. Francesca died about ten years ago and
the Chief is in the same home as Mrs. McNally. Can't imagine she's happy
about that if she notices."

They had been talking for at least an hour at that point. The pastries
were gone, the tea pot cold, and the dinner hour would be starting soon

in the café. Lori needed to drive home, and Ben might have managed to return home from his tube escapades.

"It's been good to talk to you, I hope not unsettling," Jen said.

"It's been good talking to you too. I haven't been able to really address it in a long time. What do you think you are going to do?"

"Well, there's reference to other records in the file I looked at. They'd be somewhere in the county's records storage, hard to get to, if they still exist, but since you mentioned Peter is the Chief's son, I think I should contact him and see if he can pull some strings. It'll take some time though," Jen explained, carefully creating realistic expectations. "There are some unknowns but not really big holes in terms of investigational coverage. A review process goes through and relooks at everything and tries to reframe any assumptions, as best as possible, and I can try to do that on my own."

Lori was encouraged by Jen's open-mindedness but as a grandmother she had to smile: "you won't have time you know. Thank you even just for the effort you've put in so far. It means a lot and it really has been nice just talking to you." They parted ways, Lori wishing Jen the best of luck with motherhood.

❈ ❈ ❈

Jen got back to the apartment, opened the door, and could see the very dusty soles of her husband's shoes propped up on the sofa armrest, presumably still attached to his body. He was asleep, having left dusty footprints all over the condo floor.

Her growing sense of irritation was, however, cut short when she became baffled by the density and location of said tracks. They led, in weird fits and starts, to the nursery, the door to which was closed, before re-emerging and terminating near the couch. She went over to the nursery, opened the door, and flicked on the light.

And there, in the middle of the room, with a single pink bow inexpertly affixed to the head rest, was a white-painted Windsor rocking chair, almost identical to the one Jen remembered her grandmother having. She let out a happy chirrup (which woke Ben) and then practically skipped to the centre of the room and flopped into the chair, kicking back to set it rocking and plopping her elbows down to check clearances on the arm rests.

Ben appeared at the doorway, groggy in a way Jen found intensely adorable.

"The arms are excellent! How did you do this?" she jumped up, met him in the doorway and gave him an extremely affectionate kiss.

"Aw, you know, I asked Harry to look for one."

"But it is practically identical to my grandmother's!"

"Yep, I went through the photo albums and found a picture that had the chair in it. When Harry contacted me about the bulbs, I emailed him the picture. It took him a couple weeks to track one down and it needed to be refinished. The maintenance guys at work have a shop room in the basement and they let me use it to strip it down and paint it. Last sand and coat to the bottom was this morning. He looked at the clock: "I brought it home at 3:30 and you weren't here…"

"Aw, so sorry I was out. You deserved a real welcome home for this one." She kissed him again and then went back to the chair and happily rocked away, Ben basking somewhat in her glee.

"What do you want for dinner?" Jen asked.

Ben patted his tummy, contemplating. "Roasted meat? I am pretty hungry…"

Like a magnificent hibernating bear just woken up, Jen thought to herself. "We'll go to Simpson's. On me! We should probably go there one last time before the baby arrives anyway…"

"Let me get cleaned up," which he did. Then they set out for a nice meal at their favourite fancy restaurant, one that frowned on screaming infants and small children. Much later in the evening Ben sent an email to Harry, confirming that the rocking chair had been a great success and thanking him for all his help. He also sent a brief update on the tubes, explaining what they were and that he was getting assistance accessing the data on them from his friend Sam Eide, a professor at the university.

26

Midday Tuesday Sam texted Ben suggesting a meet up in the basement lab at 5:20 that evening. He had just met a Sociology master's student who wanted to pursue a PhD. The student was already supported through a good scholarship. Her mentor, one of Sam's colleagues, had jumped on the opportunity to supervise a unique thesis and get access to the data as soon as the rumour of what Sam had made its way through the department.

Ben arrived on time, holding the last two boxes of bulbs and Sam introduced him to the student, who was already there: "Ben, this is Mandi. Mandi, this is Ben, who found and owns the media. Ben, I took the liberty of writing up a diagram of the data." Sam handed them both a single sheet of paper.

"Mandi, here is the device we've built to read the media and convert the old bytes. I'll show you how to do it — it's really easy, but we think it will take about sixty hours to complete the data haul. Do you think you have the time?"

"Yep, sure. I have a couple exams this week and next — one paper due, almost written — but over the holidays I can free up that kind of time. I'd want to have the data available to write a paper next spring."

Sam took the next tube in sequence from the first box, loaded it and initiated the read sequence, showing Mandi some important points about the machine. Her supervisor, Professor Stratenauer, then appeared and brief introductions followed.

"Mandi, it's been running smoothly since I made final adjustments, so hopefully you don't have any problems, but after your paper is handed in we'll give you a key to this room and if you can let me know when you'll be working, I can make sure I'm around and you can text me if anything goes wrong."

After a few minutes, having seen how Sam completed the read on that tube and they all chatted a bit, including about Ben's impending fatherhood, Mandi sat down to try it herself. It was easy and she had only a few questions. As the process was finishing up, she asked "you've saved the data in a file for each day, do you mind if I create a master merged file, adding the date to each line, and then putting it all together?"

"Sure, you can do that, but make sure you keep the original isolated import files as well. Better make sure to send them to Ben too since we're probably destroying his data on the tubes with the read."

"Great! There's no demographic information for this, but once I get as much as possible into one data set I can analyse the frequency and times to better understand calling habits for that period."

"Sounds like a good project!" Sam said, encouragingly.

"One other thing, how do I confirm that the data is what we think it is and understand the population pool?"

"Well, I can confirm the exchanges match those in use for the area Ben thinks the bulbs are associated with…" Sam started.

Ben continued, "I was told the data was collected off the central circuits of the Southwestern Office exchange. As far as I know, it was all the traffic on that exchange because the original intent was to analyse the data — probably much like you want to do."

"Okay, once I have the data, I might have to look into that a bit further…" Mandi trailed off, unwilling to give up on an exciting project because some details were not yet worked out.

Professor Stratenauer interjected, "as long as we can prove what the sample represents — Sam, I think we have the company archives in the library and can take a look at those?" Sam nodded "Then, I don't think you want to de-anonymize the data really, at all, it would be hugely labour intensive and the ethics approvals would get very complicated."

Ben inserted himself into the conversation, not particularly interested in academic technicalities, and knowing he should head home, "Well, it was nice to meet you both. I have to go. Mandi, I hope the data reads go well and all I ask is you treat the tubes carefully and return them to the right box when you are done." And with that Ben left, while behind him the three researchers started talking happily about various statistical analyses they could perform if the data haul worked as expected.

27

On Wednesday Jen rummaged around in the dustier corners of her email account. Eventually she turned up Peter Cadworth's old personal email address. She had last emailed him about five years earlier, although they had run into each other on the sidewalk more recently, around the time she got married, and caught up a bit then. She hoped the email account was still active and composed a message.

Hi Peter,

How are you? Ben and I are expecting our first baby shortly.

I'm contacting you to ask for a favour (not really sure if it is big or small). A little while ago I ran across an old missing child case from your dad's neck of the woods. Was thinking I could review it while on mat leave but some of the case files never made it to the records here. If they still exist they would be at the county police station storage facility. Are you able to pull any strings there? All I ask is they get sent over to us at regional headquarters and I can digitize and organize them. County would then get them uploaded to their system as well. It is the Julie McNally disappearance, October 1970.

Was also wondering about possibly talking to your dad about it, if you think that is a good idea?

Hope you are well,

Jen Mahoney

The electronic missive pinged into a virtual email account that would eventually be accessed by an old PC in a home about forty minutes' drive away. Peter Cadworth was not in the habit of checking this account more than once or twice a week. And there the message sat, waiting, for two days, but early on Friday morning after returning from his run, Peter fired up the PC and logged on.

His initial thought was happiness for Jen and Ben about the baby, and then the face of Valerie Belmont popped almost unbidden to mind:

his dad's old secretary. A jolly woman with ginger hair (white now, he assumed), who used to give him lollipops when he visited the police station as a child. The one person who would know where all the files were.

He had heard something recently about Valerie and mined his brain for a moment to remember what it was: her husband had died, and she was now living with her sister in the next town over. He heard that from her nephew, who had done his taxes back in the spring. Peter pulled out his cell phone and called the business number for the nephew, who was not in the office yet, so Peter left a voicemail.

"Hi Tom, this is Peter Cadworth. Thanks again for your work on my taxes this year. Listen, I need to get some advice from your Aunt Valerie, can you text me her phone number or if possible give her mine and ask her to call?" He closed the message with his number then composed a short email to Jen congratulating her and explaining that he would see what he could do about the files. Then he quickly showered and headed out for work.

And so it was that at 9:18 AM Carol Smitherman received a phone call from her son Tom that brightened her day, and after a bit of maternal futzing she put her sister Valerie on the phone. Valerie listened and then carefully wrote down a phone number on a pad they kept for just such occasions.

"Well wouldn't you know, Chief Cadworth's son is trying to get in touch with me!?! Haven't seen him since his mother's funeral." Valerie thought for a second. "He must be about fifty now."

"What about? Has something happened to the Chief?"

"I don't know," Valerie replied, a bit worried, "suppose I best call." Peter's cell phone started ringing in his pocket as he was on his way to a 9:30 meeting at his detachment and he stepped to the side in the hallway, slowing his gait, to answer it.

"Hello, Peter speaking."

"Peter is that you? This is Valerie Belmont. Is everything alright with your father?"

"Oh Valerie, nice to hear from you! What? No, this is not about dad. I just need your advice."

"Oh good, that's a relief," she waited patiently for him to continue.

"I need a favour. It's to do with some old files a colleague of mine is hoping to review. I suspect you are the only person who will be able to figure out where they are."

"Really?"

"Yes, it is a missing child case from when I was a baby." Peter paused a moment to pull the sticky note on which he had recorded Jen's request from his pocket, but he did not need it.

A long breath left Valerie's lips "the Julie McNally case." Across the room, Carol's head popped up, listening in greater interest.

"Yes, that's the one. October 1970. Can you help?"

Valerie paused for only a heartbeat: "absolutely. Hopefully everything is still where I left it. Could you meet us in town for lunch? At the diner?"

Peter paused, a little surprised at her eagerness. "Sure, I think I could do that for about 1 PM. Would that work?"

"Absolutely, we'll be there!" and she hung up the phone. Peter noted the repeat use of 'absolutely,' and wondered who 'we' was. He started to suspect he had gotten himself into something unexpected. He shook off the feeling out of necessity and made it to his morning meeting just in time.

In the early afternoon he was on the road heading back to his old town (and his old diner turkey salad sandwich). Things had not changed much since his childhood and he took a moment to relish that.

Living close to a large city, he had seen tremendous changes in the last twenty years, as fields disappeared and housing developments went in, including the one he currently lived in. Churches and orchards were gone, and chain restaurants and big box stores popped up. Out here that had not really happened. Maybe it never would. He kind of hoped for that but felt naïve for doing so.

He pulled into the diner a little past one, parked, and went inside. He spotted the two women immediately. Valerie, exactly as he remembered her, but with whiter hair, and a woman who could only be her sister and Tom's mother. There was a pot of tea on the table, and they had clearly been waiting for a little while. Peter leaned in and gave Valerie a peck on the cheek and a brief hug, then reached across to shake Carol's hand.

"Hi Peter, this is my sister Carol."

"Of course, nice to meet you" he said, politely enough, wondering if she was there because of his request, or despite it. "Do you both come here for lunch often?" he ventured.

"No. Hardly ever."

"Right." A waiter came over and took their orders (three turkey salad sandwiches) but once the waiter left, Peter found two sets of eyes staring at him, transfixed.

"So?" It was actually Carol, the elder and apparently more in-charge sister, who made this opening gambit.

Peter sat there looking baffled.

"Are they reopening the Julie McNally case?" Valerie inquired. Again, the two sets of transfixed eyes.

"Not so far as I know," Peter returned, wondering exactly what he had gotten himself into, and trying to backpedal a little more towards full professional discretion. He decided to interrogate them, rather than having it the other way around.

"What's the story with this case? I don't know it because I was a baby..." he trailed off.

"Well," Carol started, "it's just the biggest unsolved mystery in county history!"

"Really," Peter harrumphed, as if nonplussed, quite sure that this would elicit everything they knew, which it did. Over the next few minutes, as the cook prepared the three sandwiches in the kitchen, the entire story tumbled out.

"She was taken from the fair?" Peter said, appalled that the beloved rural enjoyment had been defiled and wondering how he had never heard

THE GIRL IN THE LIBRARY 111

of it.

"Well, we don't know for sure" Carol replied.

"It was the fair," Valerie countered. "We all sat down, you see, the next morning, and thought it through. It pretty much had to be the fair."

"We?"

"All of us. The whole secretarial pool. Even the retirees. And the dispatchers. We set up a station at the entrance and interviewed everyone who came to the rest of the fair. And we sat there, looking at the fairgrounds for days and trying to figure it out."

Peter had never heard of an investigation like that. "It was just the department? Didn't they bring in regional detectives?"

"They did, about a week in" Valerie replied, looking down at her teacup.

Then Peter began to understand. He had never heard of this case because it was his father's biggest failure. A child had been abducted from the county fair and his father failed to find her. A queasy feeling began to take hold in his guts. All cops had their failures, but they were hard to stomach. And while he was old enough to have a realistic understanding of his father — hero worshiping was long past — this was clearly an event that impacted his early life in ways Peter never perceived.

Valerie, ever loyal to Chief Cadworth and realizing Peter understood the implications of what she was saying, immediately tried to change the mood. "We'd done a good job though, Peter. I swear we covered everything. Regional couldn't believe we hadn't identified strangers who'd gone to the fair the first day, but we really had tried. Very thoroughly. Either there weren't any or the perpetrator somehow evaded detection. There are thousands of questionnaires and hundreds of completed interviews. You'll see when we get to the files."

"Okay. I expect that is exactly the paperwork my colleague is after. Where do you think it is?"

"Well, I left it in the bowels of the new station. It was still there when I retired, so unless someone's had the energy to move it somewhere else in the last seven years — which I doubt — it should still be there."

"Right. Do you know the current head administrator?"

"You bet I do. Hired and trained her."

Peter smiled. This was doable. He might even be back at his detachment at 2 PM. "Do you think you can give her a call and let her know we'll be over in twenty minutes?"

"Yup." And Valerie pulled out her years-old cell phone, dialing the main police switchboard from memory and asking to be put through to her successor. After a brief conversation in which Valerie explained she was helping the regional police locate some old files they needed access to, and which they would scan and upload to the new electronic file system (a free administrative service any bureaucrat would snap up), they arranged to meet at the back staff entrance at 1:30.

Three sandwiches were rapidly consumed, the bill paid, and they left the parking lot in their respective cars only a few minutes later.

The station was not far, and they arrived just on time, Valerie waving through her windshield to the administrator, Sharon, who opened the door to them, holding in one hand a large bunch of keys. Valerie made the introductions and Sharon's eyes flared in recognition at Peter's name.

"Cadworth? You must be Dick Cadworth's son?"

"Yep."

"Are these files for you?" she asked.

"No, no. A colleague of mine in the city asked for my help in locating the files once she realized it was my dad's old unit."

"Right. I see. Well Valerie, you show me where to find them and I'll ship them to my counterpart down at King Street."

Valerie led their expedition party, while Carol held the rear. Peter noticed Sharon handled the reappearance of her old boss (and her sister) with remarkable aplomb. Valerie led them to a set of stairs leading down into the basement and unlocked a door into a short hallway, then walked down another half staircase and into a large room filled with metal shelving units.

"When was it?"

"1970."

"The late sixties and early seventies are mostly along that back wall..."

"But not this case," Valerie replied and walked across the room to another door, which they unlocked and went through, finding themselves in a small vestibule with a sink on one wall, a mop in the corner, and two other doors.

Valerie indicated the door to their left and somewhat imperiously lifted the keys from her successor's hand, flipping through the ring until she found the one she wanted. Valerie inserted it into the lock and the bolt turned, she opened the door and pulled down on a metal string to light the single overhead bulb. It had probably been intended as a cleaning supplies closet but instead it was stacked to the ceiling with several boxes.

"They're reopening the Julie McNally case!" Carol explained from the back, breathlessly.

28

"I see" Sharon said, raising a slightly sceptical eyebrow as she turned to look at Peter.

"Now, now" Peter said, making calming gestures with his hands "as far as I know the case is not being reopened. An old friend and colleague of mine has taken an interest and she is about to go on mat leave and thought she could do an informal review while she is off."

He paused, "I don't think she knows how much material is here" and all four of them gave the pile an appraising eye. Sharon began to count the boxes.

"Well, to be honest we're sending a truck down to the city partially empty anyway and I could just piggyback these boxes on the shipment. It is going out this afternoon. How she'll have the budget to get all the scanning done though..."

Peter thought for a moment or two. He knew Jen and knew she would not give up. Ideally she would come and pick and choose what to scan but the logistics of that would not work.

"I'm sure she'll want them. Let me fill in her details on the paperwork here and that way you can get them in this afternoon's shipment, and then she'll have to figure out the budget stuff on her end."

Sharon made a note of the key Valerie had used to open the door but then she paused, looking at her watch. "We'll need to get them up to the shipping pick up within the next hour," she looked at the three of them.

Valerie volunteered: "I saw two trolleys back there." Carol turned, went back through the door, which Valerie propped open, and returned a moment later with a trolley in each hand. Peter reached up to take the highest boxes off the top of the pile and pass them along. In a few moments, the trolleys were loaded, with one almost empty box remaining on the floor, which Sharon picked up. She took the lead, and they followed her back into the large room. However, instead of heading for the stairs, she went the opposite way and down another long hallway, which held a service elevator at the end.

They all managed to fit into the elevator and got off a half floor up in a semi-industrial area with a loading dock door at one end. A clerk was sitting at a computer surrounded by other file boxes, including several labelled Evidence. Sharon was too discrete to say what those were, but Peter had the impression they might include cold case evidence being sent to the forensic sciences lab in the city, probably for DNA analysis.

"Okay, we'll need to check our records register and make sure everything here is on it and then barcode everything before we do the shipping labels. Peter, that will take some time but if you just want to give us the destination details and sign off, you don't need to stay." And the small group went over to the clerk, who opened a database that would automatically load Jen's details from a system-wide directory.

"It's going to Jen Mahoney down at King Street," Peter informed the clerk, "and I am facilitating the transfer: Peter Cadworth."

The clerk found Jen's details in the directory without problem and since Peter was not affiliated with the county Sharon put her own name on the transfer as well.

Carol, still observing from the back piped up: "Jen Mahoney? She's not from around here, is she?"

"No, Jen's from out east."

"Okay. Peter I think that's all we need from you here, although someone should give Jen and her receiving department the head's up these boxes are coming in and explain the situation."

"No problem, I can do that when I get back to the office. Well Valerie, thanks so much for your help and it was good to see you again! Carol, nice to meet you too." Both women fairly beamed at Peter, and he turned and shook Sharon's hand with a high degree of appreciation for how she had handled the situation. Then the three interlopers left the building.

Peter was back in his office just after 2 PM and he called Jen on her work line at regional headquarters, but she was away from her desk (probably, he thought, at an infernal meeting), so he left a message: "Hi Jen, Peter here. I have had tremendous luck with the help of dad's old secretary, Valerie Belmont, and the county investigation files for the McNally disappearance are winging their way towards you as I speak. There's a lot of them though, so you probably should tell your receiving department. The chief administrator at county doesn't think you can get the budget for scanning, but I told her you'd manage somehow..."

Peter paused, scratching his forehead "...And about talking to dad, to be honest he's got dementia and he's in a care home and I have no idea how it would go. Maybe we should talk again if your review turns anything up?" And with that Peter hung up his phone and got on with his day, vague plans for the weekend starting to form in his mind. Tomorrow, he would take the dog to the local conservation area and on Sunday, he would go visit his father.

29

Jen exited the second of two infernal meetings at 4:10 and was back in
her office five minutes later checking her voicemail when Kristin
Johnson, Senior Records Administrator, appeared at her door, looking
noticeably irritated. Jen heard Peter's message while looking at Kristin
and could guess what had happened. She hung up the phone.

"Jen. A huge pile of boxes has turned up on the loading dock and
there is no active case code to match them to, but you are listed as the
recipient."

"Sorry about that Kristin, a colleague just left a voicemail regarding
those, they were shipped in record time, otherwise I would have warned
you."

Kristin, somewhat placated, "well, what do we do with them with no
active case code?"

Jen had initially intended to get them delivered to her desk but sensed
she needed to evaluate the situation "how about I come down and take a
look?"

Kristin nodded, and as Jen struggled to get out of her chair, asked
"when's the baby due?"

"Next week."

Kristin, who had two children herself, was not unsympathetic and
her irritation started to drop away as they made their way towards the
elevator.

"What will you be able to do with these with the mat leave coming
up?"

"Well, it's an old cold case and I thought I'd scan them and review them at home while I was off. It's a missing child."

"No, really?" that pulled at Kristin's heartstrings.

"Yes, disappeared 1970 and absolutely no sign of what happened to her."

Kristin shuddered on hearing one of her greatest fears, "are the family still around?"

"Yes, the mother is. No siblings. I met with one of her friends though. Believe it or not she was probably taken from the county fair in front of hundreds of people."

Kristin shuddered again, and then the doors opened, and they walked a short distance to the shipping receiving bay. There sat a pallet, stacked rows deep in file boxes, wrapped round in plastic to keep everything together.

"Hmm. There's no way I'll be able to scan that before I go on leave."

"It's not a reactivated case? There's no budget code?" Kristin asked.

"No, there's no budget code. It's unfortunate because I've been really lucky in terms of getting them to dig the records out. A friend out there actually tracked down the old Chief's secretary and she has somehow managed to magic them out of storage and ship them here."

They pulled some of the plastic off the top and opened a box, revealing a stack of the questionnaires the secretaries had used while manning the front gate. These had *'Not at Fair on Friday'* scrawled across the top and were bound with a desiccated elastic band.

"Interesting," Jen said, "you see, all the secretaries set up stations at the fair entrance and asked questions of everyone going in for all the days following the disappearance."

"Really? All the secretaries?"

"Yep, and the dispatchers. These boxes are probably mostly the questionnaires, canvassing notes, and the interviews that the police then conducted once they identified people who might be witnesses or have information."

"Where are we going to put it all?" Kristin asked.

"Well, I think we can squeeze it in my office. I won't be there anyway. I can come in and scan when I have time."

Kristin, mother of two, thought to herself, *you won't have time*, but an idea was forming in her mind and she said nothing.

"Okay, we have some old trolleys around here somewhere, I'll go find one, we can load it up down here, and you can just keep the cart in your office for a few months."

"Sounds like a plan, thank you."

30

On Wednesday nobody came to pick Cassie up from doggie daycare. Cassie found herself sitting alone, well past six in the evening, on the sculpted synthetic-turf dog run that was the pride of the midtown facility. It got later and later, and Cassie's tummy was grumbly, when, unexpectedly, her dog-walker came through the sliding doors. Clapping both her thighs, the dog walker invited Cassie over by name for some friendly head scritches. Cassie trotted over but wasn't fooled. Something was definitely not as it should be.

However, seeing no better option, she followed her dog walker, whom she quite liked, and found she was invited to jump into the dog walker van, which she did not often ride in, and Pootles (the dog walker's Special Dog) was in there too. Cassie gave a good sniff to the van, and to Pootles, who was nonplussed, and determined everything might not be normal but it was okay.

They travelled in the van for a few minutes and then they got out onto a sidewalk Cassie had never been to before. They trundled up some wooden steps and through a door and they were in a home. Cassie could tell it was a home by the furnishings and smell. Pootles seemed very comfortable here and picked up the pace heading down the hallway, so Cassie followed. Soon, she could see why Pootles was energized: there was food (in quite a nice bowl) in the kitchen.

Cassie's tummy was even more rumbly now, but that was clearly Pootles' bowl and Pootles' food, so Cassie looked up at her dog walker for guidance, thumping her tail against the floor.

"I bet you want some dinner too, dontcha?" said the dog walker, to which Cassie did a small whinge and offered a big expectant smile. The dog walker went over to a cupboard, got another bowl, and filled it with kibble and plopped it down under Cassie's nose. While Cassie started munching away on the slightly strange food that nonetheless tasted perfectly fine, the dog walker found a suitable water bowl and set it down beside her as well. On seeing that, Cassie wondered where Ben and Jen were and how long she was expected to stay at Pootles' house and got a little anxious.

However, she was more interested in eating. Soon Pootles, who'd had a head start, finished her own diner and then something extraordinary happened. The dog walker went to what Cassie assumed had to be the balcony doors and slid one open. But it wasn't a balcony. It led to a park, *attached to the home.* Pootles trotted through the doors and into the park like this was nothing in the world, but Cassie sat there for a moment, baffled.

"C'mon girl, time to play outside" said the dog walker.

And Cassie left her bowl and went up to the magical opening and looked outside and went through and found herself in a delightful small park with grass and bushes and everything anyone could ever want.

Pootles flopped down just outside the door, somewhat bored, but Cassie leaped with joy down the steps and started sniffing everything maniacally. Pootles was intrigued by Cassie's reaction to her backyard and managed to roll over, get up, and go over to see what Cassie was so excited about. Pootles began to grasp that Cassie didn't quite understand backyards, so she very patiently waited for her to calm down and then gave her the full tour.

Pootles showed Cassie the good smell corners, which Cassie rubbed herself against (a lapse in etiquette Pootles decided to forgive, as something strange was clearly going on in Cassie's family and who was Pootles to judge, really). She ended the tour at the Dog House and with certain head gestures implied that Cassie was allowed to take a look inside, which she did, discovering the incredible sight of an enclosed dog bed *in the park.* What a delightful and novel idea, Cassie thought.

Around about then it was getting thoroughly dark and much colder, and Cassie was a bit worried about what would happen next. Then she saw Pootles go to a corner of the yard and pee. Cassie followed her lead and only moments later the dog walker opened the door and called "Pootles, Cassie" and the two dogs hustled to get back inside where it was warm.

Pootles led the way back down the hall towards a room near the front door and turned in a little circle as if to say: "pick your spot." Which Cassie did, finding a very nice pillow dog bed in a corner, under the window, not unlike where her dog bed was at home.

And on thinking of home, Cassie wondered again where Jen and Ben were, but being a reasonable dog, decided not to panic unless there were definite signs that something was wrong. Obviously, someone had asked the dog walker to come and pick her up at doggie day care, and that had to be Ben or Jen. Cassie did her best to have a good night's sleep, listening to Pootles' snoring, which was somewhat soothing.

In the morning, the dinnertime process repeated itself, but they got to stay outside for hours. Extra water bowls and food bowls were placed just outside the door and frolicking and napping ensued. At 12:30 there was the call for "Pootles, Cassie" and they once again trundled back into the house but this time they went straight down the hallway and out the front door, and back into the van. And they drove a little bit and stopped, and the dog walker got out and went somewhere, and then the van door opened and there was Sherman.

Sherman was an old bruiser of a bulldog and he looked at Cassie, and looked at Pootles, and looked back at Cassie, and was surprised. *That's not how it's supposed to be*, thought Sherman, *we pick up Kevin, then Frick and Frack* (as Sherman called the Pomeranians) *and then we park the van and then we pick up Cassie and go down to the lake path. No, this isn't right at all.* Sherman didn't like for things to be unexpected, and this alteration put him in a grumpy mood.

The dog pack had its walk (with a few whispers about *what was happening with Cassie's family*?) but was generally devoted to enjoying the bright sunshine day. Cassie wondered if she would go back to the apartment after this walk like normal, but that was not what happened, instead they went back to the van and returned to Pootles' house, where they had a late lunch and went back outside to the home-park. And as the sun drifted Cassie followed Pootles' lead in moving to take naps in the warm spots.

Finally, the dog-walker came out, holding her phone in her hand and clapped both thighs and said: "Your daddy's coming to pick you up!" and Cassie knew to be overjoyed. And a little while later a gate in the fence around the home-park opened, and there was Ben, and it was glorious. Cassie barked and ran up to him but then ran away and started trotting in circles around the perimeter of the home-park to show Ben how wonderful it was and maybe it would be a good idea if they got one of these home-parks too.

"She loves the backyard," said the dog-walker to Ben, who just laughed to see her so happy. And that was when Cassie noticed that Ben was exhausted. Exhausted, but happier than Cassie had ever seen him. So, Cassie settled down and went over and Ben leashed her collar, and they went through the gate and Cassie looked back at Pootles, who looked relieved, because she had the impression that whatever was going on with Cassie's family, it wasn't bad.

And Ben put Cassie in the hatchback, and they were in the condo parking in no time and then up the elevator and into the apartment. The first thing Cassie noticed was the living room was all funny, the coffee table was pushed aside, and the couch had expanded into a bed and there was a suitcase near the door that Cassie had never seen before and it smelled strange. Then Cassie saw the old lady. It was the nice old lady that she had visited with Jen! The one who'd gone with them to the stone park! And Cassie was very excited to recognize the nice old lady and went up to her and said hello very enthusiastically.

"Cassie, my girl, you are a big sister now!" the nice old lady said, and Cassie didn't know what she meant but knew it was important.

And then Ben left again, and Cassie and the nice old lady sat quietly, and Cassie could tell they were waiting. Waiting for something big to happen. And then they waited some more, and finally there were noises in the hallway and Cassie could hear Ben *and* Jen talking and the front door opened very slowly and cautiously, and Ben came through and gently grabbed Cassie by the collar and then Jen came through very slowly carrying a bundle with a big handle that was full of very soft and fluffy blankets.

And in the middle of the blankets was the most beautiful puppy Cassie had ever seen.

31

The Monday morning meeting for administrative staff at King Street regional headquarters was coming to an end when Kristin Johnson announced that Jen Mahoney had her baby late Wednesday (a girl, seven pounds two ounces, named Clementine). Jen had not, it appeared, gotten quite everything sorted before the maternity leave started.

"She was working to reopen an old cold case. A missing little girl from 1970 out in the county. Thought she could review the investigation files while on leave. She managed to get the county files sent here — there's a lot — but there is no budget for it, and she couldn't scan it before she left. Now, obviously she's not going to do anything for a few weeks…" all the parents in the room laughed at that suggestion "… but I had an idea. If we each take a box and volunteer to scan a file or two early in the morning or before we leave each day, we can get it done."

Pretty much everyone in the room nodded. "Great, I'll set up an electronic file structure and come around with the cart to drop the boxes off to each of you at the end of today."

❊ ❊ ❊

On Monday evening Jen's mother was folding laundry on the kitchen counter while her daughter took a much-needed nap in the bedroom. Her son-in-law had staggered out bleary-eyed a few minutes before to walk Cassie.

She paused a moment and popped into the nursery to boggle a bit at her beautiful sleeping granddaughter, before returning to the kitchen, hoisting the laundry to her hip, and then making her way around the apartment to tuck the items away in appropriate places.

She had made up a few casseroles and placed all but one into the miniscule freezer, forming the firm opinion they did not have enough space in this condo. The remaining casserole was a lasagna that was now bubbling away in the oven and filling the small home with delectable smells.

By this point the new family unit was up and running and she would shortly be more underfoot then helpful. She would feed them dinner, stay the night and in the morning reluctantly head off on the journey that was too long to allow her to see her daughter, and now her grandchild, more than once or twice a year.

She was very attached to her own home, the one she'd grown up in and where she'd raised Jen with the help of her own mother after her husband died, but maybe the time had come to sell up and move closer.

This thought of moving to be nearer had just crossed her mind when Ben and Cassie reappeared.

"Oh, that smells good," said a grateful Ben, coming through the door after Cassie, who trotted right up to Grandma, as she now knew her. Ben washed his hands at the kitchen sink then grabbed the stack of plates and cutlery already on the counter and took them over to their small dining room table, where he deposited them in roughly the appropriate places and went into the bedroom to wake Jen.

He gently shook her shoulder: "Jen there's lasagna." He paused a moment, judging that further encouragement was needed, "it smells good." She opened an eyelid and gingerly sniffed the air, recognizing her mother's cooking and finding the willpower to get up.

"Ok. Be there in a minute. You guys start without me." Ben returned to the living area, too hungry to ignore her advice, while Jen rose and made her way into the bathroom to run a washcloth over her face and clean her hands before changing into a fresh dressing gown, which had somehow appeared on the hook in the bathroom. Ben had started eating by the time Jen made it to the table, although her mother had not.

"Mom, this looks great, thank you so much."

"There are more casseroles in the freezer. Enough to get you through a couple of weeks with leftovers." Ben was cheered by this news, but Jen suspected what was coming next and felt a surge of panic, "I think I'll take the midmorning train home tomorrow."

Jen's eyebrows shot up in protest, but her mother continued: "You'll be fine. And I am taking up too much space here." Jen looked around at the war zone that was their living room and the pull-out sofa her poor mother had been sleeping on for almost a week.

"I see your point."

"You can call me whenever you need to but she's doing so well! Wish you'd been such a good sleeper at this stage." Ben looked askance at the idea that the shrieking demands for milk and comfort emanating at regular intervals from the nursery was 'sleeping well' but he knew better than to complain out loud. Jen had just finished eating a modest slice of lasagna and a bit of salad when Clementine woke up and decided it would be good to eat along with the rest of the family, so Jen went to the nursery, leaving Ben and her mother alone at the table.

"How are things at work?"

"Good, good. I can take more vacation days next week if needed but right now it looks like I'll go back on Monday."

"Quite a short commute you have now, isn't it?"

Ben, finally grasping where the conversation was headed, knew what she wanted to hear. "Right now, yes, but we are thinking of buying a house out in the county soon."

Jen's mother smiled, "that sounds like an excellent idea."

Ben, seeking a bit of levity, "we have to move soon anyway, Cassie's seen a backyard, and now the balcony just doesn't cut it."

32

P eter Cadworth's black Labrador Posey sat patiently at the side of his bed and thwumped her tail gently against the floor. Dad would be waking up any minute and if Posey had done her calculating right, today was Conservation Area Day. Peter opened his eyes and looking into her adorable and expectant face, smiled. Conservation Area it was.

He got up and filled Posey's bowl to the brim, then made one of his rare hearty breakfasts of blueberry pancakes, bacon, sausages, eggs, coffee, and cranberry juice, with a fried tomato. They munched away in silence, interrupted only by two birds twittering insistently at each other on the birdfeeder outside the kitchen window.

Peter briefed himself on the Saturday news, reading one long article on his phone and double checking the weather before deciding what to wear. A couple of moisture-wicking layers, a fleece and a jacket should cover it. He pocketed some gloves and donned a light knit hat and his hiking boots.

Clipping on Posey's extendable leash, they bounded into the SUV and then rolled backwards down the drive before Peter turned the car onto the road and they were finally headed towards their destination. Posey sat upright; her eyes glued out the windshield waiting for the yellow-painted park gates to appear.

While the glorious fall colours had peaked a week or two before, there were still some red-brown leaves on the trees and the grass was not completely dead. In the blue-white sky, the clouds were a benevolent fluffy cream rather than the ominous grey they took on when filled with snow. With almost no breeze, the air had an inert quality; the growing season was over, and nature was preparing to rest. When they got out in the parking lot, Peter noticed that sounds were sharp and travelling far.

Posey nosed around a bit then chose the entrance to one of the longer hiking trails. Peter liked this trail as it ran across the top of an escarpment with panoramic viewing platforms, then down into a valley of cedar and pine, running along a small creek and incorporating a marshland boardwalk at the end before finally returning to the parking lot. Posey trotted, taking long stops at her favourite smells, which she knew were about to hibernate for the winter.

They had just emerged from the cedar valley and Peter was standing on the boardwalk surrounded by dried out cattails when his phone rang. It was his father's care home. These calls were instantly anxiety-inducing. He breathed in once and held it before answering, praying this was not the call he dreaded.

"Hi Peter, it's Ellen."

"Hi Ellen, is everything okay?"

Knowing family members were often unnerved when their number popped up, Ellen cut to the chase: "your father's having quite a bad day, Peter. He's very upset that he's not with your mother."

Peter sighed, half relieved, and half resentful at his father's disease. "I'll be there as soon as I can."

"Thanks so much," and she hung up.

This had happened before, and they had a little routine they followed to try help settle his father down without resorting to the more hard-core medications. It was a good thing he had had such a robust breakfast as it would probably be a delicate and stressful afternoon.

Peter took one last look around at the beautiful stillness and breathed the calm in for a few moments before he and Posey picked up the pace to get back to the car.

They arrived at the home soon enough and Peter checked in, leaving Posey with the lady at the desk who was very fond of such pet-sitting opportunities. Ellen turned up immediately and said his father was in a quiet room they called The Study, alone.

"Hi dad," Peter said calmly on opening the door and finding his father crumpled into a wingback chair next to the cold electric fireplace. "It's me Peter," and as he said it he looked his father directly in the eyes and smiled warmly.

Dick Cadworth looked up at his son, confused, "Peter? No, no, no, no...." There was a pause and then a baffled look crossed his father's face. "Where's Franny?" he asked, without apparently grasping that he was speaking to his son. "Where's Franny?"

Peter sat down in the other chair, looked at his father and said resolutely, but not unkindly "Mom's not here at the long-term care home, dad." And as he said it he gestured around the room with his hands, causing his father to look up, through bleary eyes, and glance around at his surroundings.

"Not here?"

"No."

"At the care home?"

"At the care home. We are at the care home."

"The care home" his father said, at the beginning of acceptance if not full understanding.

"And you are Peter?"

"I'm Peter."

The light started to glimmer in the reaches of his father's eyes. He was beginning to understand that he was not where he expected to be. If Peter could modulate his own responses to his father's statements and they were not interrupted in this little room, his father might slowly become less agitated.

On a good day he might even genuinely remember. Peter kept the conversation going with some well-worn topics that tended not to cause problems or upset him further. After about an hour there was a genuine click of recognition and a sudden clear statement: "Your mother's gone, isn't she?"

Peter paused, surprised for a moment at his own relief in seeing the father he had always known reappear, "Yes, mom's gone."

"When?"

"About ten years ago," Peter did not bother giving him more detail than that, in his experience it could agitate him further.

"Ten years!" this seemed to shock his dad considerably.

"Do we ever, go ... to visit her?" Peter was not sure if his father fully understood she had passed and needed a moment to think how to respond carefully. In the interval his father's canny perceptual capabilities re-emerged and he managed to anticipate Peter's conundrum.

"Do we ever go to the cemetery, I mean?"

"We do," Peter answered, quickly "we used to go when you were feeling up to it. We can go to visit her if you would like to."

His father seemed to think a moment. "I think we should. I'd like to be with your mother for a bit."

"No problem," Peter said, and he got up and stood next to his father's chair to help ease him to his feet. They hobbled out into the hallway and catching Ellen's eye, Peter said "we're going to go out to visit mom for a bit."

Ellen looked at them both, and performing her duty-of-care, asked "Are you sure?"

"Yes, we're sure."

"All right then, fresh air it is. Just a sec and I'll get his cane." She ducked behind the counter to retrieve the stick they knew to take away from him when he got upset. She passed it over and when Peter placed it in his father's hand muscle memory kicked in and he instantly seemed more stable and more mobile. They went around the desk and the woman on duty looked up and handed Posey over, to the delight of his father.

"Posey old girl, how are you?" his father said scratching her behind the ear with his free hand. Great, Peter thought to himself, *I swear he cannot remember me, but he remembers the dog*, and he had to laugh at that. They were out of the facility and into the SUV quickly, Dick showing an unexpected lightness of step, given his infirmities.

In a short while they pulled into the cemetery gate and Peter drove up the lane, parking at a convenient pull off. He let Posey out of the back and then went around the vehicle to help his father out, Dick swatting away the offer of assistance and one-two stepping his way to the ground by himself. Peter walked over to his mother's grave and took a moment, but then as his father caught up he left him alone and went to find the dog.

He caught Posey starting to pee on the side of a granite obelisk and managed to redirect her aim before too much damage was done. Taking a short lead from his jacket pocket, he snapped it onto the collar loop, and they made their way back towards his mother's resting place.

His father had wandered farther afield by that point — Peter knew many people buried here were familiar to his dad and decided not to interrupt his reminiscences. Peter took a moment to clear some twigs and leaves from his mother's stone while Posey sat respectfully at a distance.

Posey got up and lumbered over to his father, which fortunately caused Peter to glance up. His father was turning in a circle, suddenly more unsteady, and had made his way to the lane. He was no longer looking at the stones and Peter had a sinking feeling. "Dad?" There was no response.

"Dad?"

His father turned at that "What?" He looked dazed, but after a moment his face cleared. "I think we should go now."

"Sure dad."

Peter reached out a hand to brace his father's elbow but then thought better of it. His father stumbled somewhat on the return but with a bit of fiddling at the door handle eventually managed his way back into the SUV. Peter whistled for the dog and she jumped into the back seat. Peter, sensing his dad was feeling disoriented, quickly got them out of the cemetery and headed back to the home before his father's anxiety levels could rise.

Out on the familiar county road, he could sense his father calming down.

"How're you feeling now dad?"

There was a pause. "Fine. I'm fine. Are we headed home?"

"We are headed back to the care home." Peter said, carefully ensuring his father had the right frame of reference.

"Right. Right, of course." There was a pause. "I miss your mother."

"I miss her too dad."

"Life is not the same without the people we love."

Peter winced a bit at that. It was true of course, but there was an undercurrent of depression to the comment that worried him. His father was looking out the window, but Peter did not think he was seeing much of the present day rapidly passing before him.

As they pulled into the parking lot Peter remembered Jen Mahoney and her missing child case. He knew now was not a good time to ask his father about the past, particularly a traumatic case with a poor outcome. On some level, Peter knew the opportunities to bring up something like that were going to be increasingly few and far between.

33

Lori Sorenson Wheatley stood at the photocopier inside the public library, a large, slightly dusty scrapbook in hand. She put her library payment card into the required slot and then, brow furled, figured out how to adjust the page size and magnification so she could copy the irregular pages, on which were pasted yellowed newspaper clippings. Within a minute or two she had the settings right and set off rapidly. Five minutes later she had a stack of pages and she tucked those and the book back into her canvas tote bag, retracted her card, and went upstairs.

She had not seen her old friend, the reference librarian Sarah Carmine, in some years. Lori had rummaged around her attic a week earlier, eventually finding the scrapbook containing clippings of all of Julie's articles published in the local paper.

On realizing the library was the convenient place to make a copy, it naturally occurred to her that she should catch up with Sarah. They had arranged that Lori would stop by while Sarah was working, and they could take some tea in the library staff room.

Lori reached the Reference Desk and her old friend got up and gave her a big hug then led the way down a short hallway to a little room with a sink, small counter and tiny café table positioned next to another of the library's glorious old deep-set windows. Lori took a seat and gazed out at the nice landscaping which had almost entirely replaced the decrepit old parking lot.

Sarah put the kettle on. "Have you heard they are reopening Julie's case?" Sarah asked.

"Funny you should mention that. I met with a young investigator in the city, and I'm here today to photocopy Julie's old articles to send them to her. How did you hear?"

"Well, I heard from Bonnie, who is friends with the sister of Chief Cadworth's old secretary. The whole town knows. And there was a couple in here around the time of the fair and they saw the case in the paper on a microfilm reel. Are they something to do with your investigator?"

"Believe so. Pregnant?" Sarah nodded. "She's quite nice but I don't know how much she'll be able to do on the case with a new baby. It's their first."

Sarah brought two cups of tea over to the table and set them down, taking a seat herself. She sighed, "it would be good to know what happened," she said, meaning it would settle an old and noxious anxiety.

Lori nodded, "it would be good to know where she is. Doesn't make sense that we still don't know."

They both shook their heads in unison.

"How're your kids doing?" Sarah asked Lori, who gave her the full maternal update and then countered with "And your son?"

"He's out west now. Very happy with a new job in the tech sector."

They smiled at each other and held tight to these more comforting thoughts.

It was not until Friday that Lori managed to put the photocopies in an appropriate envelope, affix sufficient postage and get her package of Julie's old articles into the mail, addressed to Jen Mahoney at her condo in the city.

34

Mandi the grad student submitted her last essay and grabbed some lunch. Afterwards she stopped by Sam Eide's second floor office, as arranged, to pick up the key to the basement laboratory.

"Think I can put in a few hours later today" Mandi said to Sam, promptly heading back out the door on her way to a one o'clock class.

The class, being late in the semester, was not very onerous, and Mandi left with her energy levels intact, grabbing a snack and a coffee before heading back across campus. She went through the departmental main door, which was a looming neo-gothic stone arch. Then, up a small flight of stone stairs much used and somewhat eroded in the middle. On reaching the top, she turned left and entered a narrow and discreet portal opening into the long tunnel-like staircase down to the basement.

It was poorly lit and sepulchral, once providing narrow access for staff hauling in the coal deliveries needed to run a Victorian building. A newer entryway with a service elevator and large doors to the basement now existed, and that worked well for the cafeteria workers and building maintenance staff, but it was all the way around the other side of the large building adjacent to the parking lot. The small number of people heading to the basement from main campus inevitably chose to risk their ankle bones and use the narrow historic stairway instead.

On reaching the bottom Mandi made her way through a warren of hallways, pausing twice to reorient herself and make sure she was headed in the right direction. Sam had succeeded in securing the lab-closet mainly because it was so isolated and difficult to reach that no one knew it was there, and those that did could rarely find it. Having reached the lab, Mandi pulled out the key, opened the door, turned on the light, powered up the equipment and got to work.

An hour or so later and she had found the rhythm of the data transfer work and her focus wandered a little. She could hear the old pipes in the building creaking and odd little snippets of conversation as people walked through nearby hallways or past vents that transferred noise to her location. She was isolated but cozy enough. In her own mind, she was like Mulder and Scully in their basement FBI office.

Mandi successfully transferred several tubes and saved the individual files to disk, immediately attaching them to an email and sending that to Ben before she could forget. She did not expect to hear back from him, now they had the new baby.

Then, she took a few minutes to create a new file structure, adding the rows from one file plus a column with the date, and then repeating the procedure to assemble all the data in one place. It was exciting, looking at thousands upon thousands of rows of data accumulating, ripe for analysis and quite possibly a noteworthy paper. Mandi closed everything down and locked up the office, taking a moment to add the key to her personal key ring so she would not lose it.

Then she navigated her way back through the hallways and up the narrow staircase. The campus was starting to quiet down for the holidays and classes were ending, with exams occurring in the large auditoriums farther afield. When she emerged into the outside, which was cold and dark this time of year, she was alone.

35

Ben set off for work early Monday and as the front door closed behind him, Jen sat at the table and wondered how to plan her day. It would be good to get out of the house for a bit. They had first taken Clementine out in the stroller on the weekend, avoiding crowds but getting a little fresh air. With winter likely to take hold any day now and the holidays almost upon them, Jen was sure the first three months of the mat leave would be mostly an indoor proposition. The three of them, Clementine, Cassie, and Jen would have a cozy winter, with a slight risk of cabin fever.

Cassie emerged from the nursery, having completed her half-hourly baby check, and came up to Jen to report that everything was fine and wonderful and beautiful. Cassie was besotted with Clementine and taking her nanny duties very seriously. Jen got up, went into the nursery, and watched her daughter's wonderful little pink face as she snoozed, quite comfortable for the moment.

Jen got dressed, spotting a small stack of summer thrillers on the bureau she had never gotten around to reading. They were suddenly of greater interest. Even though she was fairly exhausted, and her thinking was not tremendously clear, she regretted not getting the Julie McNally case files scanned before going into labour.

Assuming she could keep on top of the cleaning and feeding (including herself, Cassie, and Ben) she would not mind having something to pick up and do in the odd moments here and there when Clementine was truly settled. Clementine was still sleeping when Jen returned from the bedroom, so she took a couple of minutes to reorganize their front closet, moving the parkas and boots to the nearer spots and tucking away summer items. She rummaged about until she had found all their old hats, scarves, and gloves.

Then she went to the linen closet and extracted a baby tuque, sweater, mittens, and booties, gifted by her partner Sumeet and his wife. She stowed those in the net basket on their nifty combo baby seat-stroller, ready for when they were heading out.

Clementine woke up with a pip squeak, a noise that brought Cassie immediately crib-side. Later in the morning, after everyone was fed and burped, as needed, Jen bundled the little group into all their gear, and they headed out to the hallway and down in the elevator.

The concierge on staff in the lobby, a young guy named Louis, gave them a big smile, and leaned over the counter to look at the baby, causing Cassie to park herself between him and the stroller, panting and grinning happily as her beautiful sister was appropriately adored, but also within biting range. Louis seemed okay though, in Cassie's opinion. Not a bad idea to have him manning the front door.

Then they were through the doors and outside and it was like passing through a vacuum seal. Jen swung the buggy left and they were on a quiet tree-lined street in no time. They passed the postal delivery truck pulling up to the back service entrance of their building and Jen gave a little wave to the driver, both as a fellow public servant, and to be sure he could see the stroller and the dog.

It was an unusually warm day, this late in the fall, and the leaves — bright reds, oranges, and yellows, many fallen on the ground — seemed cheerful rather than gloomy. A breeze caused everything to rustle, pleasantly obscuring normal mechanical city noises. Cassie's ears perked up and Jen took a good deep breath, letting a little of the stress of new parenting slide off her shoulders. They rolled and trotted their way towards a small parkette. On arriving, Jen found a good bench and settled in while Cassie inspected the perimeter.

Clementine was asleep, apparently taking the new and expansive surroundings in stride, and Jen pulled out the thriller she had taken from the pile in the bedroom earlier and placed in a pocket on the stroller. She read for over half an hour, stopping to sooth the baby when she awoke, and to respond to Cassie's intermittent security reports with head pats.

Eventually, they headed back home.

Once they arrived back at the building Jen was reluctant to return to the apartment. Remembering the mail truck, she realized they had not picked up their post in several days. She manoeuvred the little group into the tiny mail alcove and with some difficulty popped the box open, wherein she found a large manila envelope crammed in under some flyers. Extracting it with some difficulty, her eyes locked onto the return address: Lori Wheatley. With that in hand she returned to the condo with more enthusiasm, quickly leaving Cassie to her own devices in the living room and settling Clementine back in her crib.

Jen sat on the sofa, peeled the envelope open, and the stack of photocopied news clippings slid into her hands. It was immediately clear that Julie's presence in the community was noticeable in the year before her disappearance. There were interviews with most of the town notables and reports filed from all the community events and festivals, as well as pieces on school trips and the accomplishments of her elementary school compatriots. Jen started reading, and for the first time could hear the voice of a missing eleven-year-old girl.

36

Mandi loved having the campus to herself over the holidays. The quiet and stillness was unprecedented in her experience. Every outside view seemed like a period drama with superb cinematography. She puttered around picking up coffee or a snack at the few remaining open food kiosks (but without having to wait in line) or at the vending machine near the staff lunchroom in the basement. Able to completely control her own schedule she worked when energized, took breaks as needed, and stopped only when she really had to sleep (or security kicked her out of the building). If this was life as a researcher she looked forward to many happy years without boredom or fatigue.

She left the cool gray winter afternoon behind as she entered the stone portal of the main doors. No one was manning the security booth at the moment and there was a handwritten "Be back in five, please wait" notice propped up on the counter.

The holiday sign-in sheet was nowhere to be seen. Mandi waited a minute or two, shrugged and went to the stairs. Her winter boots gave a sloshy echo on the stone and she made her way even more carefully than usual down the treacherous incline. She squeaked for a fair few steps on the linoleum of the basement corridor but eventually moved quietly again.

There was no one else there — the basement seemed completely abandoned — and she had to admit to herself that the stillness in these corridors had transitioned from pleasant to creepy.

In her eagerness to get the data transfer done she was not about to let an irrational sense of foreboding put her off work for the day. She opened the closet-office door, switched on the desk lamp, and powered up the computer.

Unbundling from her winter gear, she sat down and set to work. The machines whirred away, and a faintly irritating hum came from the desk lamp, very close to her face in the tiny office. The noise had probably always been there, but was more obvious now, without the usual sounds of people trickling in from the air vents.

She placed her phone on the desk with her favourite playlist on to take the edge off. With the door ajar, the music echoed off the cinder block hallway, announcing her presence to any wee beasties living in the walls and floors.

Hours passed. When dinner-time hunger pains hit she pulled an energy bar and drink combo out of her backpack and started nibbling. While crunching away, and with the music playing, she did not hear footsteps approaching. She sensed the presence of another person just a moment before a light tap-tap of knuckles hit the door; Mandi flinched, nearly jumping out of her skin.

"Hullo!" a man said.

He was large, taking up most of the doorway. Mandi could not quite make out his features as his face was in front of the hallway lighting and well above the desk lamp. But he had grey hair, which instantly struck Mandi as odd, given most of the people she interacted with on campus were young. He was not wearing a security uniform and he was completely unfamiliar.

Mandi reacted in a way she had learned long ago, concealing her alarm, adopting a pleasant demeanor, and flashing a smile that, if he had noticed, did not reach her eyes: "Hi. Can I help you?"

"I think you can! I think you can!" He said, without introducing himself, and rocking back and forth on his feet with a degree of excitement that was very off-putting.

"You must be the grad student working for Professor Sam Eide?" He continued, without bothering to wait for her reply, "could I take a look at this data you've got?"

Mandi thought quickly. She needed him to back off out of the doorway.

Realistically, she could not push him out of the way. Adopting a naïve and girlish expression, she raised an eyebrow and replied "Oh, I work for Professor Stratenauer, actually. You know, I am not authorized to show anyone…"

She moved her wheelie chair over, blocking his view of the computer monitor, wondering what he had already seen over her shoulder, and took hold of one edge of the door, applying a light pressure that he could not fail to sense in the hand held up against it.

He paused at that, and the excitement seemed to drain out of him. Fortunately, as he took a moment to reconsider his strategy, he stepped backwards. "Right, right, I see," and as he did that, Mandi was able to slowly and gently press the door closed in his face. She very quietly wheeled forward and turned the lock.

After a moment, she sensed he had walked away on the other side but could not be sure. With the door locked, she reached out a shaky hand for her phone and quickly called Professor Stratenauer. It did not ring. Down here in the basement, she had no signal.

37

S he was a little shaky. Every instinct told her this was an odd situation, and she should not go out into the hallway by herself. She looked around the office closet but there was no intercom, buzzer, or alarm system on the walls.

Searching more thoroughly she found a landline phone jack in the baseboard behind the desk next to the Ethernet connection, but she had no phone to plug into it.

She had the computer though, and it was on the Faculty network. She logged into her faculty account and checked the email directory to see if building security had an email address. Unsurprisingly, they did not seem to. There were some corporate addresses for building security managers but none of them would be around at this time of the evening.

She sent an email to Professor Stratenauer, trying not to sound panicked.

Hi Professor Stratenauer,

I'm working in the lab – getting a bit late here. A man I don't know just turned up at the door wanting to take a look at the data. I told him I was not authorized to show it to anyone and closed and locked the door. The thing is, I am alone, my phone has no signal and I am not sure what to do.

Thanks, Mandi

Seconds later, a reply arrived.

Hello,

I am out of the office...

"Crap" she said aloud; she did not need to read the whole thing. She remembered. Professor Stratenauer was out in the country with her family until the New Year.

Mandi copied the email she had just sent into a new window addressed to Sam Eide and hit send. Then she waited, nibbling a bit more on her energy bar for comfort.

Fortunately, Sam's work emails were received on his phone, which was generally in his pocket. While he was crossing a noisy street when the initial ping came in, only a minute or two later he pulled out his phone to check the time and saw the notification.

Sam was slightly alarmed by the message. He tried calling Mandi first, and when the call failed to connect, he ducked into a doorway and composed a reply.

Hi Mandi,

Sorry to hear that you've had a scare. I am about 15 minutes away. How about I come back to the college, get security and we come down to rescue you? SE

When the email arrived on the desktop Mandi practically cried with relief.

That sounds great! Thank you so much. There's a phone jack here but no phone...

She relished a big bite of her energy bar as her nascent fear quickly turned to relief, and then irritation at being stuck in this ridiculous situation.

Sam made his way back to campus and found Jerry, the night watchman, sitting in the security kiosk, feet up, with his headphones on. Sam waved to get his attention.

"Hi Jerry"

"Hi Professor Eide"

"Listen, I've got a grad student working in the basement and she's had a bit of a scare. Will you come down with me to help her out?"

"That can't be right Professor Eide, see there's nobody in the building right now," Jerry pointed to the near empty login sheet now displayed on the desk, on which everyone who had entered that day had also signed out.

This was the sheet Jerry had been handed at 5 PM when his shift started. Sam paused a moment, pulled out his phone, and checked. He was sure the messages were from Mandi and genuine.

"I see the sheet says no one is here ... but I am pretty sure we do have a problem..."

Jerry liked and respected Sam, and as much as the idea that there could be someone in the building who was not on the sign-in sheet violated his worldview, he knew better than to quibble.

"Okay." Jerry put the *Security on Patrol* sign up and grabbed his bundle of keys. Unlike his predecessor, when they left the security kiosk Jerry remembered to leave the sign-in sheet in an accessible place on the counter.

In no time they were standing at the locked door to the lab. Sam knocked gently. "Mandi, it's Sam. I'm with Jerry the security guard. Do you want to open the door?" There was a click and the door opened with Mandi standing there, slightly wide-eyed, but clearly relieved.

Jerry, a bit baffled at this turn of events, knew instantly what needed to be said in this situation: "You are not on the sign-in sheet young lady."

Mandi looked irritated and chagrined at that. "There was no sheet!" she snapped.

Sam raised a hand to mediate and asked, simply: "What happened?"

"Well, I got here about three — there was no security in the booth and a note said 'be back in five' but I waited, and no one showed up — so I came down and started to work. I had the door open. About forty minutes ago this man is suddenly knocking on the door." She continued with a recap of the conversation that had passed.

"What did he look like?" Sam and Jerry asked in unison.

"Well, I couldn't really make out his face because of the light. But he was large, and he had gray hair."

The description puzzled Sam and Jerry even more. Sam went into the lab and sat in the chair to see it from her perspective. From there he understood her point about the light.

"I can't think who it could be Professor Eide," said Jerry, from the door.

"No, me neither. Anyway, I think you should stop working for now. Show me this phone jack?" Mandi pointed and he bent over to look under the desk while Mandi started gathering her things.

When he got up, she was logging off the computer. Sam took the empty energy drink can and bar wrapper in hand and passed them to Jerry for eventual disposal. "Is this all you've had to eat?"

Mandi, suspicious her experiences were about to be written off as hysterical hypoglycaemia said, defensively "I had a big lunch."

Jerry raised an eyebrow at that, but he knew what protocol dictated, "okay, so I should go upstairs and write this up in an incident report. Dunno what happened on the afternoon shift with the sign-ins... Are you folks heading home now?"

Sam said "yes I think so. Mandi which way are you headed on campus?"

"Out the back gets me home fastest."

"Okay, I'll walk you out. Maybe you'll remember another detail and we can figure out who this was."

Mandi nodded. They locked the office up, checking twice that it was secure and heading out the rabbit warren of hallways while the thudding footsteps of Jerry going up the stairs retreated behind them. Mandi was a bit taciturn in response to being uncharitably judged. Sam could sense a motivating good-will gesture was required. "The food truck on the far side of the parking lot is still open, how about I send you home with some dinner? I think Professor Stratenauer would expect me to make sure you don't get scared off a career in research."

Mandi looked up, grateful at the offer. In truth, she was hungry, and all the energy stimulants she had taken that afternoon were not helping her nerves. She nodded and her demeanour started to ease. They passed no one in the hallways and only three cars were sitting in the parking lot. The food truck, positioned in a circle of light from a streetlamp, appeared like an oasis in the desert of snow. They went up to the window and Mandi ordered a veggie burger and fries. Sam caught her eyeballing the vegan brownies as well and without asking, said "add a brownie" to the cook/

cashier and pulled out his wallet to pay.

They stepped back to wait, and Sam had an idea, although he would be surprised if it worked. Using his phone, he pulled up the faculty biographies website, which included headshots.

"Here, can you scroll through that and see if it could be anyone there."

"Sure" and she started looking. She paused once or twice but the verdict was delivered within a minute or two: "no, I don't think it was a faculty member."

Her answer was not surprising. He knew his colleagues well and while there were a fair few wingnuts (and even one or two people who, in his opinion, were very unreasonable and unpleasant), he did not think this was likely to be a faculty member. For one thing, everyone had done mandatory anti-harassment and sensitivity training and this sort of isolated after hours involuntary encounter was exactly the thing they had all been trained to avoid by university lawyers and bureaucrats.

However, there were also a host of people attached to the faculty in more peripheral roles. A grey-haired post-doc would be unusual, but not entirely impossible.

"How old do you think he was?" Sam asked.

Mandi thought for a moment, "hard to say, but the impression I got was he was old. You know? Like at least in his fifties, probably even sixties…"

Sam chuckled a bit, thinking back to when fifties seemed old. He took his phone back. "I'm going to send Professor Stratenauer an email just to let her know you are okay. I don't think you should come back in to work tomorrow."

The hackles of Mandi's ambition were instinctively raised by the inevitable delay this strange, unwelcome intrusion had caused, but her sense of self-preservation had the upper hand and she nodded meekly in agreement.

"If we do some things to make the lab safer, do you think you'd want to continue? I can get a phone installed, hopefully this week. We'll put a peep hole in the door – which I think you should always have closed. And we'll need to be a bit more rigorous about signing in and ensuring security knows you are there in future."

She thought for a moment. "That sounds good. I think I'll be okay. And I want to get it done sooner rather than later."

The order was up at that point, and Mandi reached over to the counter, sticking her hand into the steaming bag to grab a few fries. Before closing it up to keep the food warm, she offered some fries to Sam, who refused.

They left the parking lot and started walking towards the main campus thoroughfare. When they reached it there was more activity, a few groups of students out and about attempting to have an enjoyable evening despite the cold and preternatural quiet.

"I think I'll be okay from here," Mandi said, "thanks again for the food."

"I'll let you know when the phone is hooked up and we'll set up a meeting with the security team before you are back down there by yourself."

She nodded at that and turned left, offering a brief wave goodbye with her free hand. Sam watched her go and once she was far enough away not to see his face clearly should she glance back, lines of worry started crossing his forehead.

Instead of immediately heading home, he sat down on a bench and monitored her progress, making sure she was safe for as long as it was in his power to do so.

Bad things happened on college campuses. He had spent decades on them and while he did not have much direct experience of real danger, he had heard stories. He also worked from time-to-time with law enforcement on cases requiring his expertise, which had included some truly dark and disturbing things.

Bad things happened in the world generally, let alone on college campuses.

The office they had been able to get for the tube project had not seemed so unsafe before the holidays, but under the current campus conditions, there was another colour to it entirely. He mulled the suspicion this could have been a bad or clueless man who tried interacting with Mandi simply because she was alone and vulnerable.

But thinking back to the conversation she recounted, the man had started off by mentioning Sam himself. And he clearly had an idea about the dataset. That was, if anything, reassuring.

Sam tried to map out who could possibly know about their project at this point. Given that he asked around to find Mandi to work for them to begin with, it was not surprising word of what they had seeped out through the grapevine.

The idea that this was a socially inept postgraduate — and possibly one from a generation that did not know any better in terms of interacting with women — seemed very possible. Sam wondered if he should send a quick note to Ben Mahoney about this interloper and his interest in the tubes. He pulled his phone out and had input Ben's address into the destination field on a new email before he thought better of it. They had the new baby and there was nothing Ben could do anyway; best not to bother him.

38

Kristin Johnson crossed the last item off her list and smiled. One week to Christmas and her shopping was done. She sipped some coffee, tucked her hair behind her ears and started ruthlessly clearing her inbox. She refused to head into a new year with any outstanding items bogging her down.

Scrolling down, a clutch of automated processing emails appeared. These messages were sent out by their information management system when certain project tasks were completed. In this case they indicated files Jen Mahoney needed for her missing child case review had completed scanning.

Kristin opened the system application and clicked on the project name. A long list of boxes and files appeared and there were green check marks next to each of them. It looked like everything was done.

A few hours later, the workday was finishing, and Kristin got her cart and rolled around the floor to the various offices and cubicles where she had deposited Jen's boxes weeks before. She reclaimed them one by one and, using her master key to open the door, parked the full cart back in Jen's office. She went back to her own desk and composed a quick email.

Hi Jen,

How's the baby?

We have a Christmas present for you. A group of us here all pitched in the last few weeks and scanned your boxes when we could. Believe it or not it is all done! I've just sent everything to upload to the existing casefile number so when you login next time you should see it all.

Hope everything is well and Happy Holidays,

Kristin

And with that she turned off her workstation and left for the day.

❋ ❋ ❋

Several blocks away Jen was struggling to wrestle the Christmas wrapping paper out of the space it happily occupied at the back of the closet for the last year. She emerged victorious and dropped the wrapping paper on the bed, then went to grab the scissors and tape.

Clementine was sleeping and Jen took a moment to collect the shopping bags of presents and bring them to the bedroom, where she had enough space to wrangle with the giftwrap. Within a half hour she had a small pile of festive packages, mostly for Clementine and Cassie.

Ben had brought their tree up from storage the night before and set it up in the corner of the living room; Jen artfully placed the packages underneath. This time of year, it was already dark outside and while they had not added decorations, she took a distinct pleasure in turning on the tree lights and instantly brightening up the room.

She went to the kitchen to make a cup of tea and start dinner. Her phone was on the kitchen counter and she spotted Kristin's message notification. Jen set the water boiling then read the email with interest, loading the files in her work app. There they all were. Thousands of scanned items from that heap of boxes: it was a veritable seasonal miracle. She composed a quick reply to Kristin.

That is a great and unexpected Christmas present. Thanks so much to everybody who worked on this and to you for making it happen. Happy Holidays!

And she attached a picture of Clementine with a Santa's Elf filter that she had sent to her mother the day before. She would not have too much time to look at it over the next week, but the full case file would be there when she was ready.

Just then Ben came through the door.

"Something smells good."

"I made three batches of Christmas cookies today. Mom confirmed she's coming down here for Christmas. She's booked a hotel room though.

Says she wants to use the pool, but really she knows we can't fit her and the Christmas tree into the living room. Have your parents gotten back to you?"

Ben helped himself to a shortbread cookie from the plate on the counter, and responded through crumbs: "Yep, they were thinking of driving in on Boxing Day to see Clementine and do some shopping."

Ben's parents lived a good two-hour drive outside the city. They both took a moment to wonder how they would be able to handle the holidays when Clem got older, and she wanted to be with all her grandparents at Christmas.

"The tree lights are looking good. I'll go downstairs and get the ornaments." And he took the set of keys that opened the storage room and the padlock on their locker and headed for the basement.

39

The day after Boxing Day, Jen sat at the kitchen counter with her foot in Cassie's fur, in the same position as when they returned from visiting Bob Micklethwaite's grave back in the fall. Today she was eating reheated turkey, mashed potatoes and stuffing, roast vegetables, and a neat little rationed portion of the remaining cranberry sauce.

There were still some cookies and cake left. It was snowing outside, cold but with little wind, and Clementine was tucked up in her crib, surrounded by an assortment of new soft toys and blankets. Cassie was chewing on a rawhide Ben's parents gave her the day before.

Snowy weather and piles of carbohydrates could be good for brain work, with the help of a little coffee, and Jen had set up a French press for that purpose, although it was mostly decaf to ensure the caffeine would not make Clem fussy later.

As it steeped, she opened the Julie McNally case file on her tablet. She needed to review the questionnaires collected at the fairground gates in the days after Julie disappeared. Those were as close as she could get to interviewing the people who had been there at the time.

Given that these were handwritten, they were not currently searchable with the application software, but as she read, she could add tags. The key thing, she figured, was to tag all the names that appeared. At some point, she would start tracing the whereabouts of specific people of interest across a given timeline.

Each questionnaire had started out as a mimeographed form that someone had obviously knocked up pretty quickly on a typewriter. The blue ink looked like a notice Jen might have brought home from kindergarten.

Across the top there were three slots for *NAME*, *ADDRESS*, and *NUMBER*. She poured a large mug of coffee and held it in her left hand, sipping frequently as she read. She hovered over every name, then clicked and typed it in. Within an hour she had read over forty questionnaires and added probably two hundred tagged names to the file, which was a kind of progress.

Clearly, the community was very invested in figuring out where Julie was right from the beginning. The response on every form in the first batch Jen reviewed contained no apparent irritation. While to some extent these responses were filtered through the police dispatchers and secretaries who were recording what people told them, it was clear everyone had the right priorities and were more concerned about finding the girl than any inconvenience the investigation was causing.

There was also a strong undercurrent of fear, although more so from the adults than the children, who probably had not grasped the severity of events.

As Jen got deeper into the interviews it did not take long to unearth a useful nugget. As soon as Jen saw the recollection described on one questionnaire, she remembered Lori Sorenson telling her '*an older couple behind us and behind them I remember there were rowdy boys...*'

And here was one of the boys, on Saturday attending the fair with both his parents, and reporting that he remembered seeing a group of girls, possibly including Julie McNally, while he had waited in line at the gate with his friends the day before. His name was Jeff Dalrymple and on the form he listed the three buddies and identified the man in the couple ahead of them as Mr. Bromwich from the hardware store.

Jen searched the file for Bromwich to see if his first name was otherwise listed but it was not, so she settled for tagging "Mr. Bromwich." Then she accessed a tool in her app and spent an hour setting up a special map overlay on top of modern satellite imagery of the fairgrounds. She used some pictures found online, an old pdf map of the fairgrounds from a few years previously still hosted on the county website and her own memory to add in as much detail as possible.

Once persons of interest were defined, she could add them to the map at specific locations with associated time points. The accumulated data could be reviewed in a text timeline or as a map animation which would show people as dots transported from location to location while a clock progressed in fast forward at the bottom of the screen.

Having started on the map, she progressed no further with the questionnaires that afternoon and concentrated simply on plotting Julie, her friends, and now the Dalrymple boy and Mr. and Mrs. Bromwich onto the map. If she wanted to do this with everyone in the file, it was going to take weeks, possibly even months. She had the time, but there was no guarantee it would lead to any new insights.

40

L ate on a dark mid-January evening, Jen smeared one last dollop of cleansing facemask onto her cheek, poked her phone timer and then picked up her toothbrush. Ben, sitting up in bed a few feet away, was browsing the internet and checking emails. He was nattering in an absent-minded and pleasant way, updating her with news about their friends, particularly egregious political happenings, and the current weather predictions.

She was tired (the facemask more for reducing the puffiness under her eyes than cleansing her pores) and only picking up every second or third point in his running commentary.

"Ah, Mandi's finished with the tubes. I'll have to bring them back here. Where do you want me to put them?"

Jen sighed. The stupid tubes. She had completely forgotten about them. *Well, they were not going back on top of the bookshelves, that was for sure.* She paused, thinking a moment, and concluded they were possibly useless and deserved to be trashed. She spit out enough toothpaste to enable word formation.

"What was even on them, anyway?" she said over her shoulder.

"Didn't I tell you?" Ben was surprised that she did not know; surely he had mentioned it. Although, thinking back to the baby's arrival, it was distinctly possible he had not.

"It's a phone log. They're all excited and going to do a big analysis on calling patterns back in 1970."

In the bathroom, Jen stared at her own reflection in the mirror. Her eyes grew huge. She spit out more toothpaste foam and, toothbrush in hand, turned to directly address her husband from the bathroom door.

"What did you say?"

Ben was startled by her sudden and emphatic engagement, wondering if he had done something wrong.

He looked at her and repeated somewhat meekly and apologetically: "It's a call log."

Jen's head titled back ever so slightly, and her knees bent somewhat. "What are you saying? Are you saying you have a log of some of the calls made in 1970? The names and times?"

"No." Jen's agitation seemed to abate when he said that which was a relief. She started to turn away to rinse out her mouth.

"No, we have a call-log of all the calls in the county for 1970, but it is only times and *numbers*."

Jen heard that and the wheels in her head went into overdrive. She turned again towards her husband but could not immediately think of what to say. The timer on her phone pinged and she lifted one finger, indicating she would return to the conversation in a few moments. At the sink she wet a washcloth and vigorously scrubbed off the face mask. She needed to see this data.

Jen left the bathroom and deliberately made her way around the bed, all the while Ben stared at her, baffled. She sat down, robe and slippers still on, her back straight and barely nestled against the pillow.

"Can you show me what you are talking about?"

Ben was surprised. "Sure." He closed some windows on his laptop and clicked on one of Mandi's email attachments.

"See, this is the data once it's been converted from primitive bits and then split into fields. Mandi and her supervisor and Sam analyzed it and determined it is the calling number, the receiving number, and a time stamp which pretty much must be the call start time, they think, based on how the recording rig was set up. They did all sorts of analysis and basically the data seems to be intact."

"Right, okay. How do you know the date?"

"Oh, so Mandi just puts the date stamped on the tube in the file title. She's assembling everything into one big dataset that will have a field for the day as well, but I don't have that."

Jen paused, and then with no explanation she got up, went into the living room, and returned with her tablet. She stood at the door waking the tablet up and accessing her work app. Ben remained baffled. Jen, still looking at her tablet and scrolling, wandered forward and dropped cross-legged at the end of the bed, from where she addressed Ben without looking at him: "Do you have the file for October 8th, 1970?"

Ben clicked and opened the main folder where he had archived the files Mandi sent over the last two months. He sorted them by title, opening 19701008. "Yep."

"Okay, okay," Jen was very excited; she clicked a few more times, clearly seeking something deliberately. Ben could not see it, but she had pulled up Mrs. McNally's initial missing person report. In a form field at the top was the McNally's home number. "Okay, okay," she said again, "can you do a search for 645-1723?"

Ben did exactly that. In that moment, he began to understand that all the time his wife had spent on that tablet in the evenings had something to do with the county. In 1970. In October.

In an instant he realized she had been looking into that case from the microfilm reel. The one with the missing kid. Slightly irritated at being kept out of the loop, he suddenly felt he had the moral high ground in this situation and became more straightforward. "Find says seven instances. First one is outgoing at 7:48 AM."

"Okay, it won't be that one, what is the next?"

"Incoming at 8:15."

"No."

"Outgoing at 9:37. Followed by incoming at 10:02."

"Neither of those. It will be late afternoon."

"Next one is incoming at 4:49."

"That could be it. What are the last two?"

"Both incoming at 8:15 and 9:32."

"It's not those. It is the 4:49."

"Oh, it is, is it?" Ben managed to make eye contact with Jen and raised an eyebrow. She looked slightly sheepish but ignored him, for the moment, getting up and opening the bedside table to retrieve a block of post-its and a pen. "I'll explain in a minute. Now, what is the calling number at 4:49?"

Ben harrumphed slightly then read it out: "448-9287."

Jen did more scrolling and poking, pulling up the first interview sheet for Lori Sorenson. The Sorenson home number listed at the top did not match. Lori had been right all along; she had not called Julie on Thursday.

Jen could text search the entire massive set of investigation files and the person associated with 448-9287 would pop up. If it was not Lori who called Julie the day before she went missing, whoever did was probably significant to the investigation. All her police instincts told her so. With her hand trembling slightly, Jen input the number in the Search box.

41

The processing daisy wheel rotated on the screen for more than a minute. It was efficient software, but a large number of scanned documents needed going through. When it finally produced a result, Jen was completely deflated.

Zero. There were zero instances of that number in the file. She tossed the tablet on the coverlet dismissively. Ben gave her a moment, and then asked: "what is going on?"

"Remember that missing child case we saw when we went to the county library to look at tube-man Bob's obituary?"

"Yes," Ben wondered if he should reveal he had figured that part out by himself.

"Well, I've been reviewing the case."

"No kidding? When have you had the time to do that?" he said, carefully withholding all judgement. He was tempted to whimper a bit about devoting her attention to other things, but then she had been a good sport about the tubes.

"It wasn't hard to get our records on the case and I started with those, but then I discovered there were a pile of interview files still at the county. Remember Peter Cadworth?"

"Sure."

"Well, his father was the chief out there for decades and Peter managed to get those files sent down to us for scanning. They arrived just before Clementine was born and I couldn't do it, but believe it or not, a whole bunch of people at work chipped in and did it together.

"I've had a massive amount of information to work with for the last month or so and that is what I do during the day when Clem is sleeping.

"One of the outstanding questions in the investigation is who called the missing girl, Julie McNally, late in the afternoon on the day before she disappeared.

"Her mother came home from getting her hair done and had the impression Julie was hanging up on a call with her best friend, Lori.

"Lori always denied calling Julie on Thursday and her number does not match that one in your call log. According to the search I just did, that number you gave me does not appear anywhere in the casefile — and it is gigantic."

He was mildly impressed at the scale of the thing and that she had managed to keep this from him for so long.

"Let's see what you've got." He picked up the tablet, she used touch ID to open the interface and showed him the investigation files lined up in their special structure. As a systems administrator it did not take him long to understand what he was looking at.

"So, they just perform optical character recognition on scans of the old typescript files?"

"As far as I know, yes."

"Any chance it just has a poor read of the text and that is why it can't find the number?" as he spoke he fiddled with some of the viewing options and managed to pull up the underlying data layer as a text file.

They browsed through it. Clearly it did not always correctly identify the original text, as evidenced by some nonsensical character assemblages. "Maybe we should just search on the last four numbers, it could easily be messing up the hyphen." He did that and got no hits.

"Well, I guess that leaves the prefix." Ben input '448' in the search field. There were four hundred and seventy-three instances.

"Hmmm." Jen pulled the tablet back towards her lap, stuck the sticky note to the bottom and checked it against the first instance in the electronic file. No match.

Ben retreated to his own computer and the internet. For the next hour and a half, as Ben started to nod off next to her, and with two breaks to attend to Clementine, Jen checked every single phone number the software could identify as having the 448 prefix.

None of them matched 448-9287. As far as she could tell, the initial search was correct. The only option for double checking now would be to read every single page of investigative material herself. That would take forever.

"Arggh," Jen muttered, and Ben woke up a bit at that, "you know I bet if I had a name for that number to work with I could find something in here somewhere…"

"I remember Mandi's supervisor saying something about that. That they weren't going to de-anonymise the data because of ethics…" Ben semi-suggested, groggily.

"What was she thinking of doing?" Jen responded, also slipping towards a tiredness where thoughts were harder to grasp and articulate. "At work we'd do a reverse number search."

And on saying that she remembered a line from a movie seen long ago, set in Los Angeles in the 1950s, in which an old-time copper says: *'Would you grab a reverse directory and shag a name and address for me?'*

"You know they used to have paper copy reverse directories back in the day. If there are any left from the 1960s and 1970s, where do you think they are stored?"

"Dunno. Good chance we might have some at the university. I could ask around at work tomorrow." He offered generously, if somewhat incoherently with his face smashed into the pillow. He turned his head towards the air: "you know, do you think it's odd that there's Bob, with his call log, dying suddenly just as a police investigation needed to track down this phone call?"

And just as he said that Clementine started crying.

42

The next day, Ben completely forgot to go to the university library and ask about old reverse phone directories. But by Thursday he remembered, and, after wolfing down a sandwich for lunch he walked over to the main campus library and went straight to the reference desk. He pulled out his employee library card in case it was needed. "Hi, I am looking for reverse phone directories for the 1960s and 1970s. Can you tell me if we have any of those?"

The librarian thought a moment. "You know, directories are not part of our collecting mandate. They tend to be considered local history and the municipal library system handles that — we send the history students over to the main city branch fairly often... I'll check though."

She did some searching on her computer and after a moment or two gave him a rueful glance. "Nope, none here. You should try the Reference desk at the city main branch."

"Thanks anyway," Ben smiled and shrugged, then turned around and went back to work. He had only the vaguest notion of where the municipal library was but pulled out his phone, did a map search and formed a plan to stop in there after work. He was determined to find what Jen needed for her investigation.

At five he left his office, sent Jen a text that he would be late for dinner and got on transit, which was fortunately not completely packed, given he was heading farther downtown while most people were going the other way.

The municipal reference library was a mid-sized red-brick 1980s block with a large bronze sculpture out front next to a reflecting pool in desperate need of a cleanout and power-wash. Two homeless people with carts stacked tightly full of their worldly goods sat on the wooden slat and concrete benches near the entrance.

Ben pushed through the brown-tinted revolving doors and entered a terracotta-tiled foyer glinting dully under thirty years of accumulated floor wax. The smell brought him right back to the institutional buildings of his childhood.

The carpet was a slightly faded blue and ran not only along the floors but formed a textile wainscoting. It was pinned tightly to the curvy modernist stairway off to the right, above which an old sign with white lettering indicated the Reference section was on the second floor.

Ben went up the stairs and made his way towards his second Reference desk of the day. He smiled at the librarian, and repeated his earlier request, practically word for word.

"Hmmm. Reverse directory? That is interesting. We for sure have all the telephone directories — they are over there where that yellow sign is — but I if I remember correctly, we don't have any reverse directories. Let me ask a colleague who should know." She picked up the phone, dialed an internal line, and after some pleasantries repeated Ben's request.

There were various mumbles from the other end for a minute or two.

"Right, right. That makes sense. Unfortunate. Well, tell the budget overlords the taxpaying public needs this information! Hmmm. What should he do? Right. I'll let him know." The librarian finally put the phone down and looked up at Ben apologetically.

"Okay, so we used to have a few reverse directories — not many and probably not even for the years you needed. They tended to get deposited here whenever Emergency Services did an office clean-out. Anyway, we don't have a lot of space to spare so wherever we can we deaccession. Now, we are in the process of digitizing all the telephone directories and putting them online. Someone upstairs" she gestured to the powers above, with more than a hint of frustration "decided we could chuck the reverse directories because anybody who needed that function would be better served by just text searching the scanned normal directories."

She paused. "However, our budget has been cut so the digitization project is suspended, and we've only scanned the directories up to 1947."

Ben looked at her, flummoxed by the complexity of the situation. He had enough wits about him to remember how hard it had been for Jen to know if the text searching on her work file was even doing its job correctly, but he decided not to criticize.

"Anyway, my colleague Phil thinks there are two places that can maybe help you. One would be the phone company itself — we have no idea who to contact there — and the other would be the archives of the regional police force. He says they would have been the primary users of the original directories — they were usually very restricted — and would have kept them in storage for a good long while. Maybe not fifty years but you never know..."

This was turning out to be harder than Ben had thought, although at least both of her suggestions held promise. Jen could presumably get into the police archives if needed, but his first thought was to see what his own department had in the phone company archives they had acquired, and that Sam had used to reengineer the tubes.

"Okay, well thank you for trying" Ben said and turned, went back downstairs, and headed out the door. Given his trip had not taken very long, he now faced the prospect of taking transit back up town, this time with the crush of commuting traffic. The idea held no appeal, and he got on the phone to Jen, leaving a voicemail.

"Honey, I'm stuck downtown. Not far from the waterfront, would you want to bring Clem down in a cab and we could go to the Park Restaurant for dinner?"

Ben found a clean spot on a bench which he believed was outside the territory of either homeless person and waited, hoping she would pick the message up right away, which she did. His phone rang.

"What are you doing downtown?"

"Chasing a red herring, apparently. Anyway, I can tell you all about it when you get here. Can you?"

Jen was overjoyed at the prospect of getting out of the house and had already strapped Clementine into her baby carrier before calling Ben back.

"Sure, we're out the door now." And she hung up before Ben responded, causing him to lurch off the bench and set off at a trot. He would have to walk quickly to get to the restaurant before them.

* * *

He made it to the maître-de station a minute or two before Jen arrived and managed to get them a reservation. They were whisked graciously towards a spacious booth once Jen struggled through the door with Clementine.

The Park Restaurant was a family-friendly grill, gastronomically a half-step up from a diner. Mostly traditional fare, and mostly seating on easy to clean vinyl. There was a patio in summer and good windows set into the old neo-Tudor fabric which gave patrons one of the best views of the rock garden and duck and geese gamboling space that led down to the water. There were also lots of seagulls whirling around, even at this time of year.

"This is her first trip down to the waterfront," Jen mused, looking out the window and taking off her winter gear. Ben took out his phone and grabbed some snapshots of Clementine *in situ* in front of the window, backlit by the seasonal lighting display outside.

They propped Clem, still in her carrier, in front of the old fireplace, adorned now with slightly wilted poinsettias, and took a couple of photos there as well, then they settled down and looked at the menus. Before long they had their orders in and Jen could start interrogating her husband.

"So, what have you been up to?"

"Well. I was going to hunt you a reverse phone directory for 1970 but it appears those are endangered beasts."

"Really?"

"Yep, I asked at the university library and they sent me down to the city reference library. And, get this, they threw all of theirs away because they had a plan to digitize the normal directories — which would enable searching phone numbers — but then they haven't got the money to finish the project and are stuck at 1947."

"You are kidding." Jen had to smile. "You've given it the old college try that's for sure."

"I'm not giving up yet. No siree!" he said with mock Victorian gumption, "the city librarian thinks the phone company, or the police archives will be the best bet at this point."

Jen thought for a moment "that makes sense. I wonder who I should call…"

"Give me a chance to look into the phone company archives the department has at work. That'll probably be easier."

"Okay. Thanks for doing that. You said the library has the normal directories, they still have the ones going up to 1970, but they just aren't online yet?"

"Right, they are in the reference section."

"Reference, so that means we can't sign it out?"

"No, in-library use only."

"Hmmm. So that number is in there somewhere and we just need to find it… You think the library is still open?"

Ben pulled out his phone and opened the maps, which still had the library showing as his selected destination. He pulled up the detail information. "Open until 8 PM tonight."

"Well, I wouldn't mind taking a look at one just to see what we are dealing with. I was trying to get a grasp on why the number isn't already in the file. There were almost five hundred instances of that one prefix — now some of them would have been repeats but probably not that many because the file is mostly canvassing interviews and other reports. Do you know how many prefixes there were at the time?"

"Nine. That was how we figured out what the tube data was. There were only nine three-digit sequences and they were always positioned at the beginning of a line and then again after four more digits."

"Okay, so maybe forty-five hundred numbers in the file, which makes sense because the county population would support about that number of households and you wouldn't expect there to be many commercial numbers reported on investigation paperwork. I meant to ask you, can you send me all the data files for October? I should probably check all the phone traffic into and out of the McNally residence as well as their associates and maybe if I check the unknown number I'll see a pattern that will explain who it belongs to. I've got a hunch that particular call is important but if we were investigating this today we would analyse every single call for that household plus a fairly wide network."

"Sure, sounds like a good plan."

With the dinner bill paid, they put their winter gear on and bundled Clementine back into her various baby-knits; the restaurant visit eliciting not much more than boggle eyes and some yawns. They transferred her to a harness across Ben's chest, where she was mostly tucked into his coat, toasty and warm for the time outside on their way to the library.

Light displays the city put up along the sidewalks to help the citizenry stay sane through the winter provided a certain romantic sparkle. Fortunately, it was not really that cold and the snow and ice had been well cleared so their journey was a pleasant outdoor break from winter claustrophobia. In the twilight the bronze statue and reflecting pool looked much cleaner and more welcoming than they had on Ben's first visit. They went through the doors and Jen followed Ben up to the second floor. He made a beeline for the shelves with the yellow sign. And there they were: a hundred and fifty years of city and county directories. Along the edge of each shelf was a sticker that said: *No photocopies.*

"Hmm. Wonder why we can't make copies?" Jen asked aloud.

"Dunno."

They pulled the 1970 directory off the shelf and took it over to a table. It was heavy, with several hundred frail tissue-like pages.

"I haven't used one of these in years and I forgot what the paper and the type was like" Ben muttered.

"It's awfully big."

They looked at the first page and realized the directory covered the entire greater metropolitan area.

"I hadn't thought of that. Are there any subsections?"

There was a separate commercial section and half was an address-based directory, which did not help them.

"You know, we can't be sure it was a personal number, so we're still looking at what, hundreds of pages of minuscule writing, somewhere in which is our number? How would we get through it all..."

Ben took the book over to the librarian: "Hi, I saw the signs saying we can't photocopy, why is that?"

"It's a condition issue. The paper is very fragile, and they are glue bound, so if people press them down on the copier the pages will eventually fall out."

"Right."

"You can take pictures though, with your phone. That is what most experienced genealogists do," the librarian said, assuming that was their motivation.

Ben put the book down and Jen lined up her phone camera and took a few shots. They could both see it was not going to work well. People probably had no trouble photographing a specific listing close-up but getting an entire page well-lit and into focus was another story. Plus, taking a few hundred photos was not something they could accomplish in what remained of the night. A voice came over the intercom to let the patrons know 'the library is closing in twenty minutes.' Against Ben's chest, Clementine let out a burp. They probably needed to get her back to the condo soon to settle her properly.

"Arggh. This is way harder than it should be," Jen said. Ben nodded in sympathy. Jen held the book in her hands, knowing her number was in there somewhere, then gave up and returned the book to the shelf. They set out home.

43

The next day Ben woke early and as the coffee percolated he copied the October phone files into a new folder. He opened each one up, added a column for the day, added the day in bulk to the column, and then assembled them into one large file. He emailed the file to Jen, so she would see it when she got up, and then poured himself a cup of coffee.

He popped in to check on Clementine before sitting at their little glass table by the window alone. Cassie snored peacefully behind him on her dog bed. He did a Google search, finding the best sources for county real estate listings and started browsing. Outside the sun was rising but the masses of cold grey concrete in the city resisted the warmth. He would not miss these stony mornings if they should find themselves looking out on fields and trees in the future.

He had a good sense of what their condo was worth and felt he should research what sort of buying power they would have out in the county in given areas, taking into account the financial burden of commuting. He was surprised when one of the big Victorian places near the county museum showed up in the group of houses restricted to their price range, but the listing revealed that inside it was a fixer-upper, with very outdated kitchens and bathrooms. Expensive renovations seemed like a risky proposition to Ben.

Cassie stirred, rolled over, stretched out and then got up, looking at Ben to get his attention and communicate that she was desirous of a walk. Ben went quietly into the bedroom and swapped out his pajama bottoms for a pair of jeans, then bundled himself up to fend off the cold morning and set out with the dog.

When they got back Ben showered, got dressed, ate a muffin defrosted from the freezer in the microwave and headed out for work. Jen slept through all of this, having been up two or three times tending to Clementine. She did not wake until close to nine and only then because she was starving.

She made scrambled eggs, toast, coffee, and on seeing Ben's muffin wrapper in the bin, promptly pulled two more out of the freezer, reheating one for now and letting one defrost on the counter for later. Clementine was asleep and Jen checked her phone, seeing the file from Ben in her email.

She sat down at the glass table, where Ben had been a couple of hours before. Full daylight was revealing the city at something approaching its best and brightest, given it was winter. Mug of coffee in one hand and tablet in the other she opened the spreadsheet Ben had sent and did a number of searches for the McNally's home number.

She copied those lines of data into a spreadsheet one by one, eventually ending up with over a hundred lines of information. The mystery number appeared only once in that particular sixteen-day period.

She thought she recognized the Sorenson home phone from memory but double checked it against the interview reports in the case file. She was right and added a note column to the table, typing "Sorenson" in the row each time the number appeared. There was a clear pattern of calls on weeknights, excepting Thursdays, and on week-ends after breakfast. It was the girls calling each other regularly, exactly as expected.

She went back to the top of the McNally household call log, and ran the first incoming number through the find function in the investigation case file. The number hit. It was identified as the household number for one of the neighbours who had been interviewed the night of the disappearance.

She tried the second number and got nothing, which was surprising, but then she remembered something: the fairground gate questionnaires were handwritten and there would be no character recognition for that huge stack of information. Jen sighed.

She had read through the questionnaires and tagged all the names, plotting people with useful information onto her events map, but she had done that just after Christmas, before knowing about the phone data set, and she had not tagged any of the numbers at the top of those questionnaires.

She would have to go through them again. Given that the case file would probably include most of the numbers on the McNally list eventually, it probably was not worth trying to decode the callers until she had tagged the questionnaires, especially since getting a reverse directory was proving so difficult.

She also realized this outstanding data set might contain the mystery number. The tagging would go more quickly the second time around, but all things considered, including laundry, cooking, Clementine tending, necessary naps and walking the dog, this was going to mean another week of work.

Jen took a long sip of coffee and started in.

44

The first week of February was a busy one for Ben. Work weighed heavily, and while he was getting some sleep, the baby was waking them up at least once or twice each night. That, coupled with the general malaise of winter, left him feeling worn out.

He bought Jen a box of Valentine's chocolate early, to ensure he would not forget, but ended up eating most of it in the afternoons just to get through each workday. He was pulling the last caramel dark chocolate out of the magenta and gold box when Sam Eide sent a text, reminding him to pick up the remaining tubes in their now-vacated office before someone came along and inadvertently threw them away.

Fortunately, Ben had cleared some space in the condo storage locker when he started taking the Christmas ornaments back downstairs and figured out he could stack the shoe boxes in a corner. He borrowed Sam's lab key and took the tubes home, two or three boxes a night, without telling Jen what he was up to. On Friday he retrieved the last two over the lunch hour and then late in the afternoon arranged to drop the key off to Sam at his office. He turned up and knocked on Sam's semi-open door. Sam turned and could not quite hide a small flinch at Ben's exhausted appearance.

"How're you doing? How's the baby?" Sam asked.

At the mention of the baby Ben beamed and pulled his phone out and showed some recent photos. Sam smiled; she was an adorable little button. He guessed the exhaustion was worth it.

"Listen," Ben started asking, apparently without energy for the usual courtesies, "you've seen the phone company archives, right?"

"Yep."

"Do you think they have reverse directories?"

"Maybe. I could check," Sam hesitated a moment, "but why are you asking?"

Ben, who had not really thought this through, paused a moment trying to gather his thoughts and form an appropriate explanation.

"Something's come up. You know Jen's a police detective?"

"Right," Sam nodded.

"Well normally she only works white-collar. Fraud. You get the idea," Ben said, waving a hand, "but we came across this missing child case last fall. It happened in 1970 and has never been solved. Jen pulled all the old case files and she's reviewing them while on mat leave. Anyway, there's a mysterious phone call the day before the kid went missing and we can see it in the data, but we can't identify who it is. We need a reverse directory for 1970."

"Sounds interesting." Sam thought for a moment: "well, I can get someone to look through the archive, but you won't be able to remove the directory if we find one…"

"Right," Ben thought a moment "should I just send you the phone number we're looking for?"

"Sure, that makes sense. Send the number and then I'll figure it out."

Ben smiled, and handed over the key, managing a grateful "thank you" and returning to his office to finish out the week as best he could. On the way home he bought another box of Valentine's chocolates, and a card, but this time he concealed the shopping bag in the driver's door pocket of their car, down in the parking garage where they would not present a temptation. Then he went upstairs, found the stick-it note on which Jen had written the number back in January, and sent the number to Sam Eide.

45

Sam was more than a little curious about this investigation review Ben's wife was doing, and when he received the number from Ben on Friday night it seemed to glow with potential import. He obviously did not have the case file itself, but he had seen criminal cases that ended up hinging on similar pieces of data.

Earlier in the day, just after Ben left his office, Sam contacted the faculty archivist, explaining the situation. She responded that she could look into it once the number was in hand. Sam sent the number to her late Friday night and it was there waiting for her when she woke up early Saturday morning.

The archivist accessed her work drive from home and pulled up the preliminary file listing prepared a few years before when accessioning the records. It was thousands of lines long and she did a search on 'directory', getting over a hundred hits, several of which were promising.

She sipped her coffee and was tempted to try on the word 'reverse,' but twenty-first-century summer students had prepared this list, and she was not convinced they would necessarily recognize a reverse directory as compared to a normal version if they saw one. It was clear that several 1960s and 1970s directories were in the collection and there might be something useful.

As it happened, the archivist needed a new pair of winter boots, and her favourite shoe store was just off the north end of campus. On Saturdays, it did not open until 11:00 AM. She could go into the archives now, see what some searching turned up, and then go shopping. She ate a quick breakfast before heading downtown.

The archives door opened with the click-snap of high-security metal bolts sliding backwards and a swooshing noise as the positively pressured, climate-controlled room opened to the hallway.

She wrestled out of her winter coat and hung it on a hook near her desk then went to the printer and picked up the shelf-list of directories she had sent to print remotely from home.

She walked back into the storage bay and twirled the handle to open the shelving stacks at the required row, spotting a row of printed directories, unboxed, on a middle shelf about halfway down the aisle. She pulled the first one out. It was the one for 1946. She continued, finding some directories for the 50s and 60s, but all were the standard, public-issue version.

She looked at the list, which indicated another series of volumes shelved separately, so she continued down the aisle and found three red-bound books sitting on the bottom shelf. She pulled the first one out and smiled. It was a reverse directory for 1950.

She put that back and pulled out the next one, which proved to be a reverse directory for 1960. Replacing that, she mentally crossed her fingers and hoped the pattern continued. But she was out of luck, the third reverse directory was not for 1970, it was for 1974.

She took that and the 1960 directory out of the aisle to a small nearby table, propped the 1974 directory open and pulled out her phone, opening Sam Eide's email to see which number she was looking for.

And she found it. Right there in the 1974 directory. When she traced the dotted line through to the number's assignee though, her smile turned to a look of puzzlement. She pulled Sam's email up and read it carefully, wondering if she had misunderstood something, then she sighed.

Someone had clearly made a mistake. Or maybe the number had been reassigned between 1970 and 1974. She paused a moment thinking what to do and decided to check the 1960 reverse directory to see what showed up there but when she did so, the number did not appear.

Using her phone, she sent a reply to Sam, explaining they had the 1974 reverse directory but not the 1970 and that she assumed either the number had been reassigned in the interval or, she suggested gently, perhaps someone had made a mistake and sent the wrong number for checking.

She told Sam she would happily check another number if they could send the correct one, although it might be good to try to track down an actual 1970 copy instead, just to be completely sure they were dealing with the right information. Then she returned the books to the shelf, closed the stacks up, put her coat back on, locked up the archives and set out for the difficult task of finding a good pair of new boots late in winter.

46

J en made sure Ben could sleep in on Saturday as he was looking a bit peaky on Friday night. She mixed a batch of muffins, put them in the oven, and then tidied up the kitchen. As the muffins baked she tagged what turned out to be the last few phone numbers found in the fairground gate questionnaires. All the phone numbers were now searchable in the investigation file. She did a *pro forma* search for the mystery number although she was sure she would have recognized if it had come up in the last week.

While systematically tagging the questionnaires, she had successfully identified all but four of the hundred phone calls coming into or out of the McNally household in October of 1970. Almost everyone who had contact with the McNallys that month had been friends, neighbours, or family also routinely interviewed as part of the investigation. During the week, on a hunch, Jen had gone to the library with Clem and looked up hairdressers, dentists, and doctors in the 1970 directory thereby managing to identify two more of the four unknown numbers. She suspected the others could be commercial numbers as well.

It was the smell of blueberry lemon muffins baking that eventually nudged Ben out of bed. After a shower and a coffee, he looked a lot better.

"You know, would you want to get out of the city today?" Ben suggested. "I've been checking out some real estate listings and I am sure we could hit some open houses if we just got in the car and headed out there."

"That sounds good. We're getting a little stir crazy stuck in the condo all winter." By *we*, Ben assumed she was including Cassie as he imagined Clementine could not get stir crazy yet.

They enjoyed the warm blueberry muffins and some eggs, fruit, and sausages. Ben pulled up the real estate website on his phone and mapped out a few targets. Then they got ready and headed out, a full family flotilla with baby stroller, diaper bag, and dog wearing winter booties to protect her feet from road salt.

Cassie was a bit squished in the car, but she did not mind as she nestled up to Clementine's convertible car-seat stroller to keep her safe while they travelled. Clem burped in appreciation of the companionship.

They were up the parking garage ramp and sailing into the winter sunshine before noon, and out in the country a half hour later. Jen took Ben's phone out of the console and looked at the house listings he had mapped. She poked at the links to look at the pictures and the prices.

"Hmm, things seem to be significantly cheaper the other side of town. What do you think the commute would be like?"

"No idea. We'd need to try it during the week to really get a sense of it."

"Well let's see what we can get if we do the longer drive?"

Ben nodded in agreement. Thirty minutes later he turned off the highway. There were some brand new suburbs out here and signs directing them to two builder show homes. They saw both and while it meant they could more than triple the amount of space they had now, as well as get a reasonable backyard for Cassie and Clementine, Ben was not impressed. The new construction would not have much greenery, at least for the first ten years. He could not really read Jen's thoughts but was relieved that she was showing no outward signs of enthusiasm.

They got back to the car and headed closer to town, where there was one house for sale in a suburb that was about twenty years old. This development had some nice maturing trees plus lots of well-developed and maintained gardens but as they went through the house, the twenty-year-old finishes were a turn-off. Back in the car, they decided to go to the open house for the Victorian near the library in the town centre, mostly just for fun.

It had a slightly sloped porch, where they tied Cassie to a railing and Clementine was taken out of her stroller and bundled onto Ben's chest.

Cream paint looked relatively fresh on the spindles and fretwork but was sanded down on the stairs and up to the door mat by foot traffic.

The screen door snapped shut behind them with a hinge squeak and the dull crack of old wood returning to an accustomed place. Light trickled in mullioned windows, past winter-friendly holly vines and old cedar trees, taking on a greenish quality before soaking into some Persian carpets and a very comfortable looking sofa. The house smelled like dust, vinegar, and rosemary.

The light sluiced down a long hallway, bouncing off old brass hardware polished only where hands had rested many times, before hitting a mirror at the far end. The noise of the door closing brought a real estate agent into the hallway from the back porch behind the mirror. Clearly she was not busy, and Ben and Jen felt no guilt about taking up her time on a house they were already pretty sure was too much for them.

"Hello, I'm Sarah Kimmerly, would you folks like a look around?"

Ben stepped forward first, "we're Ben and Jen Mahoney, nice to meet you." They all shook hands and Sarah leaned in looking at Clementine snoozing, "and who is this cutie-pie?" On cue, Clem opened her eyes and baby-smiled adorably. "This is Clementine."

Jen glanced around with interest at the cozy and textured décor from another era, "how old is this place?"

"Over 130 years, built in the 1880s for a local merchant. It stayed in the family for four generations. The last generation cannot keep it up and they are moving into a retirement home."

"The kitchen and bathrooms need redoing?" Ben asked.

"We anticipate the buyers will probably want to undertake a fair bit of renovation. The roof is sound but realistically it needs electrical upgrades to keep pace with typical household demand these days. How about we go upstairs first?" She turned and stepped onto the first oak tread, hand resting on an ornamented newel post.

There were some great old black and white family photos on the walls, including a bulbous portrait of one Samuel Drinkwater, who seemed likely to be the original owner. He was hanging between prints of birds, with a fine layer of dust on top of the frames and in the crevices.

When they reached the landing, they saw three open doors; the one directly ahead led to a bathroom. It had a claw foot tub and vintage porcelain fixtures. The floor was terracotta and black linoleum, somewhat scratched and faded, and glossy white-painted bead board with a chair-rail formed the wainscoting. The walls above the wainscot were an old shade of minty green. It was a big space though, and with a few thousand dollars in renovations it would make a great family bathroom.

"Are there any other bathrooms on this floor?" Ben asked.

"No, although there is a large dressing room off the primary that could be converted to make an ensuite. There are three bedrooms on this floor — two at the front and the primary is at the back."

She directed them to the two other open doors, and they popped their heads in to look around. They saw medium sized rooms with high ceilings and huge casement windows looking out through some branches towards the street.

One had a second window pointing out over the roof of the porch towards the side yard. It had beautiful old floral wallpaper and could have been a little girl's room in the 1940s.

Sarah led them down a short hallway to the back of the house and directly into a large old bedroom. There was a canopy bed, old wood bureaus and tables that had to be Edwardian. Incongruously, a flat screen TV sat on top of one of them, doily underneath.

The dressing room on the right abutted the stairwell and while it currently held clothes racks and a small office, it was large and could be converted into a bathroom with a walk-in closet.

"There's also an attic floor," and Sarah led them back out into the hallway to a more discrete door which opened onto a narrow, white-painted stairway, lit with a small square window set just below the roofline.

Ben clutched Clementine close to his chest and they carefully navigated the narrow stairs up to a big room intersected with cross beams supporting the roof. It had been painted many times and in places the current pale blue-grey was starting to peel.

It was a big space, although at the back it was stuffed with old trunks, broken furniture, and even a girl's bicycle from the 1960s with tassels still attached.

"Harry would love this place," Ben commented quietly to Jen.

"Harry MacAllan the antiques dealer?" Sarah interjected.

"Yes, I think that's him, we know him from his stall at the market…"

Sarah smiled and nodded, "yes, I think the current owner will probably bring him in for a clear out before they downsize." They headed back down the stairs, all the way to the main floor, and then she led them towards the back of the house.

The kitchen was completely out of date, but it had a certain charm. Yellowy-cream cabinets sat on a linoleum floor much like the one in the bathroom but checked with cream tiles instead of black.

"Well, it would be a gut job," Sarah admitted, "but it would be worth it. There's a ton of room. Plus, there's this pantry that's slotted in under the stairs," she pulled open the pantry door "and you could move the door into the hallway and get quite a nice little ground floor powder room fitted in."

Jen went over to look and stepped inside the under-stair closet, currently holding shelves stacked with canned goods and old mops tucked into the corner. Sarah pulled down on a ceiling light string to show the space to best advantage.

Ben, interested in the old appliances, asked Sarah a question about gas lines and electricity which left Jen alone in the tiny room. As she turned to rejoin the other two, her eye caught something on the doorframe.

There were tiny lines pencilled in with a name, date, and measurement next to each. It was the family's old height measuring chart. At the top was *Steven, 6'3", 14 July 1964*. The next several lines were still Steven, and then she could see Marilyn, 5'7" 10 October 1955, then there was a clutter of Steven and Marilyn names overlapping and further down still another name popped up: *Julie, 4'6" 8 Sept 1970.*

Instinctively her finger backtracked up the doorjamb, seeking the later measurements that should be tracking *Julie*'s growth. But they were not there. The hairs on the back of Jen's neck stood up and her hand, resting on the doorframe, shook a little.

❊ ❊ ❊

Back in the car, Jen pulled out her tablet, opened her work app and plonked "Drinkwater" into the search box. And there it was, in the background synopsis of the family. Mrs. James McNally was born Marilyn Drinkwater in 1938. Jen concluded they had just been inside Julie's maternal grandparent's house. Ben leaned over to see what she was doing. He had not seen inside the pantry but suddenly remembered the 1960s girl's bicycle in the attic.

"Is there some connection to the Mr. Drinkwater who owns it now?"

"I think he must be Julie McNally's uncle," and she told Ben about the growth spurts marked off on the pantry door but with Julie's stopping in September 1970. They both looked out the car window at the house and suddenly it seemed haunted.

"How about we go to Annie's Apple Hut for some coffee and pie?" Ben suggested.

"Sounds good." And after a moment Jen added more cheerfully, "Clem's first visit!"

Ben turned into traffic and they headed out of town, implicitly deciding they would not look at more houses today.

Annie's was not as busy in the winter. The picnic tables were mostly in storage with a few set up inside the semi-winterized fruit stall porch in a way that worked so long as it was not mind-numbingly cold.

This time of year, the pie options were restricted to apple, pear, and pecan and they got one slice of apple and one pecan to share. The coffee was as good as ever and steam rolled pleasantly off the top as they sat on a picnic bench, indoors, winter coats still on, Clem in her stroller and Cassie flopped on a mat near the door.

Ben saw an SUV pull into the parking lot and whirl around to take a spot near the entrance. Jen was tending to Clem when the man in the SUV passed them by on his way into the store, paying them no particular attention. However, when he returned after purchasing a box of tarts, Jen was looking straight at him.

"Peter!" she said brightly.

"Jen!" Peter Cadworth leaned in to pat her shoulders in a brief hug, then straightened up to shake hands with Ben, who he had met only once before and had not immediately recognized.

"This must be your little one then?" he said.

"Yes this is Clementine. We've actually just been looking for a house in town."

"No kidding, you know I grew up here? Moved closer to the city years ago but I still come to Annie's for pie," he held up the tart box, "and treats for my dad."

"How's your dad doing? I was really sorry to hear he was so unwell..." and as she spoke Ben moved down the bench and gestured for Peter to take a seat.

Peter reflected for a moment while dropping a little awkwardly onto the end of the bench "he still has good days. I don't always see those but there are a couple of really good caregivers at the home, and they keep me updated."

He tapped the tart box "I'm going to see him tomorrow and I'm sure these will make his day."

Peter Cadworth paused a moment, wondering if it was impudent to ask a new mom about work but then decided to go for it, "how's that case review you were doing turning out?"

Jen beamed and nodded in Ben's direction "we've found a new clue."

Peter was surprised and turned to Ben wondering what he had to do with it. Jen took a sip of her coffee, implying Ben should tell the story.

"I found this old box of telephone company technology. This guy at work — I work at the university — is really good with vintage computing and he figured out it was this really primitive memory that contained a phone log for the main county exchange for most of 1970. Jen reviewed the case file and realized there was a mysterious call the day before Julie McNally disappeared and now we know what it is."

"Really? Who was it?" Peter asked, looking back at Jen.

"That we haven't been able to crack yet — it's really difficult to reverse number search that far back." She took another sip of coffee and then put the cup down, "and, of course, I don't know what the implications are for the case. But, we do have an entire phone log for the household, which is something the original investigation didn't have."

"No kidding! That is something. You know what, the next time dad is at all stable, I'll try to ask him about it and pass on anything he can remember."

"Thanks so much for anything you can do Peter, and if your dad is not up to it, I understand."

47

Just as Ben and Jen were getting up on Sunday morning, many miles away Peter Cadworth arrived at the care home. The box of pecan tarts sat on the passenger seat and Posey was in the back, brought along because she seemed to have a therapeutic effect on his father. He parked the vehicle, got out and went around to grab the tarts in one hand and Posey's leash in the other and then, so encumbered, made his way inside.

Inside the door he dropped Posey's leash on the floor and propped open the box to offer tarts to staff behind the desk, both of whom enthusiastically accepted. Then he closed it again, and low whistled at Posey to follow him down the hallway to his father's room, which she did quite happily.

He knocked gently and after a moment opened the unlocked door a crack and said gently into the space beyond, "dad, it's me, Peter." He pushed the door open carefully and Posey trotted in and went straight up to his father, who was sitting inert and blank-faced at the window. Posey plopped her head in his lap. And, at that, his father snapped back to reality.

"Posey my girl!" and he ruffled her silky ears, which caused the dog to smile.

"Dad, it's me, Peter. I've brought some pecan tarts from Annie's Apple Hut," and Peter carefully placed the open box on a small table at his father's elbow. His father looked down, for a moment confused, but then instinct took over. He picked up a tart with great relish and took a determined bite. After chewing he looked up at Peter with gratitude and said "oh, that is good!" Posey wagged her tail at seeing him happy.

"How is Annie?" his father asked. Annie had died two years earlier and the hut was now run by her son and daughter-in-law, but Peter kept that from his father and just said "as far as I know, good. The hut is still the same as it always was." And his dad nodded at that.

"Your mother used to love her lemon meringue pie," his tone revealing he was lucid at the moment.

"I'll have to see if I can bring lemon meringue next time."

"No need," his father said abruptly "the pecan's my favourite." And his father looked out the window again, a little forlornly, until Posey once again flopped her head in his lap.

"You know, I ran into an old friend when I was at the hut."

"Really?" his father said over his shoulder, not really engaging with the conversation, but enjoying stroking Posey's head and getting her to wag-thump her tail against the floor.

"Yes, Jen. She was a student of mine at the academy."

His father, as a fellow law enforcement man, perked up a bit at that. "She in the police now?"

"Yes, she's a fraud detective down at King Street. But she's on mat leave." He paused, trying to pull together a way to gently broach the subject. "She's also in the market for a house in this area. As it happens, on one of her trips out here she heard about an old case of yours."

Peter could not see his father's face as he looked out the window, but his father's hands paused on top of Posey's head. "Do you remember a little girl that went missing? Julie McNally, I think her name was and it was the year after I was born…"

His father slowly and shakily turned his body towards Peter, presenting him with a look of absolute despair. Within seconds his eyes were watering, and he choked out some words "her mother's here you know. She lives down the hall. Used to be a great friend of Franny. But not anymore." A kind of chortling gasp came from his father's mouth and Peter, in concern, quickly filled a mug with water from a bottle and gently pressed it to his father's lips. He gulped it down, uncertainly. After a moment or two Peter continued "so you remember?"

"Yes, I remember. Not something that can be forgotten. Why are we talking about this?" said with irritation and growing confusion.

"My friend Jen, she's reviewing the case, trying to figure out what happened..."

"Figure it out? Figure it out after all these years...?" the concept seemed to strike his father as very novel. "How is she going to do that?"

"Well, they do a lot of information analysis these days with computers."

He father harrumphed: "computers, bah!" and as he waved his hand to dismiss the new technology he did not, and never would, understand, it shook mid-air and then fell limply in his lap as his energy escaped him.

"They've got some new information as well. They've found some old data from the phone company showing the calls going into and out of the McNally household..."

But his father had lost the train of the conversation and gone a kind of peaky-gray-white colour, his eyes trailing into the distance out the window.

"Where is Franny?" he asked.

48

O n Sunday morning Sam Eide checked his email and found a message from the archivist. He could immediately see her point and assumed Ben, in his new father exhaustion, had simply made a mistake and sent the wrong number. If not, presumably the number had been reassigned. The first thing to do was to get Ben to double check with his wife about specifically which number they were dealing with.

Sam sent Ben a text: *Archives has 1960 and 74 reverse dir. Not in 60. Odd result in 74. Can you confirm number with Jen?*

Ben, who was sitting across from Jen while they ate a home cooked brunch, told her the good news. Jen opened her tablet and read out the mystery number from her spreadsheet, which she had also memorized. Ben dutifully responded: *Jen confirms 448-9287. What's up?*

Sam received this response, went back to the email the archivist had sent and mulled it over for a minute: *By 1974 that number was assigned to the police station.* Sam followed up with a second text: *If that is the right number, the archivist thinks you need to track down a 1970 reverse directory to see where it was assigned in that year.*

Ben simply handed the phone over to Jen so she could read what Sam had written.

"The police station? What the heck has happened?" Jen was flummoxed.

Ben was also baffled: "we need to check everything we've done." And he got up to get his laptop and open the original data files Mandi had sent, confirming the late afternoon number was what they thought it was.

"I suppose it is possible something went wrong with the data read and the number isn't correct..." Ben suggested.

"That doesn't seem likely. I've got a sample of one hundred numbers over two weeks going into or out of the McNally household, I've identified almost all of them and they all make sense as part of their friend and family network."

Jen paused, then pulled out her phone "we need a 1970 reverse phone directory" and she was about to send an email to Kristin Johnson to ask her to look for one in the police archives when Ben had a thought.

"We can go to the reference library and look up the police numbers in the regular 1970 directory and see if it matches."

"Right, that would be faster." Jen used her phone to check the library's hours. "They are only open ten to three today."

In unison they began clearing up the breakfast things. Clementine needed a diaper change and then they both showered and dressed. About an hour later they were all three in the car, heading downtown. Ben negotiated a few back streets to find parking then they made their way to the library.

Once up the stairs to the second floor, they headed straight for the shelves under the yellow sign and pulled out the 1970 phone directory. They took it to a table and flipped through to identify how the commercial section worked and found the listing for the county Police.

There were several numbers listed for various divisions but as Jen's finger scrolled down the list the number appeared. Jen traced towards the left and Ben let out a slow whistle when he saw what was written there: Chief of Police.

"Do you think we should let Peter know?" Ben asked.

"I don't know. I need to think this through. We don't even know what relationship this call has to her disappearance."

Jen took a photo of the numbers with her phone then snapped the book shut. Ben took it and put it on the shelf. Then they retreated back home where Jen could read through the case file and carefully evaluate the situation.

49

Back at the condo, Jen finished making some sandwiches and brought them over to the couch to hand one to Ben before flopping down beside him. A news channel full of factoids whirred in front of them while a muted newscaster emphatically presented mostly useless tidbits of information.

Jen's brow was furrowed, and Ben took a bite of his sandwich, giving her a moment to start articulating the problem.

"I distinctly remember that somewhere in the county investigation files an officer made a note that identifying the Thursday phone call was an investigation priority..."

"Are you sure it was the county side and not the regional side that made that note? If it was regional and they failed to communicate with county, maybe the right hand just never realized that the left hand called the McNally household the day before for some reason and it wasn't significant..."

"I can check but it pretty much had to be the county because they kept asking Lori Sorenson if she had made the call and those interviews were done either down at county in the first week before regional was called in or at the Sorenson house. And Julie's mother assumed it was Lori — and then my impression was the police didn't really believe Lori when she said she hadn't called..."

"Okay, so the first step is to identify whether it was county police who identified the Thursday call event and if so, specifically which people were working on it? The whole right-hand left-hand-dropped-ball could just as easily happen within an organization as between the two police agencies."

"Right, good point. I assume the chief would have known everything that was going on in the investigation but maybe not — maybe he wasn't that kind of chief. Lori didn't think very highly of him." Jen nibbled at her sandwich.

"Really, what did she say?"

"She said that by the time he was retired everyone thought he was in over his head and the county had kind of gone to pot."

"So maybe he was just really incompetent?"

"Possibly. But even so, why did his office call the McNally's on Thursday? Sure, maybe the chief or his secretary forgot to mention to the investigating officers that the call was made but why make it in the first place?"

"Did either the chief or his secretary know the McNallys personally?"

"It's possible. Marilyn McNally and Mrs. Sorenson knew the chief's wife Francesca and they got their hair done together every Thursday afternoon. I suppose it's also possible the Chief's secretary..." Jen tapped her forehead with a knuckle, willing the name to come forward "Valerie ... Valerie Belmont, could have known them as well. Obviously, she would be working Thursday afternoons when they were at the salon though, and I'm pretty sure she must be younger. But obviously if the call had been for Marilyn, Julie would have given her the phone immediately or given her a message. Marilyn wouldn't have had the impression it was Lori on the phone. And her father did not recall that Julie gave him a message that night."

"Well, I agree, not likely to be a call for Marilyn, but she could have easily just forgotten that someone had called for her father."

"Possibly, I guess we need to know if her father knew the chief or his secretary."

"If it was the secretary there might be a reason why no one was forthcoming about the call..."

"Something illicit you mean?"

"Yep."

"Hmmm. It's possible. Might explain why there was no message. But why would she call the McNally residence expecting to get James McNally before the end of the workday on a Thursday? The timing of the call is what has bugged me since we found it — either it was someone expecting Marilyn to be there because they did not know she had a standing Thursday appointment at the salon or, it was someone hoping to reach Julie after school."

Ben took a moment to follow her train of thought "...and, if they knew about Marilyn's schedule, they might have known that was their best chance of getting Julie when she was alone..."

"Exactly. I need to figure out who in the investigation was focused on the phone call, and why neither the chief or the secretary — or anyone else who could have somehow used that line on Thursday — came forward to admit calling the McNally household."

"Sounds like a plan," Ben said, as Jen took a generous bite of her sandwich, and Ben switched the channel to an afternoon movie.

Even before the film had finished, Jen had her tablet out and was reviewing the case file, yellow legal pad at her side to make notes.

50

While Valerie Belmont's name did not appear once in the file, Jen started to suspect that some of the handwriting must be hers, given that it occurred on paperwork which would be generated by the Chief's office, such as the sniffer dog search team requisition.

Fully one fifth of the fair gate questionnaires also appeared in this hand. Jen realized that given the origin of the mystery phone call, she needed to start assigning names to all the internal activities the paperwork implicitly documented.

Reports and interviews were signed off with the officer's name, but she needed to know all the other staff at the station. The picture she had taken of the phone directory at the library provided direct numbers for specific offices and divisions but there were only a few names.

Jen sent an email to Kristen Johnson asking if she could track down the master internal directory which hopefully included partner agencies back in 1970 and would list all the staff at the county police station. Only an hour later Jen received a snapshot of the page covering the county.

With a little bit of cross-referencing Jen had identified the four secretaries and dispatchers who had manned the fair gates and knew there was a fifth hand as well. Probably a retiree or someone else the women at the station could recruit at short notice.

Now that Jen knew Valerie Belmont's handwriting, she could see Valerie generated almost all the central administrative paperwork in the case file, many items per day for the first eleven days of the investigation, and without a day off. While there were four typed memos of investigation meetings, there was also one in Valerie's handwriting that had not been typed, probably due to lack of time.

Valerie was the one responsible for recording orders issued and stated investigation priorities at these meetings. The Thursday phone call appeared as part of the staff discussion, as well as in two reports filed by investigating officers who had interviewed Marilyn McNally and, subsequently, the Sorenson family. Valerie Belmont definitely knew about the phone call and that identifying the caller was considered pertinent to the investigation. If she had made the call, she had known this and said nothing.

It was much more difficult to ascertain specifically what the Chief knew and when. It was standard procedure for the Chief to initial all reports coming across his desk, but Jen could quickly see that almost all such initials were marked "DCVB" plus a date stamp. She guessed this meant that Valerie had verbally relayed the report contents to the Chief as each item arrived. If that was how they did things back then, then it was entirely possible the call information in the interview reports had slipped through the cracks.

Jen reached the frustrating conclusion that she needed to figure out where most of the station staff, including Dick Cadworth and Valerie Belmont, were on the afternoon of Thursday, October 8th, 1970, and as that was the day before Julie was abducted and the investigation began, she had absolutely no documentation regarding their movements.

Clementine started crying and Jen got up and went into the nursery, lifting Clem out of the crib and settling comfortably into the rocking chair for a feed. She and Clem rocked slowly back and forth, and Jen forgot about her files for a few happy minutes. Eventually, with Clem settled back in her crib, Jen set about figuring out what she and Ben were having for dinner.

Ben was out at the hardware store and Jen sent him a text to see when he would be coming home. She looked in the fridge. At some point they had managed to buy a ten-pound bag of russet potatoes but that was about all they had, other than some eggs. She took two good sized russets, washed them, oiled, salted, poked them, and put them in the oven to bake. When Ben replied, she asked if he could pick up some steaks, a Caesar salad, and a bottle of red wine on his way back, which he was more than happy to do.

He came home forty-five minutes later and had just enough time to grill the steaks before the potatoes finished. Jen uncorked the wine and dumped the salad in a bowl, adding the packaged dressing. She deposited basic place settings for each of them at the counter bar stools and took an unreasonable pride in the fact they, as new parents, were managing to feed themselves a reasonable dinner.

"How'd it go?" Ben asked while breaking into his potato.

"Valerie definitely knew the phone call was a point of interest. I can't quite tell if the Chief knew or not." Jen sipped her wine and then started in on the steak when Ben placed it on her plate.

"Well, what would you do if this was a current investigation?"

"I'd interview them both, very carefully."

"From what Peter said, it sounds like interviewing the Chief is not really an option..."

"No. Valerie's probably available though, she's the one Peter contacted to get access to the old files."

"You thinking of calling Peter to get her number?" Ben asked, tentatively, wondering exactly how to broach the big question that was on his mind.

"No, I don't think I want to bring Peter in yet."

"Are they suspects?" Ben asked, pointedly.

"No, definitely not. It's a stretch to even call either of them persons of interest."

"I see. But the call was made and needs to be explained?"

"It's clear we have reasonable evidence that the call was made, Julie spoke on the phone to an unknown person, and disappeared within a day of that event. It needs to be explained, if it can be, at this point. I'm sure of that — if this were an official review it would be considered a significant new finding."

"Right," Ben sipped his wine, "so what are you going to do?"

"I think I'm going to cold call Valerie Belmont, assuming I can get her number."

"Right, is the phone the best way to 'interview her very carefully'?" Ben asked, knowing it was not and guessing what his wife would do.

"Probably not. I'll need to see if she's willing to meet with me," Jen answered carefully.

"I'm not comfortable with you meeting her on your own," he said, with a flat determination and his rarely used, no-nonsense expression.

Jen furrowed her brow and was about to retaliate with a tirade about how this was her job, and she could certainly handle herself, but then her gaze drifted towards the crib, just visible from where she was sitting, through the doorway of the nursery.

"Okay, well, what if you come along?"

"That's better. How do you want to play it?"

"Play it?" Jen asked, dubious of the gumshoe persona Ben was slipping into.

"We need a non-threatening excuse to speak to her, in-depth" Ben replied, more reasonably.

"True. How about we just tell her we're coming into town to look at houses and that I was hoping to ask her questions since the Chief's not well?"

"It has the ring of truth."

"Okay, I'll get her number and call her later in the week to arrange something."

And with that they drank some more wine, relished the robust dinner, and relaxed into the rest of the evening.

51

J en found Valerie Belmont's phone number without problem and called her on Wednesday night. The phone rang many times and was answered by a chipper-sounding older woman.

"Hi, I'm hoping to speak to Valerie Belmont?"

"Just a sec... Val, phone's for you..." there was a brief tussle audible in the background and then another chipper-sounding older woman came on to what was clearly a landline.

"Valerie speaking, how can I help you?"

"Hi Valerie, my name's Jen Mahoney and I think you helped Peter Cadworth send a bunch of files down to my office at King Street?"

"Jen! Indeed I did. How did that work out?"

"It was really helpful; I can't thank you enough."

"Oh, no problem," Valerie demurred, graciously.

"I understand from Peter that the Chief is really not very well."

"No, no, he's not. Peter implied dementia, but I haven't been to see him..."

"No, of course, not a good idea to bother him at all. Looking at the files, you seem to have been very involved in the first two weeks of the investigation?"

"Yes, yes I was. Everybody was."

"Well, since I can't talk to the Chief, could I talk to you?"

"Sure, what do you need to know?"

"Well, as it happens, my husband and I are house-hunting out in the county, and we plan to be there this week-end... Is there any chance I could talk to you in person?"

"Sure! Of course," Valerie replied enthusiastically. "Have you been to the local diner yet? It's just off the highway and they make a great turkey salad sandwich. I could meet you there just after lunch on Sunday for a coffee."

"That sounds great. How about 1:30 on Sunday?"

"That works. I expect I'll be able to figure out who you are..."

"Okay, well I'll be there with my husband and our baby."

"Got it. See you then," and Valerie hung up the phone, leaving Jen to evaluate the tone of their conversation.

On Sunday morning Ben compiled a list of more open houses they could go see, and not just for theatrical purposes, as another week in the city further motivated him to find them a larger place to live.

He was not too worried about Jen interviewing Valerie Belmont, even though, unlike Jen, he felt that, unless the call could be explained innocently, someone at the police station knew something. Even if Valerie was involved, Ben assumed they couldn't really be in danger at the local diner, out in public in the middle of the afternoon on a Sunday. Plus, apparently there were good turkey salad sandwiches and his instincts told him, likely tasty pies.

With a map in his mind of where they were heading in the morning before the meet-up, he filled a cup with coffee and some milk and went into the bedroom, putting it on Jen's bedside table and giving her a peck on the forehead, gently waking her up. Jen snorted with gratitude, struggled to a sitting position, and began imbibing the coffee, one eye after the other eventually willing itself to open and blink at the new day.

Remembering what they were up to, her focus improved, and she swung her legs out of the bed and headed for the bathroom to get ready.

They had some oatmeal, tended to Clementine and then packed everyone into the car and headed out. They made it to four house showings by 11:30, before going to the diner to eat some lunch in advance of Valerie's arrival for coffee.

Inside the diner, they got a large booth and settled Clementine into the corner, still in her carrier and, at the moment, sleeping. They both ordered turkey salad sandwiches, the waitress nodding her approval of their choice.

"Side fries, salad, or chips?" she asked.

"Chips," said Ben with gusto.

"Salad," said Jen, "I might have one or two of your chips."

"Drinks?"

"Coffee and a couple of glasses of water," Ben replied, and the waitress headed off to the kitchen.

Daylight shone brightly through the large diner windows and warmed their booth. Clementine, with her face shaded by the carrier, was particularly comfortable. The coffee arrived and Ben took the gleaming chrome sugar dispenser and tipped in a generous amount.

Jen held her cup in hand and took a moment to glance around the restaurant. It was a very relaxed and open setting. Almost everyone else there had the demeanor of a regular and was completely at ease: a good space for a casual interview.

The sandwiches arrived and gave a favourable impression, with four triangular quarters stacked expertly on the plate, crisp lettuce, tomato, and cucumber layers suggesting a smidgen of potential nutritional virtue. Ben grabbed a quarter and shovelled it into his mouth. It was the best turkey salad sandwich he had ever tasted.

"Mmmm. There's a secret ingredient in here. Can't quite put my finger on it."

Jen tried her own and knew what he was getting at: maybe some kind of special mustard or curry. She grabbed a chip off his plate with a free hand before picking up her fork to start on her salad. It did not take long to eat the four sandwich quarters, which seemed too small before they were finished, and as they worked to finish the chips and salad Ben waved over the waitress and asked for a dessert menu.

She pulled a card out of her apron and handed it to him. It had five things on it: coconut cream pie, apple pie, daily pie special, ice cream sundae and chocolate fudge cake. "The pie special today is cherry" she informed them before attending to the adjacent tables, momentarily, to fill up some coffee cups.

"If they put coconut cream at the top, it has to be good," Ben reasoned. When the waitress returned Jen had decided as well: "I'll have cherry." "And I'll have coconut cream" Ben added, returning the dessert menu. They sipped their coffee, waiting for the arrival of dessert and Valerie Belmont. Clem opened an eye, yawned, and then went back to sleep.

The door swung open, and a white-haired lady appeared. Jen, who had taken the side of the booth that faced the door for this very moment, paused and when the woman did not immediately take a chair and order her usual, instead staying at the threshold glancing around, Jen assumed it had to be Valerie and waved discretely. The woman approached and Jen waited for confirmation that she had guessed correctly.

"Jen?"

"Yes, and this is my husband Ben" Jen said, smiling. Ben leaned over, shook her hand, and said: "nice to meet you."

"Hi Ben, oh, and this is your little one?" Valerie said, warmly.

"This is Clementine," Ben said, reaching over to grab the carrier, "we've ordered some pie. How about I take Clementine over there and you two have the booth to yourselves?" and he was up and out before Valerie could disagree, so she slid into his place.

The two women shook hands over the table "so nice to meet you and I can't thank you enough for your help with the files…" Jen started.

"Oh no need" and Valerie waved a hand to dismiss any excess gratitude. "Did you try the turkey salad sandwich?"

"We did. It's excellent. What is the secret ingredient?"

"Ah, that is a big town mystery. Rumour is it's some sort of curry, but Tom — who owns this place — will take the secret to his grave" and she smiled. "The coconut cream pie is really good too."

Ben, listening discretely from across the aisle, congratulated himself. The waitress brought the pie slices over and was momentarily confused by the new seating arrangements. Jen decided to sacrifice her slice for conversational expediency and waved it over to Ben's table, where it met its fate.

"So, what do you need to know?" Valerie asked, very openly.

Jen, who'd spent several hours over the last week planning this conversation, began: "Well, I suppose the way to do this is to start with a standard debrief. If I were being brought on board say a week into the investigation, what would the run down have been at that point?"

Jen hoped this would be an easy question for Valerie. She had seen debriefing notes in the file prepared when the regional police arrived, likely typed up by Valerie, and this line of inquiry would give a sense of what Valerie could remember and potentially, if she was misleading them or concealing anything.

"Right. So, thinking back," and Valerie squinted slightly to pull at well-stored memories.

Jen took the opportunity to interject: "One thing that can help access details this far back is putting them in context, how about we run down what you did that week, starting as far back as you can remember in your routine, maybe Monday or Wednesday?"

"Hmmm, okay, so as far as I remember Monday and Tuesday that week were normal. You know, get up, go to work, come home, cook dinner, the usual blur." Valerie waved a hand to dismiss the irrelevancies that came before.

"Wednesday and Thursday were different though because we all had special duties related to the fair. On Wednesday I had to finalize the overtime staffing associated with the fair and on Thursday afternoon I was onsite to confirm parking arrangements for our staff, equipment resources like radios, and I helped with the municipal safety committee, depositing and checking first aid kits."

Jen was intrigued to realize she may not have even been in the office when the call was made. "Interesting. So, you literally saw the whole fair set up the day before?"

"Yep. I did."

"Maybe we should talk that through. What time did you arrive onsite and how complete was the set-up at that point?"

"Think I got there for 1 PM or maybe 1:30. They were still bringing rides onto the grounds through the gate at the far end of the field but almost all the arena was set up. Maybe some displays in progress. Think they were still bringing the school competition stuff in. Animals were arriving through the main gates, but all the pens were already done. I can clearly picture exactly what the area she disappeared from looked like."

Jen sat back and Valerie continued in this vein, giving a sense of who was around the day before as she spoke. "There were a couple of minor snafus I had to fix — mostly to ensure our patrol cars had space in the parking lot once the fair started. And we were missing a couple of radios for a bit, but they turned up."

"Do you remember speaking to anyone?"

"Oh, of course. I must have spoken to dozens of people. The Safety Committee Chair and Secretary, even the mayor at one point."

"Any strangers?"

"No, I didn't talk to any strangers. That, I definitely would remember."

"How long were you there for?"

"Hours. I ran into my friend Sonia late in the day and the hot dog vendor was setting up to feed all the volunteers and we got two hot dogs and watched the sunset."

A tear welled up in her eye as she spoke. "It was beautiful." She wiped at the tear, "Sonia died from breast cancer back in '88."

Jen gave her a moment while quickly searching on her phone to see when sunset would have been. They sipped their coffees and, once Valerie was composed, Jen continued, "looks like sunset was between 6:30 and 7 then. Did you actually see it drop below the horizon?"

"No. Not quite. But I remember by the time I got back to the station to drop a few things off before heading home it was dark in the station parking lot and the streetlights were on."

"How long was that trip?"

"About five minutes. So, I must have been at the fair until pretty close to 6:30 at least."

Jen shifted tone at the same time her internal targeting system started focusing on persons beyond Valerie, "what sort of activity levels did you have at the station at that time of day?"

"Oh, the place was dead. Practically deserted. The night watch just coming on. But it was very quiet."

She took stock for a moment and shook her head "we had no idea what was coming. That was probably the last normal night at that station for a long time." For a moment, they both contemplated how big community traumas seem to come from nowhere.

"Okay, getting back to the investigation round-up. A week later, where were you guys at?"

"So, by that point we knew for sure she was last sighted in the area of the animal pens — do you know the fairgrounds at all?"

"I do, we went last fall and I've found some old maps online and in the files." Jen did not mention she had access to fancy mapping software, given that Valerie was of a certain age and she could not predict her reaction to new technologies.

"Good, okay, so the animal pens were close to the incoming and outgoing pedestrian turnstiles and the main vehicle gate. Our primary concern the first week, once we had identified the final sighting and thoroughly searched, confirming she was not still there, was trying to determine when and how she'd left the fairgrounds."

Valerie paused, organizing her thoughts. "I remember reporting that by Friday we had canvased over two thousand people and had hundreds of completed interviews. No one reported seeing her outside the fairgrounds after she'd been seen near the animals. We found no items or other evidence connected to her — no blood, no clothes, nothing. As far as I know, nothing of hers has ever been found. We had no direct evidence of a crime."

Valerie paused again and Jen wondered a moment at the direction she was taking. "But by that point, I was fairly sure she was forcibly removed from the fair."

Jen looked Valerie directly in the face and slightly raised an eyebrow, inquiring, encouraging her to continue, which she did. "It's a small town, you see. I didn't know the family myself, but I had a bit of a sense of who Julie was, even before it happened. She'd written articles for the local paper. And by the end of the first week, we'd all talked so much among ourselves everyone felt like they knew her..."

Her thoughts trailed a bit and she struggled to put the next bit into words. "By Friday we were sure she was abducted and some of us were starting to accept the fact that she was probably dead."

52

Jen breathed out at that, and Valerie followed suit, raising her coffee cup, and cringing slightly as she took a sip. "It happens in fits and starts — a group of people coming to terms with something that horrible... Some of us, particularly among the women, were still in denial at that point, and others of us were being careful what we said out loud, but I was pretty sure by Friday..." She raised her shoulders defensively, spooked, remembering the eerie feeling of helplessness.

"...I was looking for any sign of violence. But we didn't find any. No evidence of a crime and no one had heard or seen *anything*. It was the strangest thing.

"I can assure you that our canvassing was extremely thorough — I'd go so far even as to say it was complete. I used a city street directory and literally crossed off every name after we'd at least completed basic contact procedures. And I starred the ones we had actual interviews from. By the end of the first month the only people not crossed off turned out to be dead or to have moved before the fair. Even some of those, I tracked them down and talked to them on the phone."

"Interesting, do you know where that directory is?"

"Well, if it is not in the files, then I am afraid I can't say. I did keep it on the shelf with the other directories and it is the sort of thing that got thrown away after a couple of years."

Jen reflected a moment and Valerie let her think, until a way of phrasing the question emerged: "If you used a directory, what about people that weren't listed — homeless or newly arrived in town?"

Instead of taking that as criticism, Valerie rolled the idea over, calculating.

"You know, that is a thought. We didn't really have homeless people living in town, not even anywhere in the county — they all gravitate to the city. However, it is not unheard of for vagrant people to pass through. The constables checked all the possible encampment sites of course, and found no one, but that is not to say someone couldn't have been in town and then of course left in the hours on Friday or early Saturday morning.

"But it would have had to be someone who had a vehicle, and how many homeless people have those? And how many homeless people wouldn't get noticed at the fair? We checked all the temporary accommodations, which is really just the motel and the few B&Bs that were operating. In terms of new people, if someone had moved into town recently and was not yet listed in the directory — especially if they moved out again quickly, we might have missed them."

However, having offered that suggestion, Valerie almost instantly dismissed it, "you'd have thought the locals would have mentioned that though. Obvious thing to point out. I suspect if anyone fit that bill the rumour mill would have convicted them almost immediately," Valerie finished, wincing at the proclivities of mob justice.

Jen's impression of Valerie was that she was being straight-forward and above-board. She seemed to have an alibi for the time of the call. What Jen needed was to transition the conversation to gather more information on other people.

"One thing I noticed in the case file was that Julie received a phone call the day before and that caller was never identified. What's your theory?"

"Right. I remember that. Bit frustrating. I think, in the end, we determined it had to be her friend Lori and she was so unnerved by the situation she just got confused about the days she'd called the McNally house."

Jen chose not to reveal that she knew Lori was not the caller. Or that the call had originated from Valerie's office line within the police station.

Jen responded, "makes sense," and carefully formulated the next question. "Okay, one last question. I can see your point about people coming to terms with it. You didn't know the McNallys, but did anyone else on the regional force? Was this personal for anyone?"

Valerie leaned back, slightly offended, and Jen justified: "it's a factor we are trained to identify when reviewing investigations, and given the town context it might be particularly important..."

While Valerie was put off by the question, this was better than the livid reaction she would have if she knew what Jen was really up to. "We're not quite complete country bumpkins out here, behaving unprofessionally, you know."

"No, I know that. Really, it is just something the review structure recommends we identify."

Valerie calmed somewhat at the thought of following procedure. "Okay, well, I can tell you I remember a few people at the station did know the family. Not many though. Mrs. McNally came from an established family in this area, and they were maybe a bit more suited to socializing with the notables — what few we have, anyway."

"She knew the chief's wife though, Francesca — they were actually great friends." Valerie stopped and her head titled to the side as she realized for the first time that friendship had not survived events.

"The chief knew them a bit and I admit, I think it was personal for him. He took it very hard. I remember that one of the constables, Tim MacIntyre, had been at school the same time as Mrs. McNally and knew her to say hello to on the street. There were also two constables and one of the detectives who had school-aged children although none in Julie's year, but they were very upset. I can't really be sure about anyone else."

Valerie continued: "I suppose it's fair to say that it did feel personal to all of us."

Jen gently brought the interview to a close, not wanting Valerie to leave on a negative note, and Ben, sensing they were heading out, bundled Clementine up and carried her back across the aisle.

With the adorable button deposited in her carrier on the table, the mood quickly shifted, and Clementine endured a few grandmotherly cheek pinches, after which Valerie left smiling. Jen maneuvered back into her coat, put on her hat, and they headed out the door, exchanging a glance to communicate that analysis would occur in the privacy of the car.

They pulled both car doors closed but Ben did not immediately start the engine "so, what do you think?" he asked.

"Three main things: one, she probably has an alibi for the phone call; two, she was convinced Julie was dead within the first week; three, she did not personally know the McNallys and assumed the call the day before had to be Lori. Fourth, I believe her. I don't think she is concealing anything. In particular, I don't think she has a sense that they did anything wrong during the investigation or that there is some kind of cover-up."

"Interesting." Ben started the engine "where does that leave us?"

"If the police station is involved, she doesn't know about it. And I find it difficult to believe anything happened at that police station without Valerie knowing about it... Except during the five hours she wasn't there on the Thursday. We've eliminated a lot of possibilities and I need to calculate what's left."

Ben, who felt that only a few explanations could fit — bad ones — stayed quiet. He knew that if left to her ruminations, Jen would eventually see it too, despite her professional loyalties. Jen looked out the window, thinking, and they did not talk much during the ride home.

Jen went to sleep that night with an image in her mind of a quiet, understaffed old police station, sitting late in the day under fading autumn sun.

Inside, fluorescent lights illuminated institutional terrazzo floors and old wooden desks stationed under well-used typewriters, but in front of empty oak office chairs. Somewhere in that station a faceless person reached for the hard, black, resinous, handhold of a phone. When they pulled it free of the cradle there was a click, followed by the dial tone, connecting that person, whatever their intentions, to Julie McNally.

53

J en had a restless night and next to her, Ben could practically hear the wheels turning in her head. When her eyes snapped open at 7:30, several rotors had clicked into firm place. Instantly wide-awake, she knew Ben was too, both under the warm covers with their noses pointing up into the chill winter morning.

"You know," Jen started, "there is only one person who is likely to have been at the station on Thursday in the late afternoon, who had reasonable access to that phone line, and who also knew Julie would be alone at the McNally house."

Ben, only a beat behind her: "the Chief."

Jen continued "He knew his wife had a standing hair appointment with Mrs. McNally on Thursday afternoon. He knew Valerie was likely away from the office all afternoon. He may have even arranged for her to be gone."

She paused, trying to both calculate and accept the implications of what she was saying. "What, in the name of god, could the Police Chief possibly want with an eleven-year-old girl? Why would he need to talk to her alone on the phone?"

"And it is pretty weird that whatever it was he didn't mention it at all during the investigation" Ben added.

"It does not seem innocent" Jen concluded.

"Nope." Ben gave her a moment to see if she would continue, "what are you going to do?"

"First, I need to figure out what could have happened, logistically, in terms of the Chief interacting with Julie."

Ben nodded in agreement, then swung his legs out from under the covers and into the cold. Stretching, he pulled off his t-shirt, threw it in the laundry bin, and went to claim the shower.

Jen, under no obligation to arrive anywhere at an appointed time, refused to relinquish the warm blankets and shouted from the bed to reach Ben's ears under the shower head.

"I can map it all out. Position him at certain time points based on the documentation and see what is, and is not, possible. I can also look for any signs in the evidence and documentation that remains of what the hell was going on."

Ben sluiced the soap out of his hair and shouted back "then what?"

"Then I'll need to talk to Peter."

Ben took another minute or two then towelled off and came back out into the bedroom. "What about Bob? How does he fit into all of this?"

Jen's eyebrows raised, "I forgot about Bob."

"You should check the phone logs to see if Bob and the Chief were in contact with each other."

Jen nodded, "can't believe I forgot that. Should have checked all of Bob's contacts before we interviewed Valerie."

"It sounds like you have a good day of work ahead of you. Promise me you won't talk to Peter or anyone else without telling me first." He leaned down and kissed her.

"I promise."

Ben headed out to the kitchen, grabbed a muffin and decided to get coffee at a café on the way to work. He was a bit concerned about his wife and what she might be about to uncover. It was a good thing the Chief was effectively immobilized in a home somewhere. He also wondered how Peter would react if they suggested his father was implicated in something horrendous.

✻ ✻ ✻

When the sun moved around, intruding through the windows, warming the floor, and kissing Clementine's little noggin into wakefulness, Jen rolled out from under the covers. Checking first on the baby, then the dog, she showered, made coffee, ate a muffin, and set up camp on the couch.

She opened the case file and searched for "Micklethwaite" and found a neighbourhood canvassing form which had Mrs. Deborah Micklethwaite written at the top, next to 589 Unity Street, followed by Deborah and Bob's household phone number.

She wrote the number down and then opened the October phone log data file and searched for it. It took an hour to pull two-hundred and thirty-odd instances out of the file. She searched for what she now knew was the Chief of Police's office number, 448-9287, and it was not listed as either an incoming or outgoing call in the Micklethwaite log.

Remembering that she had identified three of the calls into the McNally household as coming from Francesca Cadworth, she opened the McNally October log and searched for "Cadworth." Jen copied the Cadworth household number and then switched spreadsheets and searched for it.

There was one instance, October 14th at 10:05 PM.

Bob Micklethwaite had called either Chief Cadworth or Francesca at home less than two hours before he died. Jen felt a tingling shudder as a last wave of denial slipped through her body and her sights finally came to rest on Chief Richard Cadworth.

Determined now to prove what she suspected, she switched back to the case file and pulled up the scene login sheet, started by the second on-scene officer at 9:05 PM on the night of the disappearance.

Cadworth first arrived about half past midnight, which made sense in terms of communications escalating up the chain of command. Midnight was when they had completed the ground search and knew for sure they could not locate the girl and that the investigation would expand. One of the on-site officers had probably called the chief at home, informed him of the situation and he had dressed and reached the fairgrounds in a reasonable amount of time.

Jen could confirm her theory if she could find a dispatch call log in the file and after a bit of keyword searching she found two whole sets that appeared, from the scans, to be photocopies of the station dispatch register which had been copied and included for the regional police force's perusal. She was right, dispatch had called the Chief at home at 11:57 PM. She plotted him at home at 11:57 in her software.

While she wanted to ascertain his movements before that, it was not going to be easy to do, so first she checked how he had behaved on scene in the first few hours of the investigation.

From what she could piece together he issued a steady stream of commands starting about one in the morning that had systematically woken up needed staff as the night progressed. By 4:45 AM everyone who worked at the station had been called in and were either there, on their way to the fairgrounds, or performing administrative tasks at the station.

Valerie was clearly at the station in the very early morning hours where she had completed a number of requisition forms by hand, either bringing them to the Chief for his signature at the fairgrounds or perhaps the Chief had briefly returned to the station between 4:00 and 5:00 AM.

Jen thought for a moment and realized if the Chief had gone to the station, or if Valerie had, it is likely they would have needed to make phone calls, so she closed her work software down and opened up Ben's excel file for October 10th.

She searched for the Chief's Office phone and she did find a cluster of calls in the 4:20 to 4:50 window. Several of them appeared to be internal to the police station and she identified that using the internal directory image Kristin had sent.

She searched the others in her existing excel listing of identified calls and found one at 4:40 that appeared to be Chief Cadworth contacting the Mayor at home. It seemed unlikely Valerie would have made that call, so Jen plotted the Chief as at the station between 4:20 and 4:50.

She remembered he was back at the fairgrounds by dawn, when he had rallied and instructed the search group, but apparently the sign-in protocols had been abandoned by then, both because they had not located a crime scene and because so many people were involved it was impractical.

Overall, nothing about his behaviour from midnight to dawn, and through the rest of what she could reconstruct of that first day of searching, seemed unusual or inappropriate.

She switched to focusing on what Ben's call log for the Friday of the disappearance could reveal. Calls to and from the 448 number started at 9:05 AM on the Friday and there was a steady trickle during the morning which ceased for forty-five minutes just after noon. Jen, having to guess, imagined this meant Valerie was on her lunch break and no one calling in was connecting.

They started up again just before one but by three pm all call activity was starting to peter out. There was nothing between 3:45 and 5:02 PM when a single outgoing call was made from the number. Jen could not identify the second number but somehow, in her gut, she suspected it was Valerie using the phone, either for personal reasons or to tie up an administrative matter before going home for the weekend.

Jen got up and made herself a decaf coffee. She retrieved a cookie from the cupboard, took a bite, and started considering things bluntly.

If the Chief was responsible, what had he done? He would have had to be at the fairgrounds around 4:00 PM and he would have needed a way to immobilize and conceal Julie. Jen stopped her train of thought for a moment, baffled at the ridiculousness of it. *Why* could he have possibly done such a thing?

But her police training took over — wonder about the *why* later, she thought — for now it was necessary to simply focus on *how*. He would have needed a vehicle, that was clear, and he would have concealed her in the vehicle and removed her from the fairgrounds before the search began. Actually, he could not have concealed her for very long at a place like the fair so he would have had to immobilize Julie, conceal her in a vehicle, and leave almost immediately.

Jen recalled something Valerie Belmont had said about her activities on Thursday: *'I needed to resolve snafus so that our patrol cars had spaces in the parking lot.'* And Jen remembered the line of emergency vehicles parked when she and Ben left the arena from the Zamboni gate on their way to the horse barn.

Julie was last seen near the animal pens and if county tradition held, which it was reasonable to think it had, the Chief would have been within his rights to park in one of the spots Valerie had reserved, which was probably roughly where they parked emergency vehicles now, close to the animal pens.

It was also, as Jen realized, behind the arena and concealed from the view of those stuck up on top of the Ferris wheel. It was one of only a very few places that fit that parameter and in the whole of the fairgrounds, it was by far the most isolated.

However, she had no proof that the Chief had even gone to the fair, let alone that he had concealed Julie McNally in his car and driven off with her. What she needed was a log sheet of the vehicles that had gone into the parking lot to see if the Chief was there and for that matter, other vehicle holders should be considered and eliminated before she contacted Peter.

It suddenly struck her as odd that in all her review of the casefile she had never seen such a vehicle log sheet. Given her understanding that the gate was manned for security and insurance purposes, this absence was suddenly striking.

Obtaining copies of such documentation was routine police work and would have been done by the officers on scene as soon as possible, probably the evening of the first search. If they had not collected it, it would be the first example of professional negligence she had run across in the case.

Jen opened the file and did a search for 'vehicle' pulling up a huge number of hits, but she expected it to show up early and presumably on an evidence collection report, so she flicked confidently through the first couple of instances until she hit an evidence log sheet.

It was dated and timed 11:34 PM and had been submitted by the officer who was on shift at the fair that night. Presumably he had brought a bag of items back to the station before clocking out, prepared to get a couple of hours sleep before returning to work early the next morning for what he must have known at that point would be a long day.

There was a list of seventeen items he had collected at the fairgrounds, including thirteen items from the lost and found bin, three employee sign-in sheets for the carnies, the volunteers, and the municipal staff, and an item called, simply 'Vehicles.'

Jen scrolled forward and while the lost and found items, as expected given they were objects, could not be found in her scanned file copy, the three employee sign-in sheets were there, but after those sheets the evidence submission ended, and the file resumed with interview reports.

The 'Vehicles' sheet, which she was confident must be the one from the gate, was missing. And it went missing after it was taken to the police station the night of Julie's disappearance.

54

The last gear in Jen's mind rotated into its final position and she dropped in a flummoxed pile onto the sofa. The Chief of Police of a small town may have driven through the secure gate of the town fair, spotted a small child, incapacitated her and dumped her — presumably in the trunk of his car, probably his *patrol car* — then driven her out of the fairgrounds and done *God Knows What* with her?

It boggled the mind. What could possibly have inspired such a spontaneous lapse by such an authority? As soon as the word *spontaneous* trickled across her mind, she knew it was untrue. Nothing about this crime was spontaneous.

Julie insisted on going to the animal pens around 4:00 PM when her friends wanted to go on the rides. The animal pens were one of the few places on the fairgrounds with relative privacy — and close to the vehicles.

Julie received a mysterious phone call from her likely abductor the day before. Ergo, he had called her and somehow convinced her to meet him at a location near the animal pens and the cars at a specific time. This was premeditated.

For a few brief and uplifting moments Jen wondered if Julie could still be alive. Perhaps the Chief had done all of this, arranged everything, so that Julie could escape some sort of abusive or dangerous situation that never came to light.

But the feeling did not last long.

Jen thought of poor Bob Micklethwaite, and Ben's tentative, sleepy suggestion from the month before: *'do you think it's odd that there's Bob, with his call log, dying suddenly just as a police investigation needed to track down this phone call?'*

It was impossibly coincidental that there should be an unexplained phone call from the Chief's office to Julie, at the one time only a few people, including the Chief, would know she was home alone, and that Bob Micklethwaite, the one person who had it in his power to reveal the source of that phone call, should die in mysterious circumstances within the week, two hours after calling the Cadworth home.

Jen preferred the certainties of straight, evidenced, deduction but she was not so narrow-minded as to ignore an unlikely alignment of suggestive probabilities.

If he had done it, *why*? And *where* was she? The intensity of Jen's need to answer those two questions started to rise. The suspect was still alive. He was cognitively impaired, but he was alive, and he was the one person who knew the answers to those two questions.

She needed to get some air to think through how she could possibly get a resolution out of this situation. Getting up from the couch, she changed clothes and bundled everybody up for a stroll in the park.

❋ ❋ ❋

Ben had an uneasy feeling late in the day and, unable to concentrate, decided to leave work a few minutes early. He called Jen but it went straight to voicemail, which was irritating. No matter, he would see her in a few minutes if he picked up the pace, which he did, reaching their building, nodding curtly to Louis the concierge and poking the elevator button more aggressively than was warranted.

Ben, opening the door to their condo, called out "Jen?" — but met with silence. No wife, no baby, no dog, no stroller. They had gone out. He could check the garage to see if they had taken the car but gambled they had gone for a walk and decided to ask Louis when they had left and which direction they had taken. He made his way back down to the lobby.

"Hi Louis, have you seen Jen?"

"Yep, she went out about thirty minutes ago with that man."

"What man?" Ben asked, panic creeping into his voice unbidden.

"Uh, I don't know. Looked like he was in his fifties? Had a big plush elephant for the baby?" Louis said, trying to be helpful, and wondering by Ben's tone if there was reason to worry.

Ben stared aghast at the concierge, momentarily frozen by the unexpected revelation that his wife was not answering her phone and she was with the baby and a stranger. Pulling himself together, he asked: "listen, she's not answering her phone. I'm just a wee bit concerned; can you tell me anything else about this guy?"

"Well, if it's important I can go back in the security footage and show you?"

"That would be a big help, thank you." And Louis hit some buttons and pulled up the camera feed from earlier while Ben came around the desk and looked over his shoulder. He saw, from an oblique angle, a man come into the building vestibule holding a large plush toy, buzz the concierge, and make his way to the desk.

"He said he was here to drop off the toy for Jen Mahoney but before I could take his name, this happened" said Louis, gesturing to the screen. Within a moment his wife, daughter, and dog appeared at the side of the frame, moving towards the front door from the direction of the elevator. He saw his wife pull up and stiffen suddenly in restrained alarm, and at that moment the man at the desk, not yet aware of Jen, looked up towards the camera. It was Peter Cadworth.

"Shit, shit, shit," Ben said under his breath, as they watched the unfolding scene, in which Jen, trapped into unexpected pleasantries, greeted Peter, visibly recovered her composure, and received the toy with much smiling and nodding.

"What are they saying Louis? What is she saying?" Louis closed his eyes and thought back. "She's thanking him for the toy and saying they were just heading out to the park."

"Which park?"

"I don't know, but I think they went north," and he forwarded the video so they could just make out the angle at which the party left the vestibule. It very much looked like Peter went with them.

Ben left Louis without another word, pushed his way through the front door with excessive force and then stopped abruptly on the sidewalk to guess where they had gone. He pulled out his phone and tried calling Jen but again it went straight to voicemail. With the phone in hand, he opened Maps and started looking for a tell-tale green square somewhere north of the blue dot showing his current location. There seemed to be three that were close, one was due north off their own busy street, an unlikely choice. Two parks were off to the left in the more sedate residential area. Ben started walking towards the closest one.

55

The first park Ben reached was full of play equipment and tiny shrieking children. It took only one glance to confirm that his family was not among them. Ben thought Jen probably went outside looking for a quiet place to sit and this was not it, although Clementine will love this park when she gets older, Ben frantically imagined, his mind actively denying the possibility that his wife and child could be in any danger.

He walked on, taking the next right, and started meandering towards the other green square displaying on the map. Within minutes he could make out the second, equipment-free and much quieter space in the distance.

There was a path leading to a small circular area that seemed to be surrounded by benches. The back of a man's head was visible, and by weaving side to side, Ben glimpsed enough to be convinced the man was sitting directly opposite his wife.

He rushed up to the park entrance and from a new angle could see Peter Cadworth sitting in a relaxed spread-eagle on one bench, arms out wide against the back rest and legs outstretched, while ten feet across the circle sat Jen, the stroller beside her.

Between Jen and Peter sat Cassie, on her haunches. The dog turned her head at Ben's approach and gave him a look that said *you took your time.* Cassie held her ground.

Ben shrieked "Jen!" and rushed into the circle, which startled both Peter and Jen, who had been talking intently.

"What!?" Jen said, looking up, alarmed.

"I've been calling you for an hour!" Ben accused without even acknowledging Peter.

"Oh." And she pulled her phone out of the pocket on the stroller, "the battery's dead." She looked up at her husband, who was the picture of irritation, and he looked at her, glanced briefly sideways at Peter with a question in his eyes, and then back into her apologetic face.

"I'm sorry," she said, overemphasizing slightly and raising the one eyebrow Peter could not see while her face was turned towards Ben. She nodded for Ben to sit beside her. Cassie had not moved, and Ben got the distinct impression from Peter's relaxed state that whatever they were discussing, Jen had so far avoided accusing his father of abduction and murder.

Peter, somewhat oblivious to the tension in the group, thought to himself that Ben was likeable enough, but he was an unusually high-strung new father. In Peter's experience, Jen was a steady, conscientious person and he wondered if it was a case of opposites attracting.

Peter sat up straighter, paused, then clapped both hands together, sensing it was time to go. "Well, it was nice talking to you, and I hope Sunday goes well." Peter stood, reaching over, shaking Ben's hand and twiggling his fingers goodbye in front of Clementine's face, before turning to leave the park.

"Thanks again for the plushie, Peter, and see you on the weekend!" Jen called after him as he left.

Peter could not see their two faces, one streaked with consternation, as Jen and Ben communicated silently behind his back. Cassie at last let her guard down, flopping fully on the ground. Clementine giggled as Jen took the elephant from her knee and tucked it into the stroller.

It was a good thing for Jen that Ben had seen the condo security footage, as the situation warranted some explanation, which Ben demanded as soon as they were back inside their home.

"What do you mean about the weekend?" he harrumphed, simultaneously grabbing her phone out of the stroller pocket, and emphatically connecting it to the charge cord on the kitchen counter.

"Well, Peter came into the city for work and was going to drop off a present for Clem but then I ran into him in the lobby. I didn't know what to do but we got talking and somehow he suggested that I should go out and take a chance his father will be able to talk this Sunday. He doesn't think his dad has too many good days left but Peter thinks Julie's disappearance is important enough to try."

And as Jen said that, a kind of hope drained from her face and she looked up at Ben, her mouth crumpling a bit.

Ben reached out and held her.

"He's a decent man. I just can't imagine what this will do to him if we are right." They looked at each other and for a moment silently considered backing away from the situation.

It was Ben who spoke. "You know, we've gotten pulled into this thing and we don't really control it. You don't know what the Chief will be able to remember or what he will say, or even, for sure, that what you suspect is true. I think all you can do is see it out as far as you can and try to find out what happened to that little girl."

She squeezed him and dried her slightly watery eyes on his shirt.

"How do you want to play it?" she asked, mimicking his gumshoe approach from their last interrogation planning session.

"Well, what do you know about the place where the Chief is at?"

"It's a care home, Peter sent me the address in a text." They checked the charging phone and then typed the address into Maps on the tablet, looking at the building on satellite view and from street level. It was a medium sized facility and obviously housed many residents and staff.

"You know Lori said Julie's mother was at the same place."

"He's been living in the same building as the mother of the girl he abducted and presumably killed?"

Jen nodded.

"Did Peter mention anything about his dad being violent or unruly?"

"No, not exactly. I never got the sense that he was close to his father though. It was not uncommon for cops of that generation to be distant and authoritarian parents. I think he mentioned though that the nursing staff at the home sometimes have to take away his cane and that he can get quite upset when confused."

"Do you think you will be able to talk to the Chief alone?"

Jen thought for a moment, running back exactly what Peter had suggested in the park. "I don't think so, I don't think Peter would feel comfortable with that — either for his dad or for me."

"Okay, so you are going to have to interview him with Peter there?"

"Yes."

"So, you can't just come out and accuse him of anything..."

"I guess not. Guess I just have to start with the phone call and see if I can get it to lead anywhere. Peter doesn't know what we've found out about it yet..." she said, looking Ben in the eyes to confirm that, as Ben suspected, she'd held that information back in the park.

Ben looked at her and nodded slowly, the inexorable pull of this encounter propelling them forward. They spent the next hour experimenting with the equipment they would need to execute their plan while protecting Jen as much as possible.

56

Sunday brought early spring. Rain pelted down from heavy clouds and while it washed away the last of the carbon-stained snow before sunrise, the sodden earth below was not appealing. However, the air coming in through the cracked balcony door smelled clean.

They ate breakfast in eerie silence. Jen was pale and Ben was worried. He had tossed their plan around in his mind for much of the night, at one moment thinking surely no harm could come to his wife, an experienced police officer, and the next riddled with fear that his wife was about to interview someone who had quite possibly killed a child.

Breakfast done, they traded off using the shower and sink, dressing with the nimble automation of soldiers donning uniforms ahead of battle. Clementine was blissfully oblivious to the high-stakes day at hand as her diaper was changed, she had a bottle, and was ultimately ensconced in a onesie and little cap before being deposited in the car seat carrier.

Cassie, however, knew that something was up. She looked up from Jen to Ben, questions in her eyes, trying to ascertain the exact source of the anxiety that ran underneath this Sunday morning. As usual, neither Ben nor Jen had the wits to give her a proper debrief, but Cassie was used to that.

They trundled downstairs and got into the car, driving up the ramp and out into the cold morning light. The city slid past quickly and when they hit the countryside the land seemed hard and grey and unforgiving. They stayed on the highway and took a less picturesque route, reaching the care home in about forty minutes. If they ever made it out of the city, this drive would be their daily commute.

Ben pulled the car into the parking lot and parked to the left of the front door. A black SUV on the right of the door seemed likely to be Peter's. Ben opened his laptop and propped it on the console while Jen plugged a microphone into her phone and then secreted it in a pocket of her jacket, dialing Ben's laptop before doing so.

Ben accepted the call on the laptop and opened the recording application. He should be able to hear everything that was said and would text Jen once she was in the room with the Chief to indicate he was receiving, and give her an opportunity to check the phone call was live.

Jen took an older police-issue voice recorder out of her purse and put it in another pocket as a backup; she would hit the record button with her thumb once she was in position. Jen leaned into the back to kiss Clem on the head and then Ben on the cheek.

Cassie sat bolt upright, expecting her door was about to open so she could go with Jen on her mission. When Jen left without that happening, Cassie whimpered. The sound did not help Ben's nerves.

Jen went inside and Ben could hear rustling from her coat pocket as she moved. "Hi, I'm here to visit Dick Cadworth?" Jen asked at the reception.

"Hi. Are you Jen? Peter said to expect you..." the receptionist said, and while the voice was faint, Ben could hear her. Ben assumed Jen had nodded as the receptionist said: "go on in, he's in 204." And the pocket rustling started again as Jen made her way down a hallway. Within seconds the rustling stopped and there was the sound of Jen knocking on a door. Ben could not hear the reply from inside the room but made out the sound of the door opening and closing.

*　*　*

Jen entered Dick Cadworth's sunny room and as her eyes adjusted from the relative dimness of the hallway, Peter got up from a small couch and came towards her. He shook her hand and said "Hi Jen," while patting their clasped hands from the top, looking her in the eyes and nodding slightly in a way that subtly communicated his dad was lucid and able to talk.

"Dad, this is my old colleague Jen."

Jen made her way over to Dick, who was sitting in a chair pulled away from a small desk near one of the windows. A large black lab was sitting at his feet in the sun and drooling on his shoes. Jen reached out and shook his hand.

"Nice to meet you Chief and thank you for speaking with me." Dick did not smile but he grasped her offered hand firmly.

Jen continued "What a lovely big dog," mostly to let Ben know there was a dog in the room, assuming he could hear her.

The Chief leaned down and scratched the dog behind one ear and said: "this is Peter's dog Posey", and Posey opened an eye at the mention of her name and thwumped her tail against the floor but was unwilling to expend any more energy.

"Here Jen, how about you sit on the couch," Peter suggested from behind her as he moved over to a chair set against the wall near the door. Jen moved to sit down and almost simultaneously there was a ping from her pocket.

She lifted her phone slightly, still concealing the microphone, and saw the text from Ben "can hear. Dog there." The green active call band was visible to her but not to Dick or Peter.

She took the opportunity to adjust her jacket and pressed her thumb against the On button for the backup recorder. While Peter was sitting relaxed by the door, Dick was watching all her movements carefully.

"So, what can I help you with today?" Dick asked, "Peter says you have taken a look at the McNally case using computers and that you have found some new evidence to do with phone calls?"

"Yes, that is right." Jen looked him full in the face and continued "there are two phone calls that we have found that are particularly interesting." And on saying that Jen could have sworn she saw a hard glint in the Chief's eye, but in an instant he had lowered his head.

His hand moved quickly to open the drawer in the desk and for a fraction of a second Jen thought he was going for a weapon, but even before a look of alarm could cross her face, Dick had removed not a gun, but a mug.

He tilted the mug, looked inside, and then placed it on the desk. Turning to Peter, Dick asked: "Peter can you go to the dining room and ask Shirley for a can of ginger ale?"

"Sure dad," and Peter got up and left.

The second the door closed behind Peter, Dick leaned towards Jen and asked, intently, "What phone calls?"

And Jen replied, evenly and confidently, "the call you made to Julie McNally at 4:49 PM on October 8th and the call Bob Micklethwaite made to you at 10:05 PM on October 14th."

57

Dick expelled air from his lungs in a ragged stream, looking at the door through which his son would return within minutes, and asked: "what do you know?"

Jen leaned back slightly, evaluating the expression on his face, and replied "I know you called Julie McNally while alone at your office the afternoon before she disappeared, when you knew her mother would be at the hair salon. You let the investigation expend considerable resources trying to identify that call without explaining it. I know the vehicle log sheet for the fair ground gate was removed from the investigation paperwork shortly after the patrol officer brought it back to the station. I know Bob Micklethwaite was the only other living person who could identify that you made that phone call, that he called you on the 14th, probably offering to help the investigation, and that he was dead about ninety minutes later."

Dick chuckled ruefully, "two phone calls and a missing piece of paper. It's not much..." he paused. Jen let him bring the inevitable truth home, "but it is enough."

Dick leaned back, some tension dropped from his shoulders. He placed one hand on the desk, grasping the mug just below the handle and slowly turning it as he thought things through before speaking.

Jen, sensing it was important to get information while Peter was out of the room, asked abruptly "What happened and where is she?"

And that was all it took to unlock Dick Cadworth's secret. It spilled out as if he was reading from a transcribed confession, held locked behind his eyes for five decades.

"Late on the Tuesday afternoon of that week, I guess October the 6th, a city cop was returning to your neck of the woods from god knows where up north and he came down County Road 15. He spotted a car driving erratically. He pulled it over. Inside was a woman who was highly intoxicated. He brought her to County and she was booked into the cells to dry out, after which the officer assumed we would charge her. However, the woman used her phone call to contact her brother. Her brother was a man named Milo Laurenz," and Dick looked at Jen to see if the name rang a bell, which it did.

"Milo Laurenz was an old-time gangster. He was responsible for half the homicides in the city in the 1960s," Jen offered, remembering what information she could from fifth generation rumours heard years ago.

"That he was, that he was" and Dick shook his head with palpable regret. "Quite the operator, Milo. Ruthless and cunning. Nose for weakness. As it happened, I was already acquainted with this sister of his. The year before my wife Franny — who I love very much," Dick's throat tightened and his voice caught, "had been going through a difficult pregnancy."

"With Peter," Jen supplied.

"With Peter," Dick concurred, continuing, "and there was a period of a couple of months while she was hospitalized, and I was very anxious and left to my own devices. I ended up patrolling town a lot in the evenings. I assume now that it was all a set up, but at the time it happened, I didn't see it coming.

"Veronica — Milo's sister — was fond of a late night and she got herself into a couple of scrapes that summer with local ne'er do wells, first at Duke's tavern and then there was one incident over at the motel. After I handled the guy at the motel, Veronica was very upset, and I stayed with her to calm her down and we had a drink. One thing led to another..." Dick's voice trailed off and he flapped his hands as if this were sufficient to fill in the blanks.

"I get the idea," Jen offered.

"Well, it wasn't long after that I received an envelope and inside were pictures of me and Veronica that night at the hotel. There was a note saying that the photos would be presented to Franny unless I could be useful to Milo," and Dick shrugged, helplessly.

"What has this got to do with Julie McNally?"

Dick sighed. "Well, the day the city officer booked Veronica into county, she called Milo, and Milo arranged for me to be contacted so that I could intervene — I didn't even know she had been booked — and that afternoon at the shift change I went down to the cells, took her out, she was still drunk, and I hauled her out to the back parking lot where her brother was waiting, leaning against this very conspicuous sports car he had. And, before I handed her over, Veronica decided to behave very affectionately towards me.

"It only took a moment or two to get her in the car and for Milo to drive away but if anybody had seen her kiss me — and the exchange — I would not have been able to provide a reasonable explanation. I looked around to make sure we had not been seen, and I thought I was in the clear. But then I looked up at the building, and I could see Julie McNally sitting in the library window seat, watching me."

58

I t was Jen's turn to expel a tortured breath. *Surely not. Surely he had not killed a child because she had seen him professionally and personally compromised?*

Jen managed to conceal her consternation and Dick, somewhat oblivious now to her presence, continued: "I knew it was only a matter of time before Julie would say something to her mother. And while Julie may not have fully understood what she had seen, Marilyn McNally would figure it out.

"Marilyn would have talked to Bridget Sorenson and between the two of them they would have figured it out and told Franny and god help me the word would have gotten out that I was cheating on my wife and under the thumb of Milo Laurenz and I would have lost everything." Dick said this emphatically and then defiantly, willing an old and tattered justification to hold water in the cooler, more reasonable reality of the present.

Jen just looked at him.

"You see Peter was still a baby. I didn't understand how children think."

"So, you waited through Wednesday and most of Thursday until you knew you could talk to her alone and then you called her?"

"Yes. I considered my options. I decided I would call her on Thursday, and we could have a chat."

He paused, at the precipice of the point where his own malevolence could no longer be ignored, but his desire to talk was strong. "I formed a little plan. Julie had interviewed me for the local paper awhile before and

I called and told her I had a friend from the city paper who was coming into town to do a piece on the fair on Friday afternoon and that he would be willing to meet with her to talk about opportunities for her to write, maybe even leading up to a summer job.

"I said he was going to be taking pictures in the animal barns at four and that she should meet us there. I told her I couldn't be sure it would work out for her though, so she shouldn't get her hopes up, and I would appreciate it if she kept it a secret from her mom as he was a buddy Franny didn't approve of.

"I still had not decided exactly what I was going to do. It was going to depend on how many people were around. I drove into the fairgrounds shortly before four, parked in a patrol spot right at the end of the horse barn, then when it was time, I walked through the horse barn to the tack room and looked up the aisle past the pig pens."

"She came into the pig barn alone and I could see back through the horse barn that there was no one coming that way. I waved at her to come into the tack room and once she was through the door I came around behind her and snapped her neck."

He said it nonchalantly, and Jen's revulsion rose so quickly that she almost threw up.

Dick continued, defensively, "it was instantaneous. She never saw it coming and she didn't feel a thing."

Jen breathed in and out carefully through her nose. She still needed to know where Julie was. "What happened then?"

"I put her in a saddle bag that was in the tack room and carried the bag down the horse barn and put it in the trunk of my car. Then, I left the fair through the vehicle gate and drove straight to my cottage at the lake and put the bag in the chest freezer I keep there for storing fish."

"Then I drove straight back into town. It took almost three hours. I ate dinner with Franny and waited all evening for the alarm to be raised. Eventually, it was. When the time came to call in the dogs, I went myself to the McNally household to collect items of clothing for scenting and I put them in the trunk of my car where the bag had been earlier. The dogs couldn't do anything with the situation they were given," Dick said, shrugging.

Jen, hoping to get to her final answers with an oblique question, asked "What was your plan for the body?"

The use of the word *'body'* seemed to unsettle Dick Cadworth, which confused Jen. He had no problem discussing *'the bag'* but given he successfully disposed of Julie's remains, presumably, at some point, he literally came face to face with the horrendous reality of what he had done.

"At that point, I didn't have one," Dick said and at that moment Peter walked through the door holding a can of ginger ale, completely oblivious.

"Here you go dad."

* * *

Out in the parking lot, Ben said "shit" quietly under his breath.

59

"Thanks son," Dick Cadworth said, taking the ginger ale as it was handed over. Peter returned to his chair near the door while Dick opened the can and methodically poured it down the side of the mug, giving it a final swirl before letting the bubbles settle. Dick held the mug and resumed turning it, so the mug handle inched around like the hand on a clock. He continued talking.

"I figured the situation was stable as it stood for the rest of the week and of course with the investigation I couldn't get out to the lake." Peter was confused as to why his father was talking about the lake.

"Then Bob Micklethwaite called me around 10:00 PM almost a week later. He had heard through the grapevine that Julie received a phone call that might be important and that we were asking around trying to figure out who it could be.

"He asked me straight off what day and time we were interested in and I asked him why he wanted to know. He explained that he had built this device that was recording traffic on the local exchange. He started to get into technical details on the phone and I suggested we meet up for a beer at Duke's so that I could understand it better.

"And I went out and met him there. He explained what he thought he could retrieve. It had never occurred to me that such a call was traceable. However, it was clear that this device he had built was pretty specialized and that he was the only one who knew about it. He also said he had to bring the device the data was on back home because he had built the reading machine at home and that meant the telephone company didn't have the technology or the knowledge.

"Once I understood that, I made an excuse to leave the table, I snuck out the back and I cut the brake line on his car. Then I went back inside, thanked him, and told him I would be in touch the next day but that it had been a long week and I needed to go home. I knew his way home took him through the gully and I was pretty sure what was going to happen."

Peter, sitting between Jen and the door, was utterly baffled. He had no idea who Bob was, although he could infer he had something to do with the phone data Jen had found. He had no knowledge of what had happened to Bob.

Why his father thought it was okay to cut the man's break line was spectacularly unclear. Peter wondered if his dad was not as lucid as he had earlier assumed, and perhaps had spent the last few minutes prattling incoherently at Jen.

Peter looked over at Jen for guidance on what was going on and when she looked back at him there was a kind of despair and guilt in her eyes that he found deeply unsettling. Utterly baffled, Peter said nothing while Dick, aware of his son's growing disorientation, hurried on to complete his story.

"Once Bob died, it suddenly became clear what I could do. I knew when the funeral would be, and I knew they would dig out the old Micklethwaite plot at Glenwood the afternoon before. Just after midnight the day of Bob's funeral I drove out to the lake and retrieved the bag. I drove to the cemetery, went to the Micklethwaite plot, climbed into the hole and dug the bottom out an extra three feet, I put the bag in the hole and refilled it carefully."

Jen, at last holding her precious answer, asked "so, she should still be there?" And Dick nodded. Then he looked over at Peter who was still trying to understand what was in the bag they were talking about.

"Peter, son," and Peter looked up at his father "I want you to know that I love you. I love you. And god knows I loved your mother. But I made mistakes." And with that, Dick took the mug that had been ticking forward like a clock in his hands for the past ten minutes and downed the contents.

Jen leapt off the sofa, but she was only in time to grab the mug as it started to slip from Dick's spasming hand. He was on the floor with Posey, who whimpered but did not bark, and convulsing within seconds. It was over before Peter could even think of reacting. Jen lifted the mug to her nose, carefully, "bitter almonds. He's taken cyanide."

Posey got up and leaned over Dick's head, licking him despondently. Peter's instinct to protect the dog kicked in and he called her over. She went and when Peter placed both hands on her temples and kissed her furry head, it snapped him back to reality.

He looked down at his father, dead on the floor, and up to Jen "What is going on?"

"I'm very sorry Peter, but there is something you need to hear," and she took the small voice recorder from her pocket, stopping it and selected a button to play the recording back from the beginning. As a tinny version of Dick's voice started emanating from the speakers, the door opened and Ben rushed in, Cassie at his heels.

"Where's Clementine?" Jen asked.

"She's in the car. It's locked," Ben held out the car keys in his hand.

"Okay, sit with Peter for a minute," and Jen took the keys from his hand and made her way out to the parking lot.

She breathed in the cool, clean, spring air, took out her phone, stopped the call that was still running to Ben's laptop, and then called the county police station.

She asked to speak to the Chief of Police, and after identifying herself by name, with her police rank and unit, explained that she had just heard the confession of the person who committed the 1970 murder of Julie McNally and witnessed the perpetrator's suicide.

Jen explained that she knew where Julie's body should be and had multiple recordings of the confession as well as additional witnesses. She did not explain that the witnesses were her husband and baby.

The Chief asked her to identify her current location and name the perpetrator and when Jen did so, there was a gasp at the other end of the line.

"Jesus. I am sending cars and an ambulance. We'll be there within minutes."

"Right, thank you. I need to call this in to my superior. SIU may need to come out here as well."

And Jen did that, abruptly truncating her boss's pleasantries when he answered the phone inquiring about what could possibly be interrupting the joys of maternity leave.

EPILOGUE

Two days later, after Jen filed considerable paperwork and sat through an intimidating interview with the internal investigation officers, the county Police Chief called to thank her and ask for a favour.

They were hoping Ben would be willing to come with a county detective to visit Rob Micklethwaite, Bob's nephew, tomorrow. They needed Rob's permission to disinter Bob and Deborah's remains so that Julie's body could be recovered.

Once they were sure she had been found, Marilyn McNally could be notified. Mrs. McNally was still in the dark, and given her age, every day that went by without her being informed was a risk they did not want to take. She had waited too long to learn the fate of her daughter.

They also needed to explain to Rob that his uncle had been murdered and why, and no one at the county police station quite grasped what this data technology thing from 1970 was all about.

If Ben could come along to explain it, the Chief felt it would be helpful. Jen handed the phone to Ben, who agreed, but also asked if he could bring a scientist from the university who really understood the details with him. The Chief was sceptical but when Ben named Sam Eide she relented, as she had seen Professor Eide testify in a criminal case a few years before.

Ben then sent Sam a text asking him to call, which he did. When Ben explained what had happened with the case, Sam whistled into his phone, and agreed to go out to Rob Micklethwaite's the next day to help in any way he could.

＊ ＊ ＊

On Wednesday morning Ben drove over to the university and picked Sam up in the faculty parking lot. Sam was carrying a bakery box on top of which were two coffees.

"I got you a coffee and I've brought a dozen donuts," Sam said once Ben leaned over and popped the passenger door open. Sam climbed into the tiny car and adjusted the seat.

"Thanks so much for doing this, think it will take about three hours. There's a great diner out there I can take you to if we go as late as lunch."

"Sounds good," Sam replied.

And they set off, Sam asking about the baby, and making general small talk as they drove. He learned how the whole situation began because Ben and Jen were looking to leave the city for more space. Sam had a spacious mid-century apartment in midtown, but he had bought it decades earlier, before the market started booming, and when they still built apartments a reasonable size; he did not mention this out loud.

Eventually, the GPS provided the last turns directing them towards Rob Micklethwaite's farm and the hatchback set out across a kilometre or two of flat fields surrounded by ditches, now full of spring rain.

The farmhouse proved to be similar in age and style to the Drinkwater house in town but seemed much more impressive rising alone from the open agricultural landscape.

Behind it several large red clapboard barns and outbuildings, well maintained, stretched around a farmyard and paddock. As they turned in the long drive, they passed through two uneven rows of very aged and gnarled apple trees.

The house had an expansive wrap-around porch and was surrounded by yellow forsythia and lilac bushes, just a few of which were coming into bloom.

There was a sedan parked slightly askew near the door and the driver was sitting inside, talking on his phone. When they pulled up and parked beside it, the driver ended his call and got out, coming around to greet them as they got out of the car and stretched their legs.

"Hullo, I am Detective Lapworth," and he held out a hand to Ben, who took it and replied "Ben Mahoney, and this is Professor Sam Eide." Lapworth waved at Sam on the other side of the car "Nice to meet you and thank you both for your time today. I've told Rob we need to speak to him about his uncle and the family plot at the cemetery and he's expecting us for nine so your timing is perfect."

The three men made their way onto the porch and Lapworth knocked concisely on the door, which opened very quickly. Rob Micklethwaite had perhaps been peeking through the door sidelight with more than a little curiosity for the last few minutes.

"Hi Rob,"

"Hullo Barry, come on in," Rob said, welcoming them in with a broad gesture of his arm and shuffling a bit on eighty-year-old knees as he made his way through the gracious old foyer and into the Victorian parlour. The men followed and before they sat down, Rob turned and shook hands with Ben and Sam, who introduced themselves; Sam taking the opportunity to hand over the box of donuts.

Rob, who liked a donut and whose wife generally prevented him from eating them whenever she could, was greatly encouraged by the gift, which he promptly plopped open on the coffee table, grabbing one and encouraging the others to do the same before they got caught and the donuts were confiscated.

The four men sat down on the assemblage of well stuffed and upholstered Victorian furniture, donuts and tiny paper napkins in hand, and Lapworth began: "Rob, I've got some news. Now, it all happened a long time ago, so I hope it doesn't come as too much of a shock."

Rob chomped his donut and raised a bushy eyebrow.

"Well, the first thing is we think we've solved the Julie McNally case." Rob stopped eating at that, swallowed, and with great fascination said "Really? Where is she?"

"Well, that's the thing. We have reason to believe that she was killed, and the killer secreted her body two or three feet below the bottom of the grave dugout the night before your uncle Bob was buried."

Rob, understanding crossing his face, lifted his partially eaten donut and used it for emphasis as he said, "because he died the week she went missing!"

"Exactly, it's more than that though, we've got a confession indicating that Julie's remains are in your family burial plot and we are really very confident it is true. We need your permission to disinter Bob and Deborah, in order to get to Julie's body," and Lapworth opened a portfolio he had been carrying, in which was a form and a pen.

"Well, I'll be damned," Rob said "who would have thought? Who did it?"

Lapworth continued, "normally I couldn't tell you that at this stage of the investigation, but here is the other thing. The perpetrator confessed that he cut your uncle's break line the night he had his accident in the gully. Your uncle was killed by the same person who murdered Julie McNally and that person was Richard Cadworth."

Rob, flabbergasted and suddenly skeptical, put his donut and paper napkin down on the well polished coffee table. "Bullshit! Dick Cadworth was no sex pervert!"

"No, no, he wasn't. It's all a bit complicated. I won't go into too many details, but apparently Julie saw something Cadworth did, and he was afraid she was going to tell people about it."

Rob, vaguely grasping that they were now talking about corruption, intuitively found that more plausible and picked his donut back up and started eating it again. Lapworth took the opportunity to continue "and it seems that your uncle Bob was in a position to identify Dick's involvement and these gentleman here are going to explain how that was."

And Sam started speaking, beginning with high praise for Bob's engineering skills and working up to a basic explanation of how Bob's phone dataset was created and ultimately could have revealed that Dick lured Julie to her doom.

Ben explained how Bob had contacted Dick the night he was killed, unfortunately revealing he had key evidence to the worst possible person.

Then the story was brought full circle when Ben explained he had bought the tubes containing the data from Harry MacAllan the junk dealer at the Farmers' Market.

"Well!" Rob exclaimed when they were finished "Barry you need me to sign this form?"

"Yes, then we can start the exhumation. We will do it later today or tomorrow. We need to know for certain before we inform Marilyn McNally."

And Rob raised a shaky hand to his forehead at that thought. He was unsettled by the news of what happened to his uncle so long ago, but he could not imagine how Julie's mother must feel. He leaned over and signed the paper and then all four men got up and made their way towards the door, Lapworth in the lead and in a hurry to take the paperwork into town so the home stretch of the investigation could begin.

Just after Lapworth reached the porch, Rob stopped and said: "there's something you two fellows might want to see." Lapworth turned, but Rob waved him on, and Barry, trusting he was no longer needed, continued to his car, quickly driving off.

Rob turned and motioned that Sam and Ben should follow him back down the hallway, although he stopped in the parlour for a moment to grab a second donut before leading them further on, through the kitchen and then out onto the back porch.

They went down some steps and into the farmyard and Ben and Sam exchanged glances behind Rob's back. His destination was one of the low, long, red clapboard outbuildings.

It had probably once been a chicken coop and had a white door in the gable end, which Rob opened, reaching a hand around inside to flick a light switch. He motioned for Ben and Sam to go through the door and after a moment's hesitation Ben's curiosity egged him on, and he crossed the threshold. Sam followed.

The overhead fluorescent light tubes stretched a good thirty feet to the far wall, illuminating wooden shelving running along both sides of the building. Many of the lower shelves held rusted and dusty tools, buckets, some bags of farm supplies, and other similar and expected items. But the high shelves, the ones under the eaves, were stuffed with twenty or more large cardboard boxes.

Ben chuckled when he realized that about ten of those boxes were covered in printing he recognized: *Trimline handset telephones … Scandalously easy to use. The dial comes right to you. Extra long cords.*

Ben walked towards the other end of the building, carefully pulling down the last box, popping the flaps open and pulling a glass bulb off the top of the pile inside. He could see the stamp and read the number out loud "691208."

"Uncle Bob used to bring me out a box to store every year around Christmas," Rob explained.

Sam, grasping what they were looking at, pulled down the box nearest to the door, opened it up, and following Ben's lead, turned the tube to read the date stamp: "481129."

Sam turned to Rob Micklethwaite, a question forming behind his eyes.

ABOUT THE AUTHOR

J. A. Tattle

J. A. Tattle is a Toronto-based author and arm-chair investigation methods aficionado who thinks the world needs more classic detective stories. 'The Girl in the Library' is a debut novel.

Printed in Great Britain
by Amazon

13586076R00144